Novel

BackWords

THE STORY OF ELIZABETH TIMOTHY

LISA M. FOSTER

ISBN: 978-1-963569-71-1 (hard cover)
        978-1-963569-72-8 (soft cover)

Published by Warren Publishing
Charlotte, NC
www.warrenpublishing.net
Printed in the United States

For Anne Scannelly Pooser, who began the research of Elizabeth Timothy's amazing accomplishments. When Anne could no longer continue the project, she selflessly gave her research to me so that I could finish what she had begun.

I stand on the shoulders of giants.

Chapter One

He could not be dead. His pillow was still warm.

At least it felt warm when she touched it. Elizabeth could feel the heat of empirical evidence, straining to confirm a fact that she wanted so much to be true. The fact was, though, that it was her own hand that conveyed the heat, playing tricks on her mind.

Cruel tricks indeed, she thought with a beaten smile, and the rising of her cheeks forced a salty tear to trickle down into her mouth. She licked it at the corner and swept away a second rogue tear with the back of her hand, remembering a recent sermon: "If thy hand offends thee, cut if off: it is better for thee to enter into life maimed, than having two hands to go into hell, into the fire that shall never be quenched."

Cutting off her hand would not bring her husband back. And it certainly would not keep her from God's judgment.

She sat there on the bed, holding his pillow for some unknown amount of time. It was a space—neither earthly nor ethereal—where every thought but one was crowded out: he was gone.

That simple singularity bore a crushing weight. She forced herself to focus on that singularity—indeed, embrace it—allowing this one fact to dominate the many cluttered realities that sprang from it. She could not consider what survival would ask of her. Her life was all pied up, like a tray of Caslon type scattered on the floor. How would she sort it all out? Where would she begin to form the words to express it? How would she manage to put back in order each ponderous slug and move forward without him?

From her seated position she lay down on the bed and put her head on his pillow. In it she caught a ghost of his breath—warm and sticky—a curious mixture of garlic and onion. The extrication of a soul is a messy procedure done unceremoniously over time, she reasoned. It is the result of layers of scars, from gouging out memories and cutting away nuances.

No, he would not be truly dead to her for quite some painful time.

Dull drops speckled the windowsill, like blood splattering on cloth. Elizabeth drew up a chair and sat heavily in it, unblinking. Her audible exhalation was near enough to the glass to breathe brief obscurity onto the scene beyond.

Outside, a cold rain slid down the windowpane thickly, as if it were clear molasses. The crisp, cool weather of Lewis's funeral yesterday had finally, inevitably succumbed to a late December winter in the colony. *The end of one thing heralds the beginning of another*, she thought, trying to console herself.

She was pleased that his service had been attended by such great numbers, though, and most likely would have been greatly attended even in this dismal squall. Her husband was well liked—respected—although he had been a Charles Towne resident for only a few short years: a tribute to their open hearts and Lewis's reputation as a good man of business and a right proper friend—even back when he was Louis Timothée, his name when they first arrived to America.

Of course, the curiosity seekers were there as well—sycophants circling the perimeter of the church, lurking in the shadows with disingenuously mournful faces that, so overdone, belied their true intent. Elizabeth was not fooled.

Everyone is in the news business, she thought.

However, this burial business having been completed, Elizabeth knew she should be opening the shop just now. She was late—past deadline—and she was a punctual person. But immobility continued to grip her, and she allowed herself to be overcome with the desire to just stay here at the window. Hundreds of raindrops slid down the glass into each other, some rushing all the way to the bottom and back into the earth. Puddles pooled, softening the packed ground like an unfired brick not yet ready for the kiln.

Elizabeth stood clumsily and fumbled for her cloak, which threatened to release its hold of her left shoulder. She repositioned it and patted around her head for the hat that was still pinned there from the church service at St. Philip's.

It would be a muddy walk to the grave site this afternoon, she thought. Her hem would take the worst of it.

She lingered at the window just a moment longer, waiting for the blood to circulate and keep her on her feet. Tiny dark sparkles clouded her vision, but they would clear. Just a fleeting dizzy spell; it always passed. She held the back of the chair tightly. Had she eaten? When had she eaten? She could not recall. No time for that now, even if she could muster an interest.

Elizabeth smoothed her black gloves against the front of her Brunswick and willed her body to move forward—out of the bedroom and downstairs to the main room of the Timothys' King Street home where the children were under Louisa's watchful eye.

"Children," Elizabeth said in characteristic authority, looking at Louisa, Mary Elizabeth, Peter, and Charles, who were all huddled together by the fireplace, "I shall be gone for a while. I expect you all to be on your best behavior for your sister. She is to be in charge in my absence. You will listen to Louisa and do as she says."

Elizabeth turned to her eldest daughter now, knowing she was expecting much from the young girl of fifteen, her face still damp with tears from burying her father. "Lou, dinner is on the fire. Everyone is to be in bed promptly and without dispute," she said, as much to Louisa as to the other children, lest they forget that obedience was obligatory.

"When will you return, Mother?" Louisa asked.

"When I have put the newspaper to bed," her mother replied curtly, stepping to the threshold. Elizabeth called out one last directive just before firmly closing the door behind her: "Peter, I expect those shoes to be shined when I return."

Elizabeth, shivering, stepped out into the street. The sky—indiscernibly gray—was lower than usual. Suffocating. Even the birds kept clear of it, those that ventured to take flight at all. The few individuals who had business on King Street were quick about it.

She hugged her clothing tightly around her, thankful that she was wearing a high-collar dress. The winter rain peppered pools of low ground, and carriage ruts were long thin vessels holding a muddy mix the earth could not absorb. Elizabeth picked up her pace in a futile attempt to keep her thoughts from wandering to Lewis's funeral.

Several friends and business acquaintances had remained at St. Philip's, offering their condolences: I am so sorry for your loss. What a tragedy. How old was your husband? Pity. You and your family have only recently moved to Charles Towne. Tsk, tsk, tsk. If there is anything you need. God be with you. We will pray for you and your family. God, in His infinite wisdom, has a purpose. Your husband is with the angels now.

The words floated around her. She heard them buzzing, swarming, but she refused to let one syllable light upon her lips or enter her nostrils, for fear the emptiness would consume her.

Still, with all her fortitude she had smiled. She had nodded graciously, offering appreciation for their sentiment. But silently she prayed they would all just go away.

Work was what she needed now. The citizens of Charles Towne would understand if the *South-Carolina Gazette* was delayed, but she had no intention of waiting. And since it was Tuesday, December 30, she had very little time to finish setting type if she intended to make Thursday's deadline. There was the historic peace pipe ceremony to include in this edition. And, of course, the unhappy death of her husband, the *Gazette*'s publisher, Lewis Timothy.

Lewis had arrived in Charles Towne in 1734, just four years ago, with Elizabeth and the children following several months later. In that time, the Timothys had met many people by virtue of their work. Printing was a community profession, after all. What information the Timothy Print Shop did not know, many wag-tongued townspeople were delighted to provide.

The raindrops felt heavier now, vindictive. Elizabeth stepped up her gait toward the print shop.

Lewis would want her to tend to business. It is what she had always done, and what he had come to rely on. He was arguably better than Elizabeth at putting words together on a printer's stick, but she was inarguably better at keeping the books. Ben Franklin, Lewis's publishing partner in the Carolina Colony, had said so himself.

Right now, Elizabeth needed to be absorbed in work. She needed something that could crowd out every other thought. Some would talk, as some always do: How could a pregnant widow, expecting her seventh child, choose to put out the next edition of the *South-Carolina Gazette* instead of mourning with family and friends? Some might ask why she was not in reclusion for at least one year, as polite society prescribed, removing herself from all business and social situations while wearing the black costume of a mourning widow.

Elizabeth could not have cared less about appearances, and she had neither the time nor the inclination to grieve. Facts are facts. Her husband was dead, and until her eldest son Peter reached majority, she was head of household.

She knew by heart most of the stale news and ads that ran in the weekly newspaper, and much of the work for the next edition had already been done. After all, it was not as if Lewis had taken ill and had not been able to work. He had been working when he died, preparing for the next issue. Still, Elizabeth was glad there was some work left to do. Putting words together, letter by letter on a printer's stick, was just the sort of mind-numbing, rote activity she desperately needed to be swallowed up in. Like an insane patient picking at a sore, she needed something that required intense single-mindedness. Without it, she feared she might not survive the next few days.

There would be time to digest the loss of him later. The guilt, of course, would remain in her throat like a goiter, reminding her with even the most basic of bodily functions that it cannot, will never, be swallowed.

It was a short but miserable walk from the Timothy home to the churchyard. Shaking, Elizabeth stood beside her husband's fresh grave. The recently turned ground hemorrhaged rain that ran down bumps and bruises in the soggy earth. Soon this wound would scab over. But other wounds would not.

Wet and cold, Elizabeth walked quickly back to King Street. Turning the key in the lock, she stepped inside the printshop, where the familiar incense of ink and leather filled her nostrils. With a comforting, wooden thud of the door—so quick upon her entry as to very nearly catch her skirts in the process—she shut the world out behind her.

Sanctuary.

Elizabeth closed her eyes and breathed her first deep breath in days, drawing air into her lungs from the very bottom and expanding them upward until she reached the top. The air spilled over, expelled in an audibly satisfying sigh. She followed it to its conclusion until there was no more air to let go. Her head slumped forward, and her shoulders—how long had they been up around her ears?—followed.

Thank goodness most of the *Gazette* had already been laid out. Lewis had always saved the front page for late-breaking news; this was her preoccupation now.

She took account through the shop window of the fading light from a short winter day, dark from its nascence. She lit only one candle—just enough to set by—and placed it close to the typeform. She reached for Lewis's ink-stained deerskin apron and tied it around her huge belly, covering the seed that ripened within her. The high stool at the workbench took the pressure off her lower back; she could work here manageably, in the dark, loading type on Lewis's composing stick.

Elizabeth reached up to retrieve four wooden trays containing Roman and italic type and began threading characters into backward words for printing. Letter by letter, she added to the lengthening column of print, double-spaced, in her hand. When she heard the knock, she did not acknowledge it.

Dr. Dale, not waiting for an invitation, opened the door and walked in.

Expecting to find her distraught, perhaps even giving birth prematurely in the agony of her grief, Dale was surprised to find her in Lewis's apron, working.

"Trading widow's weeds for a printer's apron, Elizabeth?" he asked.

The movement of Elizabeth's ears indicated the faintest soupçon of a smile.

"Did you think you would find me lying prostrate with grief, a victim of my own 'unhappy accident,' Thomas?" she asked.

Dale ignored her question.

"Elizabeth, as your doctor I order you to come down from that stool and go home to rest. This is neither the time nor the place for a woman to be working. Not even for you."

Elizabeth turned her head toward him. Vacant eyes, like the smooth, dead orbs of a statue, stared back at him. The work did not halt; she continued to feed characters onto the lengthening column of print in her hand without even looking, as if she were asleep. Dale felt as though he was an observer in her dream: only her agile and animated hands betrayed life behind dead gray eyes.

Shock, the good doctor reasoned. Like the gentle rocking back and forth of a child whose mind cannot make sense of a horrible tragedy.

Dr. Dale had known his orders would be ignored. Elizabeth was one of his most difficult patients; it was part of what made her so endearing. If he wanted her to rest, he would have to assist her in finishing the work. Only then would she agree to return home to a chair and her children.

Sighing, he pulled up a stool beside her and sat down while she finished loading each stick onto a galley. He tied it off for her and transferred the page form to the imposing stone to be locked into the chase.

Elizabeth picked up a block of wood and a soft mallet made of deerskin, then began pounding the back of the type form to ensure all the letters would make an impression on the white paper.

"You pull and I will beat," Dale said with resignation.

Elizabeth placed a sheet of rag paper in the tympan and folded the frisket over it while Dale took up a wooden brayer and began spreading ink on a mixing block.

"I doubt I will perform this job any more satisfactorily than you would treat dysentery," he said, attempting to elicit a smile.

Long silences were difficult for him. In his field, he found he worked even harder to treat a very sick patient for fear of the funeral. He never knew what to say at times of loss. "I am sorry" sounded as if he was assuming responsibility for the death. "He will be missed" was a moot statement of fact. Still, he found himself prattling on to surviving family members like some feebleminded idiot who could not contain his tongue. Elizabeth, at least, had the decency to be unresponsive to his babble.

He locked the chase onto the bed of the press, and taking up the wooden handles of two leather-covered balls, Dale collected the sticky ink and transferred it evenly onto the type. Her doctor could not help but notice the skill and strength, paired with a certain gentleness, with which Elizabeth's ink-stained fingers adeptly pressed the paper against the type. He wondered what anger seethed beneath the surface at her husband's death. Surely she was mad at God for taking Lewis from her so suddenly, especially after his recent recovery from smallpox just months earlier. Dale wished she would throw the form on the floor. This pent-up anger was not good for the baby.

When the impression had been successfully made, Elizabeth carefully pulled the long sheet from the form. Dale helped, holding a corner as she worked her way down, pulling away the freshly printed page of wet type. As soon as the rag paper was clear of it, she turned it over to inspect her work.

Dr. Dale looked at his patient. He would have thrown his arms around her, had she not been holding the first impression of Thursday's paper. He would have held her so tightly that the tears would have been squeezed out of her. He would have pressed her weeping face into his shoulder and vowed to absorb it all until the well was dry. But Elizabeth was not that kind of woman; he knew that all too well.

"An 'unhappy accident,' Elizabeth?" Dale asked softly as he read the freshly printed paper.

Without response, she let him take the wet sheet from her hands and hang it to dry. She would never have asked for his companionship, but she was grateful to have it. The remainder of the imprints for their growing number of subscribers needed to be printed and dried before distributing. She had other help: her son Peter, of course, who was apprenticing to take over when he reached majority, and two journeymen at the press and another learning the vat and coucher work. The Negro had fled, and she was glad for his sake.

"Is there anything I can do for you?" Dale asked, and Elizabeth knew he meant it.

"Yes," Elizabeth replied. "You can tell me how I got here."

Before he could consider an answer, she continued, "How did I get here, to Charles Towne, from my girlhood in Holland? What am I *doing* here, with no husband and six children—and pregnant with another on the way any moment, in a place that is so far from where I began?"

She was on the verge of tears, but she fought through it, forcing the words from her mouth.

"How do you suppose I will manage to move forward from this, into an uncertain future?"

Her doctor considered a response. In Elizabeth's own way, she was begging him for an answer that made sense of it all. He wanted to give her that. She was an intelligent woman, as evident by the skills and acumen that had made her and her husband Lewis such favorable business partners of Benjamin Franklin. Dale knew Franklin to be a man of great intellect, and in Elizabeth, Ben had found his female equal.

No, he decided. *There is no satisfactory reply, save the one she had just printed on the* Gazette's *front page.*

And that being the case, he chose to consider the question rhetorical, rubbing her shoulders with his large hands and nodding his head in silent agreement. Whether she would admit it or not, what Elizabeth wanted now was a friend, a friend who would quietly take the first step into an uncertain future with her.

Chapter Two

"**H**urry along, children," Elizabeth said in the tone she usually reserved only for Peter.

Her arms were spread out like wings as she pushed her ducklings toward the Rotterdam wharf. She had lectured the children for weeks about their responsibilities on the voyage to America, and the consequences of disobedience.

"Louisa, grab your brother's hand," she instructed, but the boy shook off his sister's hold and stuffed his hands into the pockets of his breeches.

Elizabeth snatched the boy up by his suspenders and warned him, again, to get his attention. Peter, too distracted and busy absorbing the activities of the fish mongers and salty men, would not be encumbered with the likes of his younger sibling when there was so much to see.

Elizabeth spun around. "Peter, I will whip you where you stand, young man. In front of God and these witnesses, I swear I will."

She glanced around to see if anyone had taken notice of her son's behavior. If they had, no one was returning her gaze.

Elizabeth squared her shoulders and smoothed the front of her Brunswick, surveying the crowd. Women and girls dressed in fine millinery, gloved and buttoned up tight with whalebone corsets, remained at the top of the wharf. The men, along with boys over sixteen years of age, had been culled aside, preparing to load each family's belongings on board.

Overhead, the cry of seagulls, soaring and diving for fish, mingled with boatswains' chatter and the din of passengers' voices murmuring in a dozen different tongues. The ship slapped the water rhythmically, and the working noise of footfalls and supplies being dragged across wood planks was borne on the salty breeze.

For now, the waiting throng was orderly. The men were queued up at the water's edge of the wharf, ready to load each family's trunks into the hold of the HMS *Britannia*. Although it was a formidable ship, Elizabeth wondered if it could accommodate all the people waiting to board her, as well as the cargo the ship's mates were busily stowing below deck. Did she imagine a slight sinking of the prow with each ponderous piece of luggage brought aboard? Had every traveler gone through the same painful exercise as she and Louis? Deciding which of their possessions warranted inclusion in the trunk, and which must be left behind?

Elizabeth took stock of the crowd: mostly German Palatines—emigrants from the Rhine Valley—mingled with Dutch passengers. Many of them had no chests at all to bring aboard. Others had several, indicating that the chests most likely contained most, if not all, of the family's worldly possessions. America was the spot on a map where they had pinned all their hopes and dreams.

When the cargo had been loaded and the ship's mooring lines cast off, the tide slowly pulled *Britannia* out to sea. Briny spray peppered her face; she licked it away at the corners of her mouth despite its fishy taste. Taking a wide stance, Elizabeth planted her feet squarely and bent her knees to absorb the ship's rocking. The tug of the outgoing tide, coupled with the ship's lateral motion, made her feel a bit dizzy.

When she turned back toward the harbor, she caught the last glimpse of their home just as it shrank into the horizon. When it was gone for good, Elizabeth faced the open ocean again and fixed her eyes beyond the ship's walls to the great expansive ocean that seemed to go on forever—and made herself believe that their own possibilities were just as endless.

Patting the folds of her clothing, she reassured herself that the cache of coins sewn into the lining was still there. Captain Franklyn would collect fares upon arrival in Philadelphia. Louis had figured five pounds sterling each for himself and his wife, and three pounds sterling for each child. The fare alone came to almost two hundred forty-five guldens, but they might need to purchase items from the ship's store and would certainly need to let a room in Philadelphia. He had three hundred guldens, a few dozen stuyvers, and as many penningens tucked in his wallet and slung around his neck for safekeeping. But she knew Louis would need to secure work as soon as possible in the New World.

Britannia made her way to the port of Cowes, England, and on to the Isle of Wight by fits and starts. By sunset, their grand adventure was already bearing down hard on some of her passengers. And with each successive day, Elizabeth resigned herself to the ennui of an unchanging horizon.

"The sound of the bow breaking through water at first reminded me of gently rustling wheat fields," Elizabeth told her husband on their third morning at sea.

Louis smiled, tucking her hair behind her ear as sea breezes danced with errant locks.

"Now it sounds more like a sickle, cutting down everything in its path," she said, demonstrating a threshing motion with a small smile.

"An apropos analogy as we are cutting through the water. But do not worry, my dear," Louis said, sensing his wife was trying to be brave. "The threshers know what they are doing."

Elizabeth nodded, as much to reassure Louis as herself. "For my part, I am trying to keep the children's minds occupied by teaching a few hours every day," she said. "But I think it helps me as much as it helps them. Perhaps more."

"A sensible idea," Louis responded.

Her husband had brought along dozens of books in the family's trunk, but these were strictly off limits to Elizabeth's students. She taught from four of her own volumes, packed specifically for this purpose: the *New England Primer* for teaching the alphabet, vowels and consonants, and syllabaries, but also for introducing the young Timothées to the art of printing: recognition of ligatures, Roman and Italian fonts, type ornaments, and capitalization, to name a few. Three additional volumes were packed as well: Catesby's *Natural History of Carolina, Florida and the Bahama Islands*, volumes one and two, French nursery rhymes titled *Les Contes de ma mère l'Oye* by Charles Perrault, and *Robinson Crusoe* by Daniel Defoe. So as not to frighten the youngest among them, Elizabeth was in the habit of editing *Crusoe* when reading it aloud, especially when the cannibals pay a visit.

"My floating classroom has developed quite a reputation," Elizabeth told her husband.

"Occasionally even some sailors linger in the shadows while I am teaching the children. When members of the crew show up repeatedly, I invite them to take a seat."

Louis asked her how many accept the invitation, but she said most just shook their heads and left as quietly as they had arrived.

"There is one sailor, though," Elizabeth offered, "Johann, a German boy. When he is not working, he is present alongside the children."

"Bright boy," she added pensively.

Louis smiled at her.

"He can now correctly recite the short and long sounds of each English vowel," she reported with pride. "When I commended him on his achievement, he absolutely beamed," adding that this massive man was made to look even larger in the company of children. "I told him in German that I admired anyone who tried to speak another language. I said I myself speak several languages, and anyone who speaks at least one language other than his own is a much better student of humanity because you can converse with people from other cultures."

Louis nodded in agreement.

"But more than that," Elizabeth continued, "I made it clear that it was his willingness to set aside *his* pride in order to learn that was the main source of *my* pride in him. And then he said the oddest thing. He stared at his boots, as if he wanted to confess something, and said, 'I also can teach.'"

Elizabeth told her husband that the idea had never occurred to her, and she felt as though she had unintentionally offended him. "I said he made an excellent point, and that I was certain there were many things *he* could teach *me*."

Her husband nodded as if to confirm the revelation.

Elizabeth continued, "He said, 'We work together. You teach me English. I teach you *knotenkunde*.'"

"The German word for knot-tying," Louis responded.

"Yes, and since I do not know how to make any seamen's knots, I accepted his offer," she said. "We begin tomorrow."

The next morning Johann was waiting for her on deck.

"I insist you use English as much as possible to teach me knot-tying," she told the hulking seaman. "It may be difficult for you, but the more you speak English, the faster you will learn it."

"I try. Take line," he said, handing her a length of rope and showing her how to hold it. "This call 'bowline.'"

His German accent was as thick as *gulasch*.

"How do you spell it?" Elizabeth asked.

"Spell like 'bow' and 'line,' but all sailors say 'beau-linn.'"

"Interesting," she said, studying the length of rope in her hand. "It reminds me of Anne Boleyn."

"I do not know dis," Johann replied, looking at her and shaking his head. Elizabeth seized the opportunity for a history lesson.

"Anne Boleyn was Henry VIII's mistress and Queen of England. In the early 1500s the King of England, Henry VIII, was married to a woman named Catherine. Henry never acknowledged this marriage, however. He fell in love with Anne Boleyn and pursued her as his paramour," she told him in German.

"Paramour?" her student asked.

Elizabeth thought a moment, determining the best way to explain. Holding up the index finger of her left hand, she plunged it in and out of a small circle made with the thumb and forefinger of her right hand.

She had Johann's attention.

"She finally gave in and became pregnant," Elizabeth said, using her hands to create an imaginary ripe womb.

"This means baby?" he said.

"This means trouble … for Henry, if the baby is a boy." Elizabeth continued in German with her summary of British monarchy. "Henry needed an heir to his throne, but a baby boy would not be recognized as heir if Henry was not married to Anne. So he secretly married Anne after she became pregnant. Many months later, the archbishop officially declared his marriage to Catherine invalid, and Anne was crowned queen.

"When Anne gave birth to Prin*cess* Elizabeth," she said, putting heavy emphasis on the second syllable, "she knew she needed to work hard to bear a son. She had several children to follow, but none was a boy. The last time she got pregnant, the baby—a boy— was born too early and did not live."

A strong wave knocked into the *Britannia*, and Elizabeth and Johann staggered momentarily before regaining their balance.

"Now Anne was no longer useful to the king," Elizabeth said. "Henry needed an heir, and he had a wandering eye."

Johann's quizzical expression suggested he did not understand the phrase.

"This means"—demonstrating with her fingers again—"with other women. But he had a problem. He had been successful in getting rid of Catherine, but now he needed to divorce Anne."

The sailor shook his head, confused.

"It means to *un*marry," she explained.

Johann understood. "New queen mean baby boy."

"Yes. Good old King Henry had already found a new girlfriend, but he couldn't marry *her* until he *un*married Anne. Of course, the king was very powerful, so his court made up a story that

Anne planned to kill Henry and take over his throne. They said she committed adultery." And once again, Elizabeth demonstrated copulation with her fingers.

"But not true?" he asked.

"No one knows, but probably not true. He was king, after all, and could do whatever he wanted to protect his power. They took Anne away to the Tower of London where she was pronounced guilty. That very week they cut off her head."

She translated this information with an imaginary swipe across her own throat.

"And King Henry?" Johann asked.

"Married his lover immediately, and she was the only queen to give him a son," Elizabeth said. "So when you tell me to tie a bowline knot, I think of Anne Boleyn."

Johann smiled, acknowledging he understood.

"Here is bowline," he said, holding the length of line, one end in each hand. "Here is little Anne," he began, making a small curl in the middle of the rope, like a loop. With his right hand grasping the right side of the rope, he brought it up to the curl.

"Henry say, 'Anne, Anne, please let me in!' But Anne say, 'No, you marry me.' So Henry say, 'I will marry,' and Anne lets him in." He passed the loose end of the rope up through the curl, leaving a length of rope hanging down as a big curl at the bottom.

"Now Henry tired with Anne. He go look udder women." The sailor took the right end of the rope and brought it around the length held in his left hand. "Henry look but cannot have. He find other woman—" and with those words he threaded the right end of the rope down through the small curl again, on top of the left length of rope, and pulled it tight. "Boleyn knot!"

Elizabeth took the rope in her own hands and made the knot correctly the first time. Johann beamed at his protégé and slapped her a bit too hard on her back.

"Is good for make strong loop. Boleyn knot is king of knots, but we call queen for you!" he said.

"The queen of knots," Elizabeth said. "I like it. Teach me another."

That night Elizabeth crawled into her bunk, unable to stop practicing in her mind all the different knots and their uses she had learned. Johann was an excellent instructor, providing clear directions and then setting her free to learn by rote. He stood nearby, rolling rope, polishing brass, or otherwise completing some task that left her feeling unsupervised. But when she made a mistake, almost by intuition, he was suddenly back again, offering an encouraging comment that helped her fix the error. Always with a knot's purposes in mind, he made certain to demonstrate their uses.

Elizabeth's head was swimming with different seamen's knots as she tried to fall asleep. She had tied knots used to relieve strain on another line. Square knots were easy, but Johann made her practice those the most, because they would never slip. Figure eights, sheet bends: the rote of overs and unders, loops for bends and hitches tied up her thoughts and kept her from floating away to sleep. She lay on the bunk, trying to capture a precious moment for herself without interruption from her husband or the children, with one finger lightly touching herself.

Louis dozed sporadically on the floor with his knees bent in the compartment barely six feet long and two feet wide. In the shadows Elizabeth could see the toll the voyage was taking on his frail frame.

The black night seeped into every little space now as the sea gently pitched and rolled rhythmically like a cradle on nighttime swells. The children slept peacefully to its sway.

"Elizabeth?" she heard her husband whisper in the darkness.

"Yes," she whispered back, barely more than an exhaled breath. The sound of his voice sent a surge of tingling as she kept rubbing gently, moistening her garment.

"I miss you," he answered. The ship groaned and swayed.

She could see the outline of his figure quietly stand and move toward her.

"Shhh," he said, and gently took her hand.

Standing in the dark, her husband wasted no time. He pressed into her, communicating his mutual desire, and kissed her quietly. When their lips parted, he led her quietly to a lower deck near the bow of the ship where the boatswain's storerooms offered the most privacy.

Moving as quickly and quietly as possible, she leaned up against a waist-high stack of fifty-pound burlap sacks and lifted her skirts.

After a while, he raised himself up to look into her eyes. She was smiling the happy smile of a contented woman. He smiled back at her, kissed her cheek, and wordlessly backed away. The two lovers slipped silently back into their compartment, holding hands and guarding the secret between them like some treasure.

Elizabeth would revisit the night's events many times during the rest of the voyage, reliving it, embellishing it, even changing it completely in her mind. The imagination is a sacred place that need not be shared with anyone. Not even her husband.

Chapter Three

When crew members heard the welcome jibe of several far-flying gulls native to the Bahama Islands, a plague of renewed optimism swept over *Britannia*. The gulls' call quickly became the predominant sound on deck. One child would begin, "Hahahaha—HAH, HAH!" and the infectious laughter would spread like nettle weeds from bow to stern until the ship sounded more like a nesting colony than a boatful of humans. Elizabeth showed the children Catesby's drawing of the red-billed bird, noting his jocular call and curious webbed feet with wings longer than its tail by some two inches.

Captain Franklyn announced that the West Indies would be visible by morning. Although the ship would not stop until they reached the Carolina coast, everyone was eager to see something other than sargassum islands—even if they could not disembark.

That evening, settling the children down to sleep was more difficult than usual. Even the littlest Timothée was a curious mix of fatigued exhilaration. "Mama," Mary Elizabeth said, stifling a yawn. "Do you think we shall be there soon?"

Elizabeth smiled and brushed an errant lock of hair away from her daughter's forehead. "We shall be there when we get there, M.E.," she responded. "And we are already one day closer, are we not? Now close your eyes," she instructed, "and dream of all the exciting adventures that await us."

Eventually, each little Timothée head slumped into a deliciously deep sleep with the birds' cackling laugh echoing in their heads and sweet memories of things they had not even imagined doing yet. Elizabeth, too, drifted off to sleep and dreamed of seeing other exotic feathered creatures depicted in Catesby's volumes.

* ★ *

"HEAVE TO!"

Elizabeth bolted upright, ripped from sleep in the dead of night by the loud command. The captain had turned the bow into the wind and furled the jib, forcing the hulking vessel to slow and stop. Ship's hands tumbled out of their hammocks and were putting their backs into lowering sail.

"What is happening?" Elizabeth whispered to Louis, lest they wake the children.

"I do not know," her husband answered. "Stay here."

Elizabeth trained her ears to glean some idea of what was going on. It was strange that, after the one order that had awakened her, all she could hear now were muffled whispers. No other noise breached the silence except *Britannia*'s creaking timbers—like the croak of some massive toad—and the constant liquid lick against her heavy hull.

Elizabeth lay very still, listening. Her breathing was shallow and rapid; she could hear her heartbeat in her ears.

"This will never do," she decided after some length of time. Dressing quickly in the frock she had been wearing that day, she padded barefoot up to the deck, determined to learn some news.

Britannia's sails hung from her masts like tall trees amid their autumn decay. All lights had been extinguished on deck and below; sails were rigged to catch wind and fly, ready to be raised at the captain's word. Elizabeth, intuitively realizing that silence was crucial to their safety, crept quietly to the rail. No man whispered. Few men even moved. The ship was a hole in the water, silent as the grave. The ocean, slapping *Britannia*'s hull, sounded like the lapping tongues of a hundred blood-thirsty hounds. Elizabeth swallowed hard.

She had heard the pirate threat had been dealt with some ten years ago, but it would be impossible to say with any real confidence that there were no rogues still plundering, especially since passenger and cargo ships made the transatlantic voyage more and more frequently. Elizabeth told herself that the danger of attacking a large ship, fully loaded with cargo and passengers, was a much greater risk. But with great risk comes great reward. These criminals of the high seas seemed to be drawn to both.

A prepubescent voice whispered behind her.

"Ma'am, 'tis not safe." It was the captain's cabin boy.

"Where are we?" she asked in hushed tones.

"Island of Antego, Mum," he answered, barely above a whisper. Sensing either her apprehension or wishing to dispel his own, he added, "Not to worry, though. Cap'n Anson patrols these waters."

"Who is Captain Anson?" she asked.

"He be the commander of the HMS *Scarborough*, assigned to protect Charles Towne from threat of pirates. A young man, really. No buccaneer gets past him, though, no sirree."

Elizabeth nodded to the mate and smiled. For the first time since she had been startled awake, she took a deep, slow breath. She filled her lungs with the cool night air, drawing it down, into the bottom of her lungs, and then expelling it slowly.

The ship rolled peacefully on dark swells; wind, mingled with the sound of muffled conversations, reminded Elizabeth more of gentle white-capped waves than of human voices. She looked up, hoping to see a shooting star for good luck, but immediately scolded herself for foolishly pinning her hopes on anything less than hard work and divine intervention. Still, she allowed herself to believe that, if she saw a shooting star, perhaps it was a sign that the Almighty was there, watching and protecting.

Naught but black, though, in every direction. Clouds obscured a midnight sky that was already shrouded in the pitch of a new moon.

Britannia was hiding under God's blanket, hoping desperately to pass undetected.

An ear-splitting boom, followed closely by a strange whistling sound and the sickening smell of rotten eggs, tore through the stillness mere moments before the deafening impact of timbers splintering and chaotic screams: orders, cries, mayhem.

Men, women, and children, aroused abruptly and dazed with fright, flooded the deck in their nightshirts like a ghostly invasion. The ship's crew ran in every direction, yelling panicked orders at each other and knocking several passengers down on their faces in the inky blackness.

Captain Franklyn's string of obscenity-laced commands, bellowed from the quarterdeck, were difficult to hear above the loud crack of cannon fire and screams. "Raise the sails! William! William? Where are you? Bring the ship about! *IK kan mijn broer vinden!* Get below decks! See your gasket clear for passing! *Mutter, wo sind Sie?* Catherine, over here!"

Britannia was making sail and returning fire.

Deckhands scrambled to sort out the captain's frenetically screamed orders and comply. Elizabeth turned and ran toward the ladder at midship. It was not her safety, but the safety of the children, that was foremost on her mind. Overhead, sparks lit up the sky, revealing in oblique snatches the attacking sloop some four furlongs beyond. All the rest was ubiquitous cursing, gunfire, orders barked from opposing captains, and the chaotic multilingual screams of men, women, and children bound up in the prevailing evil. Waves crashed over the side of *Britannia* as she lurched forward, turning hard to catch a strong wind that could take them out of harm's way. Passengers caught off guard were knocked off their feet; Elizabeth's cheek slammed into the deck before she could sort out how she had ended up on the floor.

Crewmen scurried like mice let loose from the sewers, overrunning the deck and clambering up the single, large mainsail to tie off line.

"Go out on the weather side of the boom," one of the crew barked as men hauled sail, including the sheet pennant amidships, getting the clew.

"Pass the turns over and to windward," the crewman yelled as Elizabeth struggled unsuccessfully to put her feet underneath her.

From all fours she turned toward the boom just as it caught a sailor in his midsection and flung him beyond the safety of the ship's walls. The sound of the poor man's violent expectoration of air—forcibly rendered when the massive wooden boom hit his body—left little doubt in Elizabeth's mind that he would drown quickly if the impact had not already killed him. Standing, she clutched the side of the cabin and searched frantically for the overboard sailor. Elizabeth knew the shipmaster would not risk crew and cargo to fish one man out—a peril of the sea, and the heavy weight of responsibility borne by their captain.

At the same time, one huge wave, with an explosion of water as loud as gunpowder, slammed into *Britannia*'s starboard bow and buried up half the cabin. Thunderous drops of seawater showered down on her, crackling like black-powder firecrackers. As the ship pitched and rolled under the water's weight, personal belongings spilled out from below decks: pewter plates and cups, bedding, wet clothing—tangled and swirling like pale intestines slashed loose from the belly—pitched up with the ocean's fierce undulations. The floor rose to meet her. She adjusted her step to a shallower depth just as *Britannia* rolled down a wave column. Before her brain could register the fall, Elizabeth was already tumbling forward, an inert stone rolling intractably downhill. Spray pummeled her again, saturating her from head to toe. Whether from cold or fear, or both, Elizabeth's teeth chattered uncontrollably. Wet and disoriented, she struggled to regain her footing as she pushed wet hair out of her salt-stung eyes and coughed up the briny seawater that had penetrated her nose and mouth.

Another wall of water followed closely behind, but she managed to outrun it and reached the portal to belowdecks. *Britannia* was putting distance between herself and the pirate ship. The sound of cannon fire was becoming more distant and less threatening as the ocean underneath buoyed them away from danger.

Her husband, poking his head out of the ship's hold like a prairie dog, caught sight of her first and extended his hand to help her down the ladder. "Where have you been?" he coughed out, as much of an admonishment as a question. Louis was shaking—from fear or the cold seawater, she could not say.

"I went above on deck to look for you," she answered apologetically. "And then the pirates started firing at us and—"

"They were not firing at us," Louis replied, putting his arm around her shoulders. "They were firing at the *Scarborough*. We simply had the misfortune of being in the way."

Elizabeth felt her control returning under Louis's embrace. The children vied for positions to hug parts of her body.

"We were so worried, Mother," little Mary Elizabeth said, struggling to choke back her sobs.

"I shall be ever so glad to be on land again, Louis," she breathed, and in the dark they found each other's mouths and kissed passionately.

Chapter Four

When Elizabeth awoke the next morning, conditions had taken a turn for the worse. While they were safely out of range from the previous night's anarchic events, there was no escaping the weather. Angry thunderheads seemed to hunt them, snarling and circling in every direction. Dark clouds smoldered where water met horizon, and thunderheads rose as sooty billows to foreboding heights, like the Pompeii volcanoes Elizabeth imagined. Blue-green water had been replaced with a dark pool, roiling and gnashing with foamy white fangs at *Britannia*'s sides.

Elizabeth climbed up on deck to find her husband and Johann talking in low tones. As she approached, the two men ended their conversation.

"Good morning, Johann," she said, pulling close to her husband to shield herself from intermittent spits of rain. Elizabeth rubbed her arms to warm herself to no avail.

"It is frightfully chilly this morning," she said.

Johann nodded and looked up.

"Weather coming," he said, tilting his head toward the heavens suspiciously.

Elizabeth followed his gaze. "Will you be in class today?"

"No ma'am. Cap'n says every mate on deck. No lesson today."

As if confirming his assessment, the wind picked up, separating some solid substance from its solution and blowing tiny caustic drops against Elizabeth's face like a thousand pins and needles. Thunder rolled ominously through the mountainous clouds: growling, circling as if evaluating when and where to strike. Cracks of lightning cast bright white scars where pieces of sky had been sliced away.

Elizabeth shivered at the chill of the approaching storm. Her long brown hair, tied loosely in a bun, whipped across her eyes and into her mouth. Except for Johann and a few other crewmen, everyone else was belowdecks, preparing for the worst of the storm. Only a handful of passengers braved the main deck, hoping for a few more gulps of fresh air before hiding below under battened hatches. With a nod to Louis and Elizabeth, Johann took his leave, making deliberate steps toward the helm.

Still damp from the night before, Elizabeth drew her dressing gown close about her body to shield against the spattering cold drops of rain and salt water. She could taste brine in the spatter, kicked up onto her lips from wind-whipped ocean.

"It certainly is wicked weather this morning," she said.

"Yes," Louis answered, looking skyward. "We may be in for a very bad storm."

"Well," Elizabeth offered, as much to draw him out as to make polite conversation, "our water reserves could benefit from a bit of rainfall."

"We would often be sorry if our wishes were gratified," Louis quoted, immediately wishing he had simply praised her attempt at optimism. His wife was too clever to miss the reference, and he did not want to alarm her.

"'The Old Man and Death,'" she replied, recognizing Aesop's fable. "Our faggots of wood are raindrops."

Louis nodded.

"Then," Elizabeth sighed and followed her husband's gaze, "I am not so thirsty as I thought."

She moved in closer to him, snuggling under his left arm and shivering from fear now, as much as from damp and cold.

"The crew know how to bring us through," Louis said, raising his left hand up to calm her loosely tied hair now blowing ominously with each gust. "They have spent their lives on the ocean battling squalls worse than this."

It was little consolation. The storm's temerity was becoming frightening even to the crew. Elizabeth could see it in the eyes of those few who had been ordered to remain on deck, and in the hasty way they carried out their tasks. Stepping out from his grasp, she took a few timorous steps toward the rail and wrapped her arms tightly around herself.

"We have come this far," she said. "I do not believe God would abandon us now," she tried to reassure herself.

"Yes," Louis answered in raised tones to be heard above the wind, "but we best not tempt Him," he said, making his way to the down hatch.

"Time to go below."

When he turned to make sure she was behind him, he saw her obscured silhouette still standing where they had been talking, visible now only between blasts of slanted rain and sea water.

"Elizabeth!" he called out as loudly as he could, but the salt and sound burned his throat. She turned toward his voice; a gust caught her dressing gown, billowing it out behind her like the figurehead at the ship's prow. The wind howled as if carrying the baying of a wolf pack. With slow, determined steps, she was moving toward him when a thunderous wave crashed over *Britannia*'s side. The ship heaved leeward, and gale-force winds shoved the massive ship over like a breaching whale. Salt water engulfed Elizabeth, forcing its way into her throat and nose and burning her eyes. Coughing, she managed to stand, only marginally aware that she had been flung to the starboard-side rail. The wailing wind growled furiously, as if circling for easy prey.

A faint but frantic cry, barely audible above the furious storm, caught Elizabeth's ear. Looking over the side of the ship she could just make out a figure flailing in the angry drink.

"Overboard!" she screamed at the top of salt-stung lungs, but no one could hear her above the crashing wind and sea.

To her right lay a coil of line, tied off at a cleat. She grabbed the loose end, working quickly through numb fingers and sea-spattered eyes. Desperately, she flung the knotted rope over the side in the direction of the voice in the water.

Someone above her yelled, "Grab the line!"

It was the captain. From his vantage point, he could see the man in the water but was too far away to lend a hand.

Elizabeth knew the person in the water had found the line when her leg was suddenly strapped to the rail.

"Put it over your head!" she yelled as the rope cut into her rectus femoris like splintered wood.

Thick red blood leached onto her gown and was immediately pelted pink by rain and sea water. She could not move, even if she wished to. The priority at present was retrieving the lost soul from a yowling sea.

Within some unknown lapse of time, two people stood beside her, pulling the razor-tight rope away from her. She knew it had cut her leg muscle, but Elizabeth managed to stand. The crewmen worked quickly, some pulling on the length of rope to provide some slack, and the others rolling the rope down to her ankles. One mate lifted her clear and put her behind them. Then the two men heaved in unison to tow the overboard man close to the hull and then up, by inches it seemed, until he could at last grasp the guardrail of the spar deck.

Johann, wet but determined, hoisted himself up enough for the crewmen to grab his waist. With their help he managed to get one leg over the side. From there, they dragged the massive German sailor back into the relative safety of the ship, a sputtering, sopping heap of a man.

Shivering and dazed, Johann was helped to his feet as torrents of rain pelted the tiny brigade. The lifeline Elizabeth had tossed him was still tied tightly around the hulking mate, securely under his arms where he had managed to get it and keep it. Working quickly, the crewmen helped him out of the rope, and en masse, the four of them made their way by steps and lunges toward the hatch leading to lower decks.

Someone wrapped a blanket around Elizabeth's cold, wet frame, soaked with blood and rain and seawater. The deep laceration on her leg suddenly made her feel very dizzy, and she bent her head toward the floor in case she might get sick. Her teeth would not stop chattering between blue, quivering lips.

Behind her, a huge grip encompassed her shoulders. She turned and looked up into the grateful eyes of her oldest student and her youngest teacher.

"Boleyn," she said.

Johann laughed, Elizabeth laughed, and they both dissolved into tears.

Chapter Five

*B*ritannia entered Charles Towne harbor late afternoon Saturday, September 15, according to the hand-drawn Gregorian calendar Elizabeth and the children had been keeping. The weather was hot and muggy, much like the West Indies but lacking the islands' gentle breezes. Certainly not the chilly autumn of her homeland, she thought, but then quickly dismissed the melancholy notion before it could take root.

Out of a porthole Elizabeth lowered a bucket into the ocean, drawing up a pailful of sea water and promising herself that the first thing she would do on their brief stopover in the Carolina Colony would be to find a proper place to bathe. With a damp cloth she blotted her forehead and the back of her neck, allowing her gaze to wander beyond the porthole to White Point, just coming into view. Her eyes traveled down the coast, trying to determine the structures that were still just specks on the horizon. The city had a formal entrance on the Cooper River; an imposing two-story building had been built atop Half Moon Battery. Charles Towne, the port city for all the Carolinas, was quite elegant. *What a beautiful place*, she thought. *Hot, but beautiful.*

As they entered the mouth of the harbor, Elizabeth could see Johnson's Fort off their port side. Charles Towne lay dead ahead.

She cupped a hand over her brow to shield her eyes from the setting sun. Even from three furlongs out, it was clear the town bore little resemblance to the ancient cities of her home. Holland's buildings, her Hooglandse Kerks and universities, the Trippenhuis of Amsterdam, even the weavers' houses, were all mature, stately structures rising out of cobbled streets and canals. But Charles Towne had her own charm, she thought, and from what she had heard, the town was already becoming a formidable British presence for trade and government in the southern Atlantic Ocean.

Colonel Rhett's bridge, where the captain had told them they would dock, was still some distance away, but the tiny dots she had observed from the harbor's mouth now appeared as miniature people, bustling to and fro along the great length of the bastion. Beyond the bridge, Elizabeth focused her attention to the north where a church steeple ripped a seam in the heavens. It was the most imposing structure in the sky, literally towering over the city's walls like a giant monarch reigning over Charles Towne. Elizabeth felt immediately safer in its shadow as the sun set over the Ashley River, casting a cool, dark spire of respite and protection deep into the ocean on the peninsula's Cooper River side.

The possibility of stepping off the boat had swept quickly through the ship, spreading renewed vigor in passengers and crew. Even the sickest among them greeted the news with a hopeful glimmer in their eyes.

The children clambered around Elizabeth's skirts with uncontained enthusiasm at the prospect of being off the ship. Their constant motion, compounded by the pregnancy, made her feel a bit nauseated.

"Now children," Elizabeth warned, "this is a short stopover. We will be docking soon but only for a little while. We are fortunate to be able to do that, but we must remember to obey Captain Franklyn and return promptly when told."

"Yea!" Peter exclaimed, a veritable whirling dervish of a boy with so much pent-up energy Elizabeth thought he would have to be strapped to the mizzenmast to calm him down. "Perhaps we shall see some INDIANS!"

Her rambunctious six-year-old ran circles around them, yelling and whooping like the apparent savage that he was.

"Peter! Settle yourself, young man. If you continue to act this way, I shall have no compunction about leaving you on the ship while the rest of us go exploring. You will miss seeing the New World *and* any Indians we may encounter."

Elizabeth knew the waiting was the worst part for the children. Truth be told, it was just as difficult for the adults.

As the ship creaked closer, Elizabeth sat distractedly with her hands limp in her lap, watching the nearing skyline of Charles Towne. She wondered if the children would remember any of the seaside town harbors *Britannia* had passed. Charles Towne afforded them their best opportunity yet, since their sad goodbyes, to feel genuinely hopeful about the decision to come to America. The memory can be so fickle, and the mind so weak, to maintain remembrances of horrible images over those more pleasant. Elizabeth wanted her children to walk the city's streets and smell the universal comfort of suppers cooking at a hearth—meats roasting and soups boiling, familiar smells, even though this was foreign territory to them. She wanted them to hear the pleasant echoes of children's laughter as they played, of hoof and carriage striking cobbled stones, of vendors hawking produce, and of bustling city life. And even though they were not quite there yet, she wanted them to feel that they were almost home, by God's good grace. There would be time for remembering what they had left behind, and what they had endured to arrive at their new beginning. For now, Elizabeth wanted them to remember what they could look forward to.

"Wave off! WAVE OFF!"

Several men on the dock were yelling at the ship and at each other, waving their arms, running along the wharf as *Britannia* almost reached the first bridge.

"Webb! Warn them off! Tell them to steer clear, George!" screamed a man at the shoreline.

Cupping his hands around his mouth to help the sound carry farther, he repeated the warning: "Tell them it is the FEVER. THE FEVER!"

George Webb, a short, balding man with long sideburns and rumpled clothing, had been talking with another man at the end of the wharf when he suddenly sprang into action like a man accustomed to emergencies. He immediately began waving the rolled-up broadsheet that had been tucked under his arm. As it unfurled, it reminded Elizabeth of a flag, and he of an unlikely patriot, defending against an enemy with whatever implements he had available. In this case, it was just the printed word.

"Stay back!" he cried. "Turn about!"

The man seemed so insistent that Elizabeth could not help but be alarmed. Telling the children to go below, she followed her husband in search of the captain.

"What is it, Louis?" she asked.

"I do not know," he said without stopping. "Some sort of problem, without doubt," he added, breaking into a trot toward the captain. Elizabeth was right behind him. When they caught up to him, Louis asked the captain what was wrong.

"Yellow fever," Franklyn replied. "We cannot dock at Charles Towne."

Hearing this news, Elizabeth took shallow breaths. Her pregnancy was still not known to her husband, and she was determined to keep it to herself as long as possible. Louis did not need this on his narrow shoulders; if he knew she was pregnant, he would not allow her to minister to the sick. He would insist that she stop lifting things. He would demand that she rest. For the remainder of the voyage, he would give her his food, or worse, insist that the children do the same. She could barely keep her own share down now. Yet it never ceased to amaze her how men, even highly intelligent ones like her husband, could miss so many obvious cues. Even seasickness wears off after a time, and surely, he could not believe that the thickness around her waist was a result of so many excellent meals. Of course she would tell him, in due time, and he would be surprised and pleased as always. But he did not need this burdensome blessing now.

"Are we in danger?" she asked.

"I do not believe so. There is yellow fever there, and I am told infection is generally located around the waterfront. But we have not had contact with the town," Louis said. "I believe we were warned off soon enough."

They stood together, watching the coast shrink as *Britannia* came about, and turned her rudder against the southernmost city toward the open sea.

"I would have sold my soul for a hot bath," she remarked, resting her head against her husband's shoulder.

"A hot bath you shall have, my love, in less than two weeks, God willing. But it will not cost you your soul, as this one might have."

Peter ran to his parents at full bore, a stick in his hand aimed at his friend Joshua's head.

"I will have your scalp, savage!" he threatened, and lunged at the younger boy.

Louis grabbed his son by the shoulders and demanded he hand him the stick.

"Joshua will keep his scalp. You will see no redskins this day," he said.

No redskins, Elizabeth thought, *but mercifully, no yellow skins either.*

Chapter Six

When the mates announced their entry into Delaware Bay after a little over ten weeks at sea, everyone flushed out from belowdecks to find a spot at the ship's rail. *Britannia* was finally winding her way up the Delaware River toward the docks of William Penn's Philadelphia, offering their first view of the Promised Land. Wild geese flew overhead in the shape of an inverted "V" as if pointing the direction. The flock was a moving embroidery, satin-stitched to form branching lines onto the sky itself, a pale blue cloth. Their grating honks, mingled with the gulls' language of soprano squeaks and moans, seemed insistent on *Britannia* following them, and on drowning out the captain's shouted announcements. But even the welcoming gun salutes, made to seem louder as they echoed off harbor structures, were not enough to overpower passengers' weeping and singing and cheering as *Britannia* creaked her way upriver toward her waiting berth. The snail's pace of the ship was practically unbearable to the beating hearts of her human cargo. Some passengers rocked back and forth, hands clasped at their chests, as if attempting to move the ship faster with the momentum of their body weight.

Elizabeth laughed and cried while Louis, overcome with emotion, hoisted three-year-old Mary Elizabeth onto his shoulders, hoping the child's first image of their new home would be burned into her memory. The girl waved to the crowd on shore as if she were aboard a floating parade and she the grand marshal of it all.

Elizabeth doubted Charles would remember much of the scene as she struggled to hold the squirmy one-year-old in her arms, but Peter and Louisa certainly would. Louisa stood on tiptoes and snuggled close to her mother while Peter, held tightly by his father to contain the boy, whooped and waved wildly to strangers on the wharves as if they were relatives at long last reunited. The professor somehow managed to spread his arms to cover all of his family and wept.

"I wonder if they really know what to expect," Louis said, wiping his eyes and surveying *Britannia*'s passengers. "The New World is a wilderness full of wild Indians and dangerous beasts. Philadelphia is settled, to be sure, but her streets are not paved with gold, and beyond her walls is still a rough frontier."

"I am most interested in what is beyond this deck at the moment," Elizabeth gibed. "A hot bath, for instance."

"Again, with the 'hot bath,' my dear? Is there nothing else you desire beyond that?" her husband joked.

"Nothing else for the present," Elizabeth replied, "but I promise, as soon as I have soaked until I am pruned, I will turn my attention to other pursuits."

"*Moeder*, when may we leave the ship?" Peter asked his mother in Dutch.

"Peter, you must remember to use your English now," she corrected. "We may leave as soon as we are safely tied up at the dock."

"But I can see the dock now," he insisted, fidgeting at her side.

"Son"—Louis bent down to eye level with the boy to make sure he had his full attention—"we will leave when the captain gives the order. Not before."

It had crossed Elizabeth's mind to offer another day or two of lessons to keep the children occupied.

They could practice their arithmetic, she thought. If a ship left Holland with 358 people aboard and arrives in Pennsylvania with 269 people, what is the percentage of human loss? *No*, she reasoned, quickly dismissing the idea. *Let us practice only our patience at this point in the voyage.* Even she could not concentrate on lessons. Nothing except a mooring line tossed from a deckhand to a quay master would soothe that particular itch.

While the crew of *Britannia* tended to the business of docking and stowing sails and lines, the passengers—people whom the Timothées had come to know well in such humbling circumstances for so many long weeks at sea—struggled to express farewells. Elizabeth watched while some offered no words, just hugs and handshakes. Several of the men could only lock gazes for the merest moment, accompanied by upturned corners of the mouth and an almost imperceptible nod before walking away without comment. Others attempted to articulate how grateful they were, how sorry they were, how hopeful they were, but in the end, the words were woefully short of the mark.

Elizabeth looked for Johann, but deciding his duties must be keeping him busy, she abandoned the search. It was awkward, really, to have had such an intimate kinship, for so long, with so many. It was easier to leave it unexpressed. Here they were now. What had begun as a grand adventure now required them to put feet to their dreams. Elizabeth knew the hard part was just beginning.

"Welcome to America!" the professor said, his voice belying a man on the verge of tears.

The Timothées moved toward *Britannia*'s gangplank, a short bridge over so long a journey. But Louis would be the only family member allowed to leave the ship.

Captain Franklyn had prepared the sea-weary passengers well for the landing. All those who had come as indentured servants would be met by their new masters. Passengers meeting relatives could inquire at the newspaper office about their family members. Inns were available for those who could afford them; for those who could not, the Quaker Friendly Society offered shelter and food. Franklyn made it clear, however, that every passenger or representative of passengers on board was to immediately go to the courthouse to take the oath of fidelity to the king of Great Britain.

All full-fare men over sixteen years of age gathered on the deck as a group—101 men in all—to be marched en masse to the courthouse. Women, children under sixteen, and indentured passengers were culled off to the side.

"It will not take long," Louis assured Elizabeth. "I will take the oath and sign my name. I will return as soon as possible."

Elizabeth smiled and nodded, knowing the requirement and fully prepared to become a subject of the English throne. *It is just a little while longer on the ship*, she consoled herself. And then the whole Timothée family could step over the threshold to their new home.

Elizabeth let her mind wander to their last night on board; the captain had made a point of complimenting Louis in front of her, telling him he had not seen so much learning in a crossing.

"Many can sign their names now," he said, "and all of us know more English."

Louis had accepted the compliment, but he was keenly aware that most of the passengers knew it was Madame Timothée who deserved the credit.

After the captain had left, Louisa asked her mother if it bothered her that Captain Franklyn had not given her credit for all the teaching she had done.

Elizabeth chuckled, leaned over, and whispered in her daughter's ear, "There is no limit to what you can do if you do not care who gets the credit."

Putting a finger across the child's mouth to warn her not to let the secret out, she said in Dutch, "That is my secret. I give it to you for your secret too."

It was common knowledge that Captain Franklyn had let Monsieur Timothée work off part of his family's passage by keeping the official roster, but few realized Madame Timothée had done most of the work. Although the wise professor had spelled all the passengers' names correctly regardless of ethnicity, he had left blanks for each passenger's age. Elizabeth, accustomed to proofreading behind her husband, had gone around to each person and filled in the blanks as accurately as possible.

"One's work is incomplete if the i's are not dotted and the t's are not crossed," she had told him many times, hoping he would develop her keen attention to detail.

But the only thing he developed was a keen reliance on her to check his work.

Elizabeth decided she would use the opportunity to teach this truism to her husband. To that end, she left off the ages of all the Timothées, hoping he would see the error himself before turning the completed list over to the captain.

She had mentioned it again, several days before the ship had docked.

"It is a good thing I check behind you," Elizabeth said. "I wanted to see if the top journeyman in the best shop in London and teacher of French, Latin, and German could come up with his family's ages."

Louis would have filled in those blanks—with her help, of course—but now he was resolved not to ask his wife for any information at all.

The American gulls soared and dived above her like little schoolgirls in an aerial playground, bringing her back to the present moment. Elizabeth handed her husband the passenger list and watched from the forecastle as the men left *Britannia* to set foot, for the first time, on Philadelphia soil. All of a sudden, the gangplank was down, and the men dispersed into the colony's crowded streets like chickens in different directions.

Elizabeth wanted to say goodbye to her older students, to hug those who had lost relatives on the voyage, to assure fellow passengers that their families would keep in touch. But the opportunity was swallowed up in the frenetic activity of moving forward into new lives.

The shorter days of mid-September cast golden highlights on the water and the dock and the treetops, giving the city the illusion of indeed being paved with gold. Elizabeth wrapped her shawl tightly around her. Soon her husband would return, a newly sworn subject of the Crown. Perhaps he would have news of Benjamin Franklin, and of a place to take a bath.

Chapter Seven

Louis was certain he could find lodging for his family somewhere in the second-largest city in the British Empire, but he had no idea how long he could finance their stay. At Elizabeth's suggestion, he had kept the ship's log for the captain and inventoried supplies in return for part of their passage, but the surplus coins she had sewn in their coat linings would not hold out forever. As he wandered up first one cobbled street and then another, his confidence in finding a suitable room at a reasonable rate began to wane with the fading light.

Dimly lit stars, the merest pinpricks, shuddered sheepishly overhead as lamplighters, walking with purpose, began to appear on Philadelphia's streets. With wide strides they raised their long fiery-tipped poles up to the streetlamps, then swung them down again—on to the next lamp—while a thin trail of smoke from the burning wick followed behind like a priest swinging incense. As darkness closed in, the lamplighters reminded Louis of huge fireflies darting from lamp to lamp. Timothée suddenly felt like a Lilliputian in *Gulliver's Travels*: so small and powerless against the night.

When the lamplighters' work was complete, an amber glow cast shadows that spilled into the streets, transforming the foreboding, unknown territory into a paved milky way in the heavens. Louis, emboldened by the light, renewed his determined footsteps toward securing a room for the night.

Rounding a corner, he turned onto Walnut Street where the Quakers ran an almshouse. Louis had walked right past it the first time, thinking they were private residences. Six of the most commodious little houses, entered through a yard, sat quaintly off the street. He would have passed them a second time had a Quaker not been on the street at that very moment. The strange gentleman removed his hat and bowed.

"May I be of service?" he asked.

"Why, yes, if it is no trouble," Louis responded. "I require a room for me and my family this evening. I cannot pay much, as we are just off the *Britannia,* and I have not yet secured gainful employment."

"My dear fellow," the funny little man said, "step inside. We are all friends here. Follow me."

Louis accepted the invitation, following him into one of the dwellings where he found a warm, well-lit room large enough for a table that seated at least twenty new Pennsylvania citizens. The atmosphere thickened with stories in different tongues as plates were passed and cups were filled and napkins were tucked into collars or placed in laps, anxious to receive a good, hot meal. It was something most had not enjoyed in a long while, and the cheerfulness engendered by the mere thought of it was palpable. Louis, too, found his mouth salivating at the sight of roast duck, boiled potatoes, and carrots with hot tea to drink. The Quakers knew food is the lowest common denominator for bringing people together. They made no secret of providing what each soul needed at the moment they needed it: a hot meal, a hot bath, a clean room with a bed to rest your head. And by the looks of the place, their efforts were succeeding.

After making arrangements to stay overnight, Louis took his leave.

"I will return soon with my family," he told the gentleman he had met on the street. "And again, my most sincere gratitude for your invitation. A hot meal and a room are a godsend."

The man smiled and said, "It is the least I can do for a fellow traveler. It is what Christ the Savior would have us do, and so woefully short of what He has done for us."

The two men shook hands, and Louis walked to the door.

"I hope you find what you are looking for in Pennsylvania, my good fellow," the older gentleman said. "'Tis a land of opportunity to be sure. They do not call it 'the best poor man's country' for nothing."

On the way back to the ship, Louis decided it would be best to tell Elizabeth that he had gone to the almshouse to ask after suitable lodging.

"While there, making inquiries," he practiced out loud, "I was offered a room gratis for the night. And since the hour was growing late, I took it, confident that we will find more permanent lodging in the light of a new day."

He saw no need to burden her with the details. She was sure to have questions, but he could stave them off till the morning. Once bathed, fed, and rested, his first priority, he knew, was finding a job, with no time to lose. Timothée could live and work as he pleased, but he must also pay his own way.

A free night's lodging is a welcome offer, even at a Quaker shelter for the poor, he reasoned. *And in the light of a new day*, he thought, *when the darkness has retreated, circumstances will seem more manageable. Best to have a good night's sleep before tackling the giants of tomorrow.*

Chapter Eight

Elizabeth, resigned to the possibility of at least one more night aboard the ship, settled her sleepy children on pallets on the main deck while they waited for their father. She found herself envying the indentured passengers who were met by farmers and tradespeople; they would be shown where to go and whom to see and what work they must do to repay the ten pounds sterling advanced for their passage. It could take years to pay off the debt, she knew, but at least they had a place to sleep tonight. The Timothées had just completed a journey across an ocean, but there was no one to greet them by their names.

Feeling alone and so far from home, she wondered if they had made a huge mistake.

Elizabeth tried not to worry, but as the night wore on—dark, and then inky black, cold, and then bitterly cold—she found it more and more difficult to keep frightening notions from intruding her mind. What if Louis was unable to return? She was not even sure which way he had gone, should they try to find him.

The falling temperatures coming off the water bit sharply at their exposed skin. Elizabeth gathered the children into a tight-knit clutch, hoping it would provide some modicum of warmth for them, while she searched for some sign of Louis. Every man of slight build resembled her husband, but each time it was not Louis. Fewer and fewer men returned. She was weary from hoping.

She forced herself to think of happy thoughts, recalling the day she first met Louis Timothée in her father's print shop. Life has a quixotic way of making events seem like a distant memory and, at the same time, as if it were just yesterday. She had been so young, not yet having reached majority. He was so frightening as he bowed and took her gloved hand in his. His blue eyes never once blinked as he raised her hand to kiss it. She was determined to hold his gaze, though, and she did, for some time. But when his lips kissed the delicate lace on the top of her hand, she could not continue. Whatever he was saying with his eyes was more than she could comprehend.

And yet, she was intensely curious about the strange new emotions he ignited in her.

She made excuses to be in his presence at every opportunity. Louis, the much older, fair-skinned man of slim build and barely a knuckle length taller than she, worked for her father in Holland. The printing business fascinated Louis, but it was her father's captivating young daughter who interested him most. Elizabeth worked in the printing shop as well, and almost immediately Louis appreciated her quick eye for catching a printing flaw and her deft hand for setting type. He found her to be a striking, yet harmonious blend of her English and German lineage: slender, delicate facial features of the British, with the birthing hips of her Teutonic ancestry. Genteel, well-spoken, and fluid in motion as any well-bred English woman, she also possessed the hardiness and fortitude of any good German. She applied these character traits to all she set her mind to do.

As a printer's apprentice, Louis was quite gifted, but after he and Elizabeth married and the babies began to arrive, it was apparent the business could not support them and their growing family. Elizabeth's brother would inherit their father's business, of course, and Louis felt he was more suited for the academic world anyway. His greatest desire was to start a university in the new world. He was persuaded, by an American gentleman with a curious knack for persuasion, to come to America.

"Mr. Franklin," Elizabeth had said, well into their established friendship, "You are the jack of all trades," and she meant it as the true compliment that it was.

There was no superficiality to the man; when he began a new study, he dove deep. His only major fault, if it could be termed that, was that he simply was not capable of choosing just one swimming hole.

Her husband, of course, was much the same—intensely curious and a lifelong learner, two prized attributes for any good teacher. Timothée was a brilliant man in many subjects, but his real gift was in setting fire to the spark of his students' academic interests—even the older ones, like Franklin.

At the end of many a work day, Elizabeth recalled, Louis often met a group of intellectual friends at a pub; it was not long after their introduction when Louis invited Ben to join them, unaware that Franklin had no taste for beer.

"Franklin, allow me to introduce you to my chums," Louis said, explaining to his British friends that this was the Water American about whom he had spoken.

Louis had given the eighteen-year-old champion swimmer the nickname as a compliment intended to convey his athletic prowess, but the Englishmen, keen on their grog, adopted it to mean that the young Philadelphian preferred a pint of water to a pint of beer. Franklin quickly proved himself to be as comfortable on the receiving end of a joke as he was on the giving end, and he wasted no time forging strong bonds with all of them.

"My dear man," one of his new British buddies observed, "you swim in water. You drink water. I do believe you would breathe water if you could."

Ben, without hesitation, pushed his chair back and stood up. With the thumb and forefinger of each hand he grabbed the tops of his ears and pulled them forward.

"I invite each of you to observe the odd configuration behind my ears," Franklin stated matter-of-factly. "It has always seemed a bit fishy to me."

The table erupted in laughter at his quick wit.

But while the other boys grew thick around the middle, Elizabeth noticed that Franklin continued to cut an imposing figure with his height and extraordinary good looks: broad shoulders by virtue of his predilection for the butterfly stroke, well-defined abdominal muscles leading to a trim waistline, and the thighs of a marble sculpture. It was rare indeed to meet a man so handsome and also so intelligent. His blue-gray eyes held a gaze captive; his dark-brown hair and an impish smile always raised a question of true motivation when he employed his considerable powers of persuasion. Benjamin Franklin was a lady-charmer—and he was well aware of it. Yet it was Louis whom he targeted for a partnership.

When the young Philadelphian offered the older man a job, he made certain to speak to Louis's interests. Franklin knew Timothée had long considered bringing his family to the New World. He would not be wooed, however, with mere promises of adventure or success. Franklin took the time, like a lion—patient and cunning—to understand Louis's goals for himself and his family before he moved in for the kill. Some might call it being a good listener. Elizabeth called it being a good beguiler, and she cautioned her husband to beware of his new friend Mephistopheles. And yet, she could not help but be intrigued by him and his ideas too.

Ben was eager to put feet on an old dream: publishing a newspaper in German, the native tongue of hordes immigrating to the City of Brotherly Love. There was talk that German should be the official language of Penns Woods, and it was true that German was heard in the marketplace more than English. Germans already outnumbered the English, and more were arriving by the boatload. Ben was completely unable to write in German himself, but he could see the possibilities.

"Philadelphia has been ready for a German newspaper for years now," the shrewd businessman confided to Louis, "and you are just the one to write it for me. I have been looking for scholars, printers, linguists, and librarians for a long time, but I never believed I would find them all in one man."

Franklin himself was self-educated, innately curious, and driven to learn everything about anything, but he was not an academic like Elizabeth's husband.

"Knowing languages as you do will be a decided advantage," Ben assured him. "If you should want to give French lessons, I for one will be an eager pupil."

Soon Franklin had the Timothées' agreement to come to America.

"I cannot promise you a job yet, but someday I am going to have a print shop and newspaper that could make good use of the likes of you. Why not look me up in Philadelphia?"

And so, here they were. Their family had made the crossing to America, the spot on the map where they had pinned their hopes and dreams. Now the hard work of putting flesh on their dreams must begin. Elizabeth wrapped her shawl tighter around her shoulders, exhaling into it to capture her own warm breath. The children slept curled around her in varying configurations, like stepping stones in a river. She dozed intermittently, awaking abruptly every so often to make a cursory search for Louis. Elizabeth, resigning herself to fatigue, closed her eyes and trusted her ears for some evidence of her husband's return. She knew his gait and the tread of his steps. At this hour she would hear him before she could see him.

When she awoke again, a man was walking with determined steps toward her.

"Louis," she whispered.

His firm hold around her was the permission she had been waiting for, and she surrendered to too many emotions in his arms. Her whole frame shook as tears ran down her cheeks and off her chin, dripping from her nose and into her mouth.

What a mess I must look, she thought, embarrassed at the display and struggling to regain control.

But Louis held her tighter, squeezing as much of the pent-up emotion out of her as she would let him.

When she had regained her composure, he took her hand and led her to one of *Britannia*'s benches. She sat down; he knelt in front of her and put his face in her lap.

The children, aroused by the commotion, huddled quietly around them on deck, a human outcropping like barnacles on *Britannia*'s hull.

"Elizabeth, we are *home*," he said, and for the first time, she knew it was true. "I am a bona fide citizen of the commonwealth now. But there is so much more good news to tell."

He told her how he had been sworn in and, still wobbling on sea legs, had wandered the Pennsylvania streets looking for temporary shelter. He told her he thought about returning to the ship immediately after taking the oath of allegiance, but he did not want to leave them alone on the ship while he surveyed the area for lodging, and it would have been cruel to make the children walk up and down unknown streets so late at night. He told her that all around him the luckier of their fellow immigrants were being greeted by relatives and friends. He described the guttural eloquence of their German—certainly not as beautiful as his own French, so lyrical and refined, but German was strong and right for forceful greetings, like those of explorers and adventurous spirits. He told her he felt like a conquering Hun among such strong language. Had he heard, as well, a suggestion of Russian in the streets? Truly Philadelphia rivaled any European city for cultural diversity, he said.

"Oh, my love, I know I am talking too much, but you have been so strong for so long," he said. "When I left the town square, I went straight away to the Quaker almshouse on Walnut Street to inquire after one of your cousins."

He continued, adjusting the story as necessary to satisfy her curiosity without burdening her with all the facts.

"But even if a relative was still in the Pennsylvania Colony," Elizabeth said, "he would not know to come looking for us at the Quaker almshouse."

"Quite right," her husband replied, ready with a plausible fiction. "But he may have stayed there when he first arrived. I considered it the best place to inquire after him, the hour being late, but could not get any information on his whereabouts. The kind man there, however, assured me of a place to sleep tonight."

A place. To sleep. Tonight. Elizabeth could barely absorb the syllables.

Louis offered Elizabeth his hand, and together they stood up and collected their belongings. Louis bent down in front of Mary Elizabeth, motioning for her to climb onto his back.

"Hold tight," he whispered.

Louisa carried a bag while Peter managed the duffel bags and bed rolls, stacked practically above his head. Elizabeth swaddled Charles in a blanket and slung him diagonally over her right shoulder, tying the cloth snugly in a square knot. The child would sleep, warm and secure so close to his mother, with the rise and fall of her breathing as his lullaby. Elizabeth's hands were now free to carry one side of the trunk, which they would take with them for the evening, with her husband carrying the other side. The remainder of their belongings would have to stay onboard, to be delivered by a mate later.

Thus organized, the whole Timothée family stepped off *Britannia* and onto dry land for the first time in seventy-two days.

After walking a short distance, Elizabeth lowered her side of the trunk, straightened her back and massaged the connective tissue of her hands. Louis lowered his side too, and he helped the children with their bundles. He did not notice that his wife had turned back toward the sea. *Britannia* was barely visible; if not for her white sails furled against the night sky, Elizabeth might not have been able to make out the shadowy specter. She was immediately struck with how massive the ship appeared, tied up stem to stern at the dock with huge braided jute ropes the size of a man's arm. She was certain *Britannia* had seemed smaller when they had called it home on the crossing.

She began to cry again. "Elizabeth, what is it?" Louis asked, putting his arms around her as the children gathered around her, to comfort her, and to be comforted.

"Oh, my sweet love," he said, "we are safe. And we are home."

"Yes, I know," she said, wiping the tears away apologetically. "And we have yet to thank God for his provisions."

Her husband understood.

"Almighty God, Father of all mercies," he began, as his family bowed their heads, "we thine unworthy servants do give thee most humble and hearty thanks for all thy goodness and loving-kindness to us, and to all men; We bless thee for our creation, preservation, and all the blessings of this life; but above all, for thine inestimable love in the redemption of the world by our Lord Jesus Christ; for the means of grace, and for the hope of glory. And, we beseech thee, give us that due sense of all thy mercies, that our hearts may be unfeignedly thankful, and that we show forth thy praise, not only with our lips, but in our lives; by giving up ourselves to thy service, and by walking before thee in holiness and righteousness all our days; through Jesus Christ our Lord, to whom with thee and the Holy Ghost be all honor and glory, world without end. *Amen.*"

While throngs swirled around them in the darkened Philadelphia streets, the Timothée family stood resolute, an island in the middle of a sea of humanity.

Chapter Nine

In her dreams, Elizabeth was on a boat, rocking gently on ocean currents. Something was pushing against her, brushing up and down her leg, and her mind wove the sensation into the dream she was reluctant to leave. She sat up with a start, expecting to find a ship rat underneath her blanket. Instead, it was her daughter's small, warm hand touching her thigh. Mary Elizabeth stood by the bedside trying to rouse her mother.

The bed was not swaying at sea after all. The months of waking up aboard ship were over.

Rolling onto her side, Elizabeth put an index finger to her pursed lips to warn the four-year-old not to wake the others, and then pulled M.E. close for a good morning hug and cuddle. The child smiled blissfully and went limp in her mother's arms while Elizabeth, finding the warm spot again on her pillow, indulged a long, satisfying yawn.

The pregnancy would soon be impossible to hide; she considered how best to tell her husband. Her belly, already beginning to touch the tops of her thighs, rumbled as she took in whiffs of sizzling breakfast sausages and leavened bread baking in the kitchen. She thought about her family back home, wishing she could tell them that an American baby was on the way.

Pans rattled in the kitchen, and children squealed with laughter; Elizabeth sat up again, wide awake now, and satisfaction turned quickly to remorse.

"Our host is already up and about while I lay sleeping," Elizabeth said quietly to herself, and she quickly swung her legs over the bedside and fumbled for her dressing gown.

Suddenly someone entered the front door of the house and walked with purpose toward their bedroom. Louis burst into the room, already talking.

"... And while I was standing there," he continued, "determining the best direction to take, I felt a tap on my shoulder. I turned 'round, and a rather tall gentleman was standing behind me. He said to me, 'Begging your pardon, sir, but are you Professor Louis Timothée?'"

Louis was pacing back and forth, scratching his head and gesturing to embellish his story.

"Who was he?" Elizabeth asked as she climbed out of bed to put on her dressing gown.

"You know him as well as I! He is a burnished brown-headed man of middle years with light blue eyes and an unmistakable smudge of printer's ink on his ear."

"I know that smudge!" she said. "I have seen it many times on you. Ben must have had an itch!"

She flicked his ear with her thumb and forefinger.

Her husband smiled and continued his story. "He said, 'Louis, it is I, Benjamin Franklin. Captain Franklyn of the *Britannia* said I would find you here.'"

"And what did you say?" Elizabeth asked.

"I said, 'My dear, Mr. Franklin! Of course, I remember you!' I recognized him almost immediately, the only excuse for the delay being my incredulity at seeing him *there*, standing behind me at the Quaker house, on the very next day of our arrival. I admit I must have stared at him for some number of minutes with a bewildered look on my face. I was caught completely off guard, Elizabeth! The same young apprentice printer from the colonies who, a world away, taught your brother to swim in the Rhine River. The same incorrigible man who had borrowed most, if not all, of my books in London at one time or another—still as brash as ever—and who is now a Philadelphia businessman, was standing there next to me! It has been some six or seven years since we last spoke, but the moment he smiled, Elizabeth, I tell you truly, the twinkle in that impish chap's eye positively transported me back to our youth. And I snatched his hand and shook it furiously!"

Louis continued to pace as if he were plowing a row over and over again, and then demonstrated how he had wrung Franklin's hand almost off the poor fellow's arm out of sheer delight at seeing him.

"And I attempted to explain that I was caught so by surprise to find him there, at the almshouse where we are staying, and that I had intended to seek him out as soon as possible. I tell you, Elizabeth, I was beside myself with incredulity! I had hopes of asking after him and perhaps discovering some bit of information after several days or even weeks, but to have been found by HIM, and so soon after our arrival, God's hand, it is. God's hand!"

Her husband, exhausted from his recount, chuckled at his own theatrics and collapsed onto the bed. Elizabeth sat down too, dumbfounded and amazed at her husband's wonderful news. The children clambered around them both, wide-eyed at the unfolding theatrics.

Louis shook his head and smiled.

"Why, that old Water American!" he said, scratching his head. "It has been years, Elizabeth, and he is not the young man I remember."

"Nor are you!" she said as she retied her dressing gown around her thick waist. "Is he still swimming a mile every day?" she asked.

"Likely not, by the looks of him," Louis responded. "He is a bit more portly than I recall. But I tell you, Elizabeth, we spoke as if no more than a week had passed between us. Providence. Divine Providence it is! We chatted a bit longer before parting, but he insisted that we drop 'round tomorrow at their home. He wants you to meet his wife, Debby!"

Chapter Ten

Debby Franklin, a round-faced woman whose figure had long since succumbed to too much of her own good cooking, met the Timothées at the door with a warm welcome, ready to take charge of the children. Mr. Franklin was playing with his little son, Will, who was toddling around the kitchen on tippy-toes and laughing the sort of laugh that gives a baby hiccups. Ben wasted no time, however, in scooping up the lad to greet the Timothée family as soon as they stepped over the threshold. Debby's mother, Mrs. Read, a thicker, gray-haired version of her homely daughter, was in the kitchen making biscuits for the noon meal for them and their boarders. She offered a flourishing curtsy and a floury hand when introduced.

Seated at the big dining table was Captain Franklyn of the *Britannia*. Another gentleman stood beside him holding a beautiful dressing table mirror. It was as if they all had been awaiting the Timothée family's arrival.

"I paid the Franklins a visit earlier this morning and told Ben I had imported him a printer," Captain Franklyn said with his mouth full of food. Pushing his chair back to stand up halfway, he extended his hand to Louis. "And he went immediately to find you."

"A pleasure to see you again, captain," Timothée responded and shook his hand.

To the other man he introduced himself. "I am Louis Timothée, new to Philadelphia from Rotterdam."

"Very nice to meet you, Mr. Timothée. I am Thomas Godfrey, just here to deliver several resilvered mirrors."

"Godfrey here is the best in Philadelphia," Ben added. "He is an amazing glazier, and a right fine tenant too."

"Oh, Mr. Godfrey, do you rent rooms here?" Elizabeth asked.

"No, ma'am, not any longer," Godfrey said, casting a glance toward the kitchen as if he was waiting for the woman of the house to relieve him of his delivery. "But I did at one time."

Elizabeth followed his gaze and saw a grimace cross Debby's face at the mention of it. But Ben, smiling in her direction from across the room, was obviously an instant cure for anything that ailed her.

"Thomas Godfrey practically raised his family in these rooms," Ben offered.

"'Tis true," Godfrey replied curtly. "I will take my leave now, Mr. and Madame Franklin."

Before Elizabeth could say so much as "pleasure meeting you," he was out in the street with the door closed behind him.

"The Timothées thought they were looking for me," Ben announced, steering the conversation back on course, "but *I* was looking for *them*. Professor, when can you come work for me at the *Pennsylvania Gazette*?"

Speechless, Elizabeth and Louis stood looking to each other to answer the question appropriately. Ben always was one to come to a point quickly, but the Timothées were a bit out of practice with their friend's ways.

From the kitchen Debby yelled, "Oh, Mr. Franklin, can you not at least offer them a chair and a drink before diving directly into business?"

Ben ignored her completely and clapped Louis on the back, almost knocking him to his knees. "Did you not know that the Fourth Estate is a brotherhood all its own?"

"Well, no, I, I mean …," Louis attempted to reply.

"Do you not fancy yourself a mechanic, Mr. Timothée?" Captain Franklyn asked.

"I am prepared to work hard to achieve my preferred station in life, yes," Timothée responded.

"Mr. Timothée fancies himself a great many things, Captain Franklyn," Ben interjected, "not the least of which is a teacher and philosopher. But he knows the value of manual labor, especially as a craftsman who takes great pride in his product. And the quality of his work is undeniably both utilitarian and utopian."

"Too kind, Ben," Louis answered. "And to your question captain, I do fancy myself a mechanic of sorts, one who builds *ideas* out of the raw material of words."

"*Printed* words, my fellow," Ben was quick to add. "That is where the livelihood resides. Ideas may be spoken or even handwritten, but all too often they leave the belly empty!"

Debby arrived with another platter of drumsticks, hard-boiled eggs, steamed broccoli, and potatoes.

"Why, Mr. Franklin," she announced, "one would think you have had to eat enough of your own words to be satisfied."

Ben relieved her of the platter, sat it on the mahogany table, and gave her a bear hug that lifted her off her feet.

"Quite right, my dear," he said, and smacked a kiss on her cheek. "But my point is that it is the *printer* who distributes the ideas."

"*And* who makes the quid on selling them!" Captain Franklyn added.

"Who is *paid* for the honor," Ben corrected, with a low bow and exaggerated genuflection to his sparring partner.

Captain Franklyn would have the last word. "Ah, my friend, we are nought but shameless peddlers, you in news and gossip and advertisements, and I in human cargo."

"Oh, but what a propitious partnership, my friend, that I sell a report of people and you sail to re-port people," Ben retorted with a wink. "Inventory, by any other name, would smell as sweet."

"Too much rhetoric for this old sea dog," the captain conceded, wiping his mouth and laying his napkin on the table. "I must be off. Mr. and Mrs. Timothée, I bid you good day. Your chest will be delivered here by nightfall. Ben, always a pleasure, and I shall call 'round again before *Britannia*'s return trip."

And then, calling out to the elder Mrs. Franklin, he offered his best compliments, accentuated with a burp.

Ben grabbed the captain around the shoulders and walked him to the door.

"And as always," he said, "I thank you for the news from abroad, my dear fellow. I shall make a front-page accounting of it tomorrow."

"Do not think it will not cost you," Captain Franklyn said. "One more of Debby's meals before sailing for Maryland. That is my fee."

"With pleasure!" came the female response from the kitchen.

While Franklin saw his guest to the door, Louis turned to Elizabeth and made an exaggerated face with bulging eyes and a wide grin that showed his molars. His wife smiled broadly, grabbed his hand, and gripped it.

When Ben returned, the Timothées had composed themselves enough to follow their host into the parlor. Ben wanted to hear about their voyage. Louis obliged with enough details to satisfy his curiosity, and promptly turned the conversation back to Ben's proposition.

"You mentioned the *Gazette*?" he asked, as more of a statement.

"Ah, yes," Ben began, "when we worked together in Europe, you had aspirations to be a bookbinder right away. Is this still true, or would you entertain the notion of replacing my man Whitemarsh as a journeyman printer here in my shop?"

Louis looked at Ben quizzically. "What happened to Whitemarsh?"

"I have sent him to South Carolina to publish the newspaper there," Ben replied. "The Assembly has offered one thousand pounds to fulfill the role of printer for the colony. Three other men have petitioned for the job: a chap by the name of George Webb, along with Thomas and another man named Eleazer Phillips from Boston."

Louis was never so glad that inner thoughts could not be heard. To discover that Franklin's journeyman had left the colony for work elsewhere, vacating his position here with the estimable Mr. Franklin—a man who had untold business connections and was faring quite well—was too much to hope for. The availability of Tom's job meant Louis could work directly with Franklin in the print shop, a rung or two up the business ladder than if Tom still occupied that position.

Not wishing to insult, Louis asked as diplomatically as possible which one of the three petitioners was likely to be awarded the position. All three were not needed, of course, and if either Webb or Phillips was chosen, then Whitemarsh might logically be expected to return to his old job in Philadelphia.

"Whitemarsh, with complete certainty," Franklin said, dismissing the notion. "No one else is up to the task. It is not a lucrative venture, at least not yet, and the only way to make it work is a partnership, with pooled resources. I have been told that Phillips is favored to be chosen, but the governor in South Carolina knows full well that Whitemarsh is backed by me, with my printing press and supplies.

"Besides, Thomas Whitemarsh was trained by me. He and I worked together in London, and he worked for me here in Philadelphia until this opportunity arose. This carries much weight in the southern colony, where they have had a devil of a time getting a proper royal King's Printer in place. No, clearly Whitemarsh is the logical choice for the position. The governor practically begged him to come to Charles Towne. He is on his way there right now," Franklin said.

"It is unfortunate that you have not arrived sooner," Ben continued. "Now that was the kind of setup you would have liked perhaps, Professor Timothée, especially with your Dutch training. We received a royal broadside printing job here concerning the need for a printer in the Carolina Colony. The ad came in a long time ago, and unfortunately, I did not have the ready cash at the time to pursue it. But they kept coming in. The royal government made a generous offer for a printer to come to Charles Towne. Tom and I figured the town could use a newspaper like the *Pennsylvania Gazette*, and he was raring to go. By then, we figured we could do well to form a partnership: I would supply him with the press and letters, and he would set up shop there, returning a portion of his profits to me."

"We tried to stop at the Carolina Colony, but they would not let us dock. There was fever there," Louis said.

"Yes, and there are other dangers, as with any frontier—rattlesnakes, pirates, hurricanes—but Thomas told me he had heard worse about Philadelphia before he came here," Franklin said. "I daresay the chap will fare quite well, but I am sorry he was not here to greet you. Terrible timing, that. But it does not assuage the fact that I am in need of a journeyman printer. And for that position, my dear Monsieur Timothée, I would like to install you, if we can come to equitable terms. I can use you immediately, and I already know the quality of your work, if newspaper printing is not too dreadfully beneath you."

Louis waited the requisite few minutes, with head hung low as if reflecting on the disappointing news that Whitemarsh was no longer in Philadelphia.

He wanted to blurt out *yes* right away, but not wishing to appear desperate, he said, "May I be permitted the night to think about it? My wife and I would like to consider your kind offer."

"Of course!" Ben laughed. "We can discuss it when you come down for breakfast since you and your family are staying with us now. We have not yet rented the rooms recently vacated by Whitemarsh."

It was said so matter-of-factly that the Timothées looked at each other as if one of them had made the bargain without telling the other. Both Louis and Elizabeth were poised to object, but Ben would not hear of it, and when he called Debby and her mother in to argue the point for his side, the Timothées knew they were beaten.

"I have already arranged for your remaining chest to be delivered here. Franklyn will have it brought 'round posthaste," Ben said as if there were no choice in the matter.

"Your living quarters are over the print shop," he added, apologizing in advance for its proximity to the square and a noisy market. "You will be wanting to vacate your room at the Quaker house now. Another boatload of Palatines arrives any day!"

Chapter Eleven

When Louis accepted Franklin's offer of employment the next morning, Ben was so overcome with enthusiasm that Debby insisted they both leave the house.

"I do not need the two of you underfoot talking shop while I am trying to get breakfast on the table," she said, and to that end she gave them an errand and two Timothée children to take with them.

Walking along as if they had not a care in the world and happy for the excuse to be away from the house, Franklin and Timothée chatted amicably before Ben brought up his latest venture.

"Timothée, it is an indisputable fact that you are a first-rate printer with all the marks of a gentleman, including a command of classical languages," Franklin began. "I recognized your skills when we were both journeyman printers in England, and I told you then that you bore the characteristics of someone ideally suited for writing and editing a newspaper in German."

"'Twas a long time ago, my old friend. I assumed you had forgotten about it," Louis said. "What was it? Around 1725? A few months before you left England for home? I liked the idea six years ago, and I like it still. I recall the strong first impression you made back then."

Both men had been employed by the same printing house just outside of London: Louis worked in the section where fine books were bound and Ben mostly in the composing room on pamphlets. Although Timothée was at least ten years older than Franklin, they had become friends almost immediately. Their backgrounds, temperaments, and many of their interests were quite dissimilar, but Louis and Ben found they shared a love of learning, regardless of the subject. Their appreciation for the bound volumes containing the sum of man's knowledge was more than enough to create and maintain a strong relationship.

"I remember my wife's assessment of you," Louis said. "You were no more than eighteen years old at the time, already a champion swimmer and shrewd businessman. She said, 'Mr. Franklin is certainly no fish out of water.'"

Ben looked at him as if he was not sure whether to thank him or not, but Louis was quick to explain.

"She meant that it seemed there was nothing you could not do once you set your mind to it. She could not help but be intrigued by you and your ideas. And more importantly, she noted that when you began a study, you dove deep."

Ben smiled with relief and studied his shoes in humility.

"I asked her if she could think of one uncomplimentary thing to say about you," Louis said candidly. "Her response was 'Ben's only major fault, if indeed it can be termed that, is that he simply is not capable of choosing just one swimming hole.'"

Ben chuckled. "You and I share that particular weakness, Timothée," he said.

Then, with a deferential wink, he added, "You are intensely curious and a lifelong learner, two prized attributes for any man."

The two walked along, reminiscing about their days in London.

"Do you remember the pub?" Louis asked the rhetorical question, finding occasion to produce his own wink.

Ben smiled.

"Ah, yes, the public house. So kind of you to include me with your chums," he said.

"I may have made a different decision, had I known then about you what I now know," Louis chided with a laugh. "You always had some strategy in mind. None of the chaps in London could ever beat you at chess. You were always several moves ahead."

Ben chuckled at the memory.

"Then for old times' sake, shall we term this move 'The Queen's Gambit?'"

"And what pawn do you offer in return for your stronger center?" Timothée inquired.

The answer was as bold as 36-point Caslon, delivered with a flourish as if Ben had written it on a huge imaginary placard in front of him: "Your name as 'L. Timothée, Editor,' on the masthead."

Franklin waited a moment, watching his opponent's reaction before continuing.

"Now as you no doubt are aware," he began, "Philadelphia is replete with Palatines, many of whom have yet to master the English language. In fact, there are so many of their own countrymen here, it is plausible that German will become the dominant tongue.

"I have the print shop, and I have already secured the type," he continued, knocking down one objection after another as he positioned himself for checkmate, "and now all I require is someone to write the newspaper for me. I am completely unable to write in German myself, but I can see a business opportunity here, and with each wave of Palatines hitting our shores, the success of such a venture appears more and more self-evident."

Louis paused as if considering the offer. He knew Ben already knew what his answer would be, but the good professor did not like to think he was so easy to deduce. He wondered what ulterior motive Franklin might have.

"Do you believe a German newspaper could be profitable?" he asked. "The Palatines are exceedingly hard workers, but they are chronically difficult to separate from their earnings."

Ben wasted no time in responding.

"Undoubtedly," he said. "They will welcome a broadsheet printed in their tongue. Many of them are well-established business men and have political aspirations."

"So these subscribers, in your view, are prominent people in the community?"

"If they are not now, they soon will be," Franklin responded, giving Louis the upper hand.

Whether profitable or not, a newspaper in their own language would be enough for the growing German community in Philadelphia to know that young editor Franklin was interested in their welfare. Ben would be poised well among them when they needed someone to speak for them in local political meetings. Franklin may have won the match to Louis's mutually agreeable defeat, but he had shown his tell. Louis would not forget it.

"I accept the position," Louis replied. "With gratitude."

The two men shook hands and, with business concluded, turned their attention back to the children. Louis's oldest daughter, Louisa, was swinging a sack of apples, which were soon to be made into delicious turnovers. Peter toted an early pumpkin, for which he would accept no help carrying.

"I want to tell Mrs. Franklin I did it all by myself," he defiantly announced.

"She told him before we left that if he managed it on his own, she would bake it into a pie, and he could have the largest slice," Ben confided to Louis, out of his eldest son's earshot.

"How is it you came upon such a welcome helpmate in Debby?" Louis used the subject change to ask diplomatically, knowing full well of Franklin's predilection for skirts. "I never would have thought you the settling-down type."

"It is quite the story," Ben began, "but not suitable for printing, if you understand my meaning."

Louis nodded his agreement to keep the conversation confidential.

"We have been man and wife barely one year," he announced, and turned toward Louis to watch his intellectual friend do the arithmetic.

"So you married her to spare her the shame of a child out of wedlock?" Louis asked. Little William was well past the one-year mark, and most likely closer to two years old.

"No, not exactly," Ben replied. "I married her to spare her the shame of a husband who had deserted her. And she married *me* to spare me the shame of a child out of wedlock."

Louis's look conveyed more shock than he had intended, and less incredulity than he would have preferred.

"Come, come, my dear boy. You knew me in my younger days. Do you really think the appetite has decreased that much in a handful of years?"

Ben clearly knew his own shortfalls, but Louis had thought that perhaps with age had come greater discretion.

"If you would rather not ...," Louis offered, but his friend shook his head.

"Quite honestly, I should like to talk about it," Ben said. "For all its twists and turns, the plot does have a happy ending. I had hopes, as most young men do, to marry well. I was quite serious at one point with the niece of the wife of Mr. Thomas Godfrey, the glazier whom you met yesterday. The courtship progressed, to all parties agreeable, until I made it known that I would require enough money to pay off my remaining debt for the printing house as a part of the marriage contract. It was a paltry sum, which I owed, but Mrs. Godfrey informed me that their inquiries had revealed that the printing business was not a profitable one, and so they denied this tenet of the treaty. I was told quite plainly that a printer was synonymous with a pauper, and that if I expected to find my fortune between a woman's legs, I should surely look elsewhere than their niece.

"I am certain Mrs. Godfrey wagered that my relationship with her relative had progressed too far to discontinue, but I made it clear that she had calculated incorrectly. I never returned to her, choosing instead to renew an old courtship with Deborah who, coincidentally, was likewise as ready as I to trade the flicker of hope for the flame of reality. I shall never admit it to Godfrey's wife, but she may have been more correct than even she was aware. Printing can be a meager way of life, and realizing this, I resigned myself not to expect money with a wife.

"Debby's husband abandoned her, but because she is untaught, she never bothered to have the marriage annulled," Ben continued. "Her errant husband was rumored to be dead, but of course, this could not be confirmed. Life, and our own shortcomings and bad decisions, do have a way of beating the illusions out of a man. And, I suppose, a woman as well."

Ben paused briefly in the street to explain.

"To be clear, we are not officially married in the eyes of God and the province of Philadelphia. There were rumors that this man had a wife who preceded Debby. She is said to be living in England, but while it could not be confirmed, a union between us would be looked upon as invalid. The cad also left behind many debts, which his successor might be called on to pay."

"A sound decision," Louis said, nodding. "And what of the boy?"

"When William was brought to me, I brought him to Deborah. To her eternal credit, she has never publicly discussed the boy's heritage. I can without equivocation say I did not marry for money, since I am not legally married, and since Debby came with no money. Neither did I marry for love or, perhaps more to the point, for lust, because the boy's mother is not my wife. But I can report that there is an affection between Deborah and me, and we are a happy little family regardless of the consequences of our own poor choices."

"I am pleased to hear it," Louis said, struggling to find the right response. Franklin patted him on his back for the effort.

"Every woman's beauty is a flower that blooms early and quickly fades," Ben said, attempting to reason, "so that every man finds himself in similar circumstances eventually: married to a comfortable old shoe. My footwear is good and faithful, attending me in the shop and helping me remain happy and productive, contentedly planted and moving forward. I believe the relationship has given each of us most of what we were looking for. What man—or woman for that matter—gets everything they desire in life?"

Louis nodded his agreement. "Without equivocation there are worse things than poverty, and better things than sexual gratification."

Ben winked and offered a half-hearted smile.

"So, my dear fellow, as the Godfreys were renters of mine, when they quite suddenly vacated the premises, I was left with the whole house. I resolved then and there to take in no more inmates. The only 'mates' I will take in now are the sort you continentals call friends, and their lovely families!"

The two men feigned laughter at the joke, both grateful for the release of tension.

"Thank you for trusting me with your story," Louis said. "You can be certain it is safe with me."

"None of us is perfect, my friend," Franklin said. "Least of all myself. But every man should strive to be as perfect as possible."

"So you said, when we worked together in London," Louis responded. "As I recall, you were gathering a list of virtues and mastering them one at a time. How is that coming along?"

Franklin laughed. "I have collected a total of thirteen to date. And I can say with neither puffery nor exaggeration that I have mastered all but one. Number twelve continues to prove a challenge."

"Excellent work," Louis offered. "What is the twelfth virtue?"

"Chastity."

Chapter Twelve

The women worked together in the kitchen like sisters while waiting for the victual brigade to return. Debby put a pot of hominy on to boil, churned butter, and made dough to be baked later into loaves of bread and Peter's piecrust. She insisted that Mrs. Timothée take a seat at the table and shuck corn.

"I detest the task," Debby told Elizabeth.

It was light work, and Elizabeth knew it, but she appreciated both the chance to be of some help as well as to be off her feet.

Elizabeth shared with Debby her concerns about the baby she carried, conceived under such arduous conditions.

"Please keep the confidence a little while longer," she asked, "until I can determine the best time to tell Louis. I want to make sure everything is progressing normally before informing him of a new mouth to feed.

"He will be pleased, of course," she said as she meticulously sought out each and every silk on the cobs. "But he has enough to worry about right now."

Debby nodded and smiled as she kneaded the huge batch of dough, almost ready for the windowsill.

"A baby is always a blessing," she said, looking down at the little boy playing at her feet. "No matter what the circumstance."

She wiped her sticky hands on her apron and covered the large wooden bowl with a linen cloth.

"But very soon now," she added, "you will not be able to conceal it."

She raised the yeasty concoction high enough to place it on the sill, tucking the cloth under the bowl to catch the warmth of the sun.

"And no man, even the most unobservant of 'em, will fail to notice *that*." She laughed, looking down at her own figure, and added, "'Course, you can always tell him you are being fed too well. In my case, 'tis true!"

"Louis would believe it!" Elizabeth responded. "We are so grateful for your hospitality. Your delicious cooking is putting meat on all our bones. Have you and Ben made plans for more children?"

She put the last shiny yellow ear of corn into the bowl for Debby's inspection.

"I would love to have a baby," her hostess answered. "William is such a joy, and I always prayed for lots of children."

Debby was constantly in motion, and Elizabeth felt it best to stay seated while the woman of the house ran her own kitchen. The shucked ears were whisked away to a steamy pot of water. In their place, Debby offered her guest a new task.

"Do ye mind helpin' a bit more?"

Elizabeth said she was pleased to oblige.

"I will be right back," Debby said, disappearing behind a door that led from the kitchen down to the basement larder. When she returned, she had a basket full of small objects wrapped in newsprint.

"Care to help me with the tomatoes?" she asked.

"Happy to!" Elizabeth answered quizzically, taking a small round package off the top of the basket and unwrapping it. Inside, she found a beautiful plump red tomato, as juicy looking as any summer fruit.

"My!" she exclaimed. "Wherever do you get ripe tomatoes in September?"

Debby explained that they had been picked slightly green in the summer and wrapped on their stems in newsprint.

"They will keep for months in a dark, dry larder," she said.

Now richly red and ripe, the tomatoes made Elizabeth's mouth water as she gently cleaned each fruit and sliced it on a plate.

"That is certainly 'news' to me," Elizabeth quipped, pleased with her clever play on words, but Debby only nodded blankly in agreement.

By the time the men and children returned, dinner was on the table. Debby met them at the door and relieved poor Peter—too stubborn to receive help carrying the pumpkin—of his prize.

"My, what a beautiful gourd you brung me." She flattered the young boy as she hoisted it onto her hip. "However did you manage this beast all by yourself, Master Peter?"

Peter beamed with pride and looked down at his feet. Making a big show of her difficulty, Debby said, "I can barely carry it from the door to the kitchen."

She stopped at the sideboard and hoisted the pumpkin up, turning the good side out as if it were a flower arrangement.

"I shall have to leave it here for the moment," Debbie said, raising a hand to her chest and fanning herself as if the exertion had required her last ounce of strength.

"After our meal, Peter, I will require your help in getting it washed and chopped. Are you up for it, young man?" she asked, all business with the eldest Timothée boy.

"Yes, ma'am, it is a large one, that. I chose the biggest one from the stack for you!"

"That you did, Peter!" Debby agreed. "I should think we may get *two* pies from it, and perhaps even a wee bit more. Now wash your hands, all of you, and we shall have a meal."

Ben, never needing to be told twice, brushed by her on the way to the pump, wrapped his arms around her thick waist, and gave her a peck on the cheek.

"What have you for this hungry brigade?" he asked his wife.

"Mistress Timothée and me prepared a feast, we did!" Debby announced with much bravado. "Many thanks to her help in the kitchen, we have Sunday succotash chowder, salt-risen bread, and sliced tomatoes. And coffee to take the chill off your walk home."

Her pride in the midday offering was apparent, and Ben wasted no time in praising her.

"A feast indeed, my dear!" he said with his arms up in the air as if he was already blessing the bounty. "I tell you, Timothée, your landlady will soon have you fattened up like me. She is the best cook in the colonies, for my money."

"Now, Mr. Franklin," Debby responded, "you will have Mr. Timothée thinking I am a paid employee rather than a helpmate."

"I should not be able to afford your culinary skills, should I be required to pay," the quick-witted Franklin answered. "And knowing that, I decided 'twas best to marry you!"

Debby set out seven red earthenware bowls and wooden spoons on the table for the adults and children.

"Well, come and get it," the hostess announced, and no one had to be told twice.

Ben said grace over the meal, and within moments of the last consonant leaving his lips, the children were hungrily devouring Mrs. Franklin's wonderful cooking. The adults were just as complimentary to their hostess, and the table fell silent of conversation. For a moment the sounds of scraping bowls and chewing almost drowned out requests for butter to be passed or coffee to be poured.

When genuine conversation resumed, it was Ben who began it, discussing plans for his newest journeyman printer.

"I have in mind to publish a yearly volume," Franklin began, "which shall require the skills of a printer as well as a bookbinder."

Louis was intrigued.

"A project separate from the German newspaper?" he asked.

It had been no more than an hour since Franklin had presented one proposition, and now he was offering another. Louis found himself so grateful to be in Ben's presence again, enjoying the robust culture of intellectualism they had shared in London.

"Yes, entirely separate," Franklin replied. "I have been retained to publish an almanac by John Jerman, but it is a tedious and unentertaining collection of drivel upon which we can almost certainly improve. My idea is to include witticisms and sage advice, weather tables, inventions, historical information useful to the farmer and businessman—all beautifully bound in a reference book.

"Very high quality, and I have precipitously hired just the man for the job," Franklin added, with a wink, as he buttered another thick slice of bread.

"It sounds like an interesting proposition," Louis responded, with a bit more hesitation than he would have liked to communicate.

"But?" Franklin said, sensing the pesky unspoken preposition dangling at the end of the sentence.

Louis considered an answer. He did not wish to appear unenthusiastic, or even fearful of the work. He was terribly grateful for the job he had been offered, and he wanted to assure his employer that he was up to the task. But there were other aspirations he wished to pursue—aspirations he had not shared with Ben.

"My dear Franklin," he cautiously began, "I am eternally indebted to you for your hospitality, including room and board for my family as well as for the position in your print shop—" but before he could finish the sentence, Franklin interrupted.

"But you want to open a school," Franklin said. "Your beautiful wife was kind enough to tell me of your dream."

Elizabeth flushed; her stomach turned, and she laid down her spoon. She met her husband's eyes and saw the betrayal in them.

"Louis," she said, "I knew you would not mention it because you are so grateful for everything Ben has already done for us, but a language school has been something you have kept in your heart since your London days together. I spoke of it only because you wish our children to retain their multilingual ability, and so I suggested that perhaps there are others who would pay for the same education."

"Quite right," Ben added, finishing off the last of his bread and wiping his mouth with the napkin tucked under his collar. "This is not news to me, my friend. You spoke of it years ago. It was a good idea then, and it is an even better idea now, here in America. When your astute wife brought it up, it immediately started the wheels turning. Philadelphia is a city of many cultures, and there are many— young girls in particular—whose families hope to include in their upbringing the genteel culture of the Europe they left behind. My only question to you is, do you think you can handle it all? Because if you cannot, I do not know another of your intellect who can. I shall have to hire an additional man to do it, and then you will find yourself in the less-than-ideal circumstance of having competition."

"No, of course, Benjamin, I can handle everything you require, including tutoring French. I should love the opportunity to teach lessons," Louis quickly replied.

Ben stood up from the table and walked over to Louis's side.

"There's a good man," he said with a wink and a smile.

They shook hands, and Ben clapped Timothée's back as the two men walked together into the front room to hammer out the details. Louis glanced back at his wife. She met his gaze and saw in it the beginnings of forgiveness for having bruised his ego.

Tonight would be the best time to tell him about the baby, she decided.

She would begin by reminding him of their interlude aboard the ship. She would take his hand and place it on the lowest part of her swelling belly, just above the hairline. She would kiss his ear, whisper the news almost wordlessly into it while he felt her womb. She would plunge her tongue into his ear, and she would feel his desire for her rise. He would be tender, loving, careful. Then they would both lie on their backs, side by side together, holding hands and breathing contentedly. After a while she would turn toward him and describe a strong, spring baby, their first born in America.

In the light of that news, all transgressions would pale.

Chapter Thirteen

Elizabeth stood up from her mending and rubbed her expanding belly. Outside the window she saw some remnants of snow, but spring was winning the battle, and soon warmer temperatures would prevail in the Pennsylvania Colony.

By the time Easter and my fifth child arrive, she thought *hopefully, all vestiges of winter will be gone.* The cold seemed to amplify her aches and pains.

The pregnancy had been troublesome, complicated by establishing the family's new life in America, but it helped that Debby was pregnant now too. After four full-term babies, Elizabeth was used to the process, even a little bored with it. She knew what lay ahead and was not looking forward to the excruciating pain of childbirth. But Debby was a fresh perspective. She had become pregnant shortly after the Timothées arrived in Philadelphia; Elizabeth liked to tease her that they had been the Franklins' lucky charm.

Debby was clearly excited about the changes in her body, as if it were all new to her. At each stage of the pregnancy—from the first noticeable roundness in her belly to the predictable chronic backache and the first flutter kick of her unborn child—she rushed to share it with her friend.

Not surprising, Elizabeth reasoned. *Will is almost three years old, and it is a clever trick of the mind to forget the worst parts of any experience. After all, a woman's second child is not the same as a woman's fifth.*

Both babies were due within weeks of each other, and Elizabeth was looking forward to their children growing up together.

Elizabeth could scarcely have imagined their good fortune. Looking around the room, she took stock of her surroundings. How uncertain their future had been just a few short months ago. After their arrival, the Timothées had no sooner settled in to the Franklins' rooms when a better opportunity presented itself. Though Ben had been kind enough to let them use his rental property over the print shop, the rooms were dreadfully inadequate for the family of six, and the raucous discord from the streets below was less than desirable for lulling small children to sleep.

Neither Louis nor Elizabeth would ever dream of complaining, though, especially to their new employer. The Timothées had unpacked what few possessions they carried with them off the ship and had made themselves quite comfortable in the small rooms. The remainder of their trunks would be delivered as soon as Captain Franklyn could arrange it. Elizabeth had been somewhat glad for the delay since there was very little room for even changing one's mind in the tight accommodations.

But circumstances had improved just a few days later when Ben Franklin's wealthy young friend, Robert Grace, left the colony for an extended period. The Grace residence on Pewter Platter Alley was the meeting place for a group of intellectuals, including Robert Grace and Franklin, every Friday night.

"He calls it 'The Junto Club,'" Louis said. "Ben had the idea of involving several prominent citizens in a club, of sorts, that offered a forum for study and mutual improvement, particularly in the area of morals, politics, and natural philosophy," he explained. The group would be gathering at Pewter Platter that evening.

"It was Ben's project from the beginning," Louis told her. "Each member is required to write essays periodically, which they present at club meetings. Through formal discourse he envisioned a mutually beneficial edification, not only for each man involved but for the larger community and for humanity itself," he explained, adding that Franklin intended to use his own significant influence to publicize, and thereby profit from, their ideas in his public forum, the *Pennsylvania Gazette.*

Ben suggested setting aside one of Grace's rooms for the club's books. The home itself was large and accommodating, having been a tavern at one time, and its location provided easy accessibility. But its true value, to Ben's way of thinking, was a generously sized room that provided space enough for club members to house their separate collections under one roof.

Mr. Grace conceded that his friend had a point; by the time he left the colony in October, the club had placed most of their collection in Grace's grand library. More shipments from London were due to arrive sometime after the first of the year.

"Franklin, my dear fellow," Robert Grace had said the day before he left the colony, "have that man Timothée and his family installed at my Pewter Platter place while I am abroad."

Mr. Grace felt that someone trustworthy should remain on the premises in his absence, to provide custodial services for their ever-enlarging collection of books and artifacts.

"These men have entrusted the club with a substantial commodity," Grace noted. "It is incumbent upon us to insure the protection of our members' private collections. Set Louis up as librarian—shall we say on a six months' trial basis? I should feel safer knowing Timothée will be there to proctor the use of my volumes among Junto members, to be sure."

Franklin agreed, noting that he himself had no small fortune bound up in his own collection. But while Ben thought it was a grand idea to install Timothée, he did not relish losing the rental income. Ultimately, he was persuaded; Franklin would need more room for his second child, and Grace needed a trustworthy caretaker for his large estate. The Timothées moved their belongings to the quieter location and were glad for the additional space.

Care and keeping of the house and servants in the owner's absence, as well as its collective, vast library, would be an enormous responsibility on top of Louis's print shop duties. But with Elizabeth's help, he was sure they could manage.

"With you in charge," Franklin told Timothée, "Grace will have the satisfaction of knowing his affairs are being looked after by a reputable man. And we shall be able to continue our Junto meetings without interruption."

The Junto Room, so called because they fancied themselves a political group, was the portion of the Timothées' new home that housed club members' books and miscellaneous contributions, now officially under the auspices of the newly formed Philadelphia Library Company. It was the logical extension of their tenancy to make Louis librarian for the Junto club's precious book collection. Louis's knowledge of the Cambridge method of cataloging helped convince the other Junto members he was the right man for the job.

"Do not worry," Ben had told the members of the Library Company when he recommended Timothée. "If the Frenchman cannot handle it, he will have excellent help in his wife."

Of course, the librarian's job officially belonged to her husband, but the Junto members could not fail to notice how much Elizabeth helped him. Gradually, the men accepted her presence during their visits, but she knew she must remain a listener if she were to stay. They would certainly disapprove, should they ever discover how much of their scholarly material Elizabeth had not only read but also set in type. She smiled at the thought of the secret.

In addition to the regular Junto members, James Logan, a former mayor of Philadelphia, would be joining them for the dinner meeting that night. Logan, she had been told, could quote Elizabeth's favorite author, Alexander Pope, as well as she. Louis said Logan was a brilliant older gentleman, as competent and well-versed in the great literary classics as he was in scientific matters. He was a reticent man, however, and it was difficult to draw him into conversation.

"When he does speak," Louis told her, "it is usually after a libation, which loosens his tongue. But even so, he is so commanding that all the other Junto members listen intently."

Elizabeth noted that only Thomas Godfrey dared debate him. She hoped there would be an opportunity to ask Mr. Logan why he had not recommended other books by Alexander Pope, Jonathan Swift, Isaac Watts, or Isaac Newton for the library. In her father's print shop in Leyden, she had proofread many manuscripts by these men. Perhaps an occasion would arise when she could show Logan her copy of an unpublished poem by Alexander Pope, entitled "Universal Prayer." He might well be impressed to learn that the hunchbacked little man himself had given it to her during a visit to her father's shop when she was a little girl.

By the time the men arrived, Elizabeth had everything in order. She had prepared venison stew, rye rolls, an assortment of cheeses, and a plum pudding for their guests. Louisa was a great help to her mother, and Elizabeth certainly needed more help these days. She enlisted the help of her other children in laying out tin plates and spoons and tankards for ale.

Benjamin was the first to arrive, fashionably early as usual. Elizabeth teased him that he needed a place to hide from his pregnant wife.

"Quite right, my dear!" Mr. Franklin admitted. "Pregnancy is a woman's affliction with which we men, the cause of the condition, cannot commiserate."

"Nor would you wish to," Elizabeth added.

"Certainly not. Should the male of the species be required to bear young, humans would have become extinct many years ago. Besides," he offered, putting his hand on the small of her back as they walked toward the Junto Room, "you females do it so much better than men ever could. At risk of sounding pompous in quoting myself, I believe a ship under sail and a big-bellied woman are the handsomest two things that can be seen common."

Elizabeth blushed.

"Flattery, my dear friend, will get you everywhere," she countered and whispered that although meat was on the menu, he would find a suitable substitute in the dishes directly in front of his plate.

Elizabeth had recently learned of Franklin's disdain of meat, and her philosophical ponderings regarding his decision aside, she found it a welcome challenge to cook in a way that pleased him.

"Arugula and beets," she said, with a wink.

He took her small hands in his, gave her an impish, appreciative smile, and excused himself to attend to other guests.

As the men arrived, Elizabeth showed them in, guiding them to where Louis was waiting to greet them. The din of masculine voices, so much louder than the voices of the ladies and so much more visceral and commanding, gradually rose to a crescendo until it was utterly impossible to discern individual dialogues. Elizabeth hungered to hear even a snippet more, but her duties lay in the kitchen for final dinner preparations. She pulled the Junto Room door closed, lingering on the other side a moment longer. Dozens of deep-throated, muffled conversations sounded reassuring and pleasant—of powerful, educated men congratulating themselves on their club, which had become quite the formidable bastion of intellectual discussion.

When Elizabeth returned with wine, Ben was talking to Mr. Logan.

"What an honor to have you with us this evening, James," Ben said, patting the old man on his back. "Gents, when Logan here was mayor, he was the most powerful man in Pennsylvania next to Penn himself, *and* the most learned."

Mr. Logan had come to Pennsylvania as secretary and protégé of William Penn, Ben explained, and he had crossed the Atlantic several times in his service. Once tall and handsome, the blond Scotch-Irishman now in his sixties was crippled from a fall and seldom left his home.

Pity, Elizabeth thought. *Politics could use a man of his genius.*

The son of an Irish schoolmaster, Logan had a gift for inspiring young men to independent thinking.

The Junto members were more impressed with the man's library. Thomas Godfrey verified the rumor: the Logan Library was in excess of two thousand books. But the great scholar had made it clear he did not believe that Benjamin Franklin, his Junto Club, nor any other group in this wilderness was capable of intellectual discussion. And certainly not leather-aproned mechanics.

Thomas Godfrey, who was as much of a math scholar as Mr. Logan, had changed his mind. While installing glass window panes at Stenton, Logan's estate, Godfrey got the old man's attention long enough to show him one of his inventions. The young glazier convinced Logan that he was not the only scholar in the Pennsylvania wilderness. Godfrey told Pennsylvania's most imminent intellectual that the Junto Club had legally organized the Philadelphia Library Company. Further, he said, they had sufficient English sterling set aside for purchasing books.

Elizabeth finished filling the men's glasses and took a seat at the back of the room, hoping to remain unnoticed a little while longer. Mr. Godfrey proposed a toast.

"I have excellent news, gentlemen," he began. "The esteemed Mr. Logan has been convinced of our endeavor and has volunteered to willingly give his advice on the choice of books for the new library."

There was a brief moment of murmurous incredulity followed closely by clapping and congratulations, loudly praising Logan for his philanthropic efforts. Elizabeth noticed that Godfrey had earned the admiration of all original six members of the Junto, save one: Franklin.

She knew the two men were still on stiff terms since the Godfrey family had moved out of Franklin's quarters over the printing house. Elizabeth had asked Louis why there was such ill will between them.

"Ben said the man is not a pleasant companion," Louis told her. "Thomas expects universal precision in everything said, or is forever denying or distinguishing upon trifles to the disturbance of all conversation."

Whatever the case, it was clear to Elizabeth that Ben could not remain in the man's presence for long periods of time.

"I must say I am delighted that you have overcome initial obstacles to this club of yours," Logan told the group. "But I still believe the better idea is a subscription library, wherein each member pays a fee as well as annual dues," he added, looking directly at Godfrey.

"Yes, I quite agree," Thomas responded, a little too quickly.

Ben had told Louis that Logan was incensed when Godfrey borrowed several of his precious volumes, only to return them dog-eared.

After a rather uncomfortable silence, Elizabeth announced that dinner awaited them in the dining room, whenever they were ready.

Chapter Fourteen

"You would have thought Logan had offered to buy books, not just select them," Louis told Elizabeth when he came home the next day for the noon meal. "But I can see why Ben was so pleased. Thomas Godfrey says Logan also knows where to find rare volumes. It is going to be interesting to see how Logan's list compares with ours."

"First, you will need to finish *your* list in order to compare it to *his*," Elizabeth said, knowing her pedantic husband would offer some justifiable excuse.

She had reminded Louis that the directors wanted that booklist. They were getting impatient, she had told him. She had even begun a list for him. When Godfrey asked why it had not been submitted for review, Louis explained the delay to his own satisfaction: he wanted to prepare an estimable list and would not be rushed by anyone, especially his wife.

Elizabeth knew Louis was well aware that he needed her help, though he would never admit it. Not to her at any rate. If he did, he knew she would follow through on her threat to help him. She had orders to stay off her feet as much as possible, and the doctor warned that any exertion might cause the baby to come early.

Elizabeth put a plate of bread, meat, and cheese in front of her husband and turned to pour a stout cup of tea. A strong spasm caught her in her belly—a sickening sensation akin to severe menstrual cramps. She dropped the hot kettle and doubled over in surrender with an audible groan. The sudden noise startled Louis, and he spun around.

"Peter!" he yelled. "Get Mrs. Franklin!"

When Debby and her mother arrived, Mrs. Read gave Elizabeth lemon balm to numb the pain. It was weak medicine, however, and it did little to keep Elizabeth from writhing in agony. From her weak hold on consciousness, she watched herself, as from far away, calmly and meticulously setting her wild thoughts in type. She slugged each letter, as if it were tomorrow's lead: ".niap eht bmun ot deliaf sah em evag daeR ssertsiM noitcocnoc ehT"

Her mind calculated the benefits of being a printer's wife and its commensurate authority to decide for others what was—and was not—important news. The birth of her child would not make headlines, even if she ran the paper and not Ben Franklin.

Another contraction hit her, this one causing her to grip the bed clothes so violently that they were altogether removed from the bed. In her **Delirium** the muslin resembled two berms, one on each side of her thighs. She felt as if she were lying in a shallow grave, surrounded on the left and right by loose, blanched cloth.

We are not dead yet, Elizabeth's actions seemed to convey. *Quite the contrary.*

We are beginning life here, she thought, and she willed herself to hang on to that sentiment.

The word **E M E R G E N C Y** stretched across the blackness behind her eyes and rolled around and around and upside down. She refused to cry out. There would be no satisfaction in that for her, and she would not offer it to others. **Y C N E G R E M E**. She proofread the word, set in uppercase Caslon: bold letters straight out of the box her father had been saving to announce the Second Coming. **E M E R G E N C Y**.

The same word Deborah Franklin had used when she went for Mrs. Read's help: "She is a midwife, familiar with emergencies."

Elizabeth's hand slipped away as the woman toddled out the door as quickly as her thick drumstick legs would take her.

Poor dear, Elizabeth thought. She must be so frightened, knowing she will give birth to her own emergency soon enough.

But the pregnancy that had begun for Elizabeth on the passage from Rotterdam, which once seemed so tenacious to have taken root under difficult circumstances, now seemed more like a weak sprout, too soon for the harsh environment in which it had been engendered.

NO, she insisted, pushing the thought away. *This is a strong baby. An American baby, the tap root of the Timothée family, diving deep into nascent land.*

Another contraction: **SURREPTITIOUS**. The pain was worse now, forcing her back to current circumstances. She felt as if she were being **PUNISHED**, but she did not know why.

WHY is it always the WHY, she thought. The why of it was a riddle she could not unravel. She had done nothing wrong—no sin she could recall. *Why* was she being punished?

And then, she remembered a quote from Jonathan Edwards: "The way to Heaven is ascending; we must be content to travel uphill, though it be hard and tiresome, and contrary to the natural bias of our flesh."

This is my punishment, she thought.

As her own blood soaked the bedclothes, Elizabeth thought of servants punished for laziness, or working poorly, or not following instructions. She considered the worst whippings, the ones employed for those who were willfully deceitful or defiant, for those who believed it is better to enter life with one eye than to have two eyes and be thrown into the fire of hell.

This pain felt like that. Not remedial punishment, as a child being corrected would be punished. This pain felt like rage.

Men of standing will always find a way to rationalize their sins, she reasoned. She would not give them the satisfaction of hearing her cry out. She would bear up in defiant resolve, even to the last blood-soaked contraction.

Surreptitious. Surreptitious. Surreptitious. She said the word over and over to herself like a mantra. The word sounded like *delicious sirup*, for making molasses: **S U R R E P D E L I C I O U S**. Blood, so red that it is black: thick and hot.

Nothing sweet about it, though, she thought.

"I am being punished," Elizabeth mumbled.

The flesh-tearing pain made it **I M P O S S I B L E** to bear any longer.

Mrs. Read was with her now, holding her hand. Elizabeth wanted to push, but her instructions were to hold.

Hold, Elizabeth.

"Wait a little longer," she heard Mrs. Read say.

How much longer?

I N C A L C U L A B L E.

She tried to work sums in her head. If a baby travels three inches per second down a birth canal twelve inches long, how long would it take that baby to crown?

Elizabeth felt her flesh ripping with the downward momentum of the birth sac. Her body struggled against the need to extricate the baby. It felt as if someone had stuck a red-hot poker into her womb and was wildly stirring the tissue into a fiery blaze. She could not breathe. Her frantic eyes searched the room, begging someone to put an end to the misery.

"Oh, God," she begged, "please help me."

Fading in and out of consciousness was the only relief she received.

When she awoke again, she was still gripping Mrs. Read's hand, but now it felt slippery. She looked down and saw the gouges she had made in the woman's palm. She wondered briefly if she had broken her fingers.

"Get the doctor" she heard Mrs. Read say. "Tell him it is an emergency!"

Precisely right, Elizabeth thought. *That is the noun I chose hours ago.*

The satisfaction of having already chosen the perfect word gave her confidence. The baby is emerging ... emerging ... and everything else must get out of the way. Emergency. Once the water breaks, all other schedules must be put aside for life's biggest emergency. A child is breaking out of its mother's womb and into this dusty realm.

"From the realm of the universal God into this dark orb," Elizabeth muttered, remembering the poet who had stated it so eloquently. "When life is born with one first gulp of breath and then, immediately begins to die."

Who was the writer? But more important, who was the child? The very reason for all this pain. *My womb is breaking open, being torn away. A new soul clothed in flesh and blood begins the journey to the grave.*

S a r c a s t i c. As darkness nibbled away in ever-increasing sparkles, she knew she had better hurry. That headline must be set before she lost consciousness. She could hear the sparkles multiplying, like a distant ringing in her ears. She focused on the word *sarcastic*, setting it as big as the others but lowercase—*not the top, page one story. No, more fitting for the bottom of page three. The italics, the lowercase italics! Where were the lowercase italics? All piled up.*

The pain was punctuated now, with an ominous *slant ... s a r c a s t i c.* Louis had showed her the word *s*arcastic in the original Latin; its literal definition meant to tear the flesh. This baby was tearing her flesh. Louis said the word meant the pain that could come from words—cutting words that tear the soul. She felt as if the pain was cleaving her soul.

Is that how God does it? She wondered. *Is part of my soul being carved away for this child?*

No, she shook her head. *This is a brand-new soul, forced to enter this world but still desperately clinging to the presence of God. My little baby is hurting too.*

Mrs. Read was holding her hand. *How long? How much longer?* From an out-of-body scene, she watched from a distance. She was standing off to the side of the room, writing down on foolscap all the little stories she saw. She saw Mrs. Read rub her back.

"Drink this," the kind old lady with the strong, large hands said. "This is what the Indians use for times like this. It will give you strength for birthing and perk you up for later."

It was so good to have strong hands to help, so like back home when Louisa, Peter, Mary Elizabeth, and Charles had been born. She wrote down their names on the foolscap too. Elizabeth had lost a baby before, but she decided not to include it in her notes. It had been delivered too early; she had decided not to see it. At her request, she had not been informed of its sex. Some facts are irrelevant, and as such, they should hold no place on the glassy surface of her memory. Truth be told, it was really nothing more than severe stomach cramps, as if she had expelled a rotten piece of meat. She had been back at the print shop the next day.

She hoped this baby would be a boy. She was born to be a mother of men, and the mother of daughters who would be mothers of men. That is what Aunt Katherine had said about her, and her father had smiled in agreement.

"And yet my Elizabeth is my best helper," her father had said. "She is better for me than ten sons."

Here in America so many years later, she still felt that sense of pleasure at her father's praise.

The darkness closed in again.

"Madame Timothée, you have a boy!" said a muffled voice, as if underwater.

Mrs. Read placed a bundle in her arms, still sticky and mewling for milk. Elizabeth put him to her breast.

When she awoke again, Mrs. Read said, "Madame Timothée, you have *another* boy."

Louis was there.

"What shall we name them?" he asked her softly, holding her hand.

"First one John," she whispered weakly.

"John Timothée," he said. "He arrived a bit early, but he is here."

"Then perhaps we should name him Jeune," Elizabeth managed to say, using the French word for "young."

Louis breathed easier at his wife's ability to make a joke despite the difficult births.

"All babies are *jeune*, my dear," he said. "And we shall not name our first American child a French adjective. But what shall we call his twin?"

"Paul Lewis," she said weakly. "Spelled like the colonists do."

"Fitting," her husband replied. "Named for your father and for me."

"Do they look American?" Elizabeth asked.

"Yes. They look American. All red in the face and puffy."

"I am glad they are here," she said, fighting the unutterable exhaustion that kept calling her to close her eyes, and to keep them closed. "Now we can get back to work on that booklist."

Chapter Fifteen

Her husband was working late; Elizabeth knew she should be looking over those proofs, but tonight she gave into the temptation to play with her children. They would be too wide awake to go to sleep anyway if she called bedtime. Truth be told, she was enjoying the diversion as much as they.

Within two weeks of the twins' birth last year, Louis had managed to compile the Library Company's list of titles, which the Junto required Mr. Collinson to purchase. By the end of March, Franklin himself had put the letter in the ship captain's hands with instructions to deliver to Peter Collinson, Quaker mercer in London.

Two days later, the Timothées buried the first-born of their American sons.

"It is not your fault," Louis tried to comfort her. "I do not blame you."

He stroked her hair as she wept.

"The babies were delivered too early. There is work to be done, and we must not waste time grieving."

Elizabeth knew he was right. There was work. Although confined to bed, she could still read proofs for the *Pennsylvania Gazette*. And there was Paul Lewis to consider—weak but becoming stronger.

And now another child was expected: almost full term.

Elizabeth understood that the business of living had drawn her husband away from the business of dying. She had never seen Louis happier. As Philadelphia's newest language master, he was busy teaching French lessons. The library was a convenient place for his students: Louis was required to keep it open from 2:00 p.m. until 3:00 p.m. each Wednesday and 10:00 a.m. until 4:00 p.m. on Saturdays, so it seemed only logical to schedule lessons during that time.

"Knowing languages as you do should be a decided advantage," Benjamin had assured him. "I, for one, will be an eager pupil."

And the brilliant Water American had made good on his promise; he had been the first to sign up. However, although he was an eager pupil, the language did not come easily to him. The children, especially Peter and Mary Elizabeth, found it difficult to hide their amusement when Mr. Franklin tried his Yankee tongue at French.

There was also the *Philadelphische Zeitung*, a newspaper in German for the High Dutch population, with Louis Timothée's name listed as editor in the masthead. Ben wanted the first issue out in early May, making this Louis's highest priority. If they could obtain enough subscriptions, they would publish another in June. Printing and job orders continued to pour into the *Gazette*, and as journeyman printer, Louis was busy setting type for Ben's weekly newspaper.

There was also the almanac and several fine books that required Timothée's considerable bookbinding abilities. And Franklin had been promoting Louis's journeyman's skills in the columns of his newspaper: "Office near the Market, next door but one to the Plume of Feathers on Front Street," he advertised, "where ads are taken in and book binding is done in the best manner."

"When that brash young Benjamin Franklin said he had enough work to keep me busy," Louis told Elizabeth a few days after the funeral, "I had no idea he meant 'round the clock."

But Elizabeth knew it was exactly the tonic her husband needed. Elizabeth knew she would be happy again too. She knew that work was the best thing for her now, even confined to bed. She had been able to help with the proofs for the *Pennsylvania Gazette*.

Chapter Sixteen

While Louis was working, Elizabeth was using the time to play with her children. She knew they would be too wide awake to go to sleep if she called bedtime soon. And truth be told, she was enjoying the diversion.

"Sing a song of sixpence, a pocket full of rye, four and twenty blackbirds baked in a pie," Elizabeth chanted as the children giggled and clapped to the meter. "When the pie was opened, the birds began to sing—was that not a dainty dish to set before the king?"

Elizabeth mimicked exaggerated gestures to illustrate the rhyme, which amused them all into belly laughs.

"The king was in the counting-house, counting out his money, the queen was in the parlor, eating bread and honey."

The children took up the pantomime, pretending to gobble up the tasty treat and rubbing their stomachs.

"The maid was in the garden, hanging out the clothes. Along came a blackbird and SNIPPED off her nose!"

Elizabeth lunged at the nearest child, pretending to take Louisa's nose with her fingers. The room erupted in laughter, and all the children fell onto the bed, begging Elizabeth to do it again.

"Say it again, Mama," Peter implored, a bit more boisterous than necessary. "Say it again!"

When Elizabeth pitched her voice in a lower key and recited the words in German, three tickle boxes toppled over again. Despite the commotion, or perhaps because of it, little Charles and Paul Lewis continued to sleep blissfully, bundled tightly in their cradles.

"No more tonight," she informed them at last. "It is late, and my little blackbirds need to go to sleep before someone comes along and bakes YOU into a pie."

"Mother," Mary Elizabeth asked, "what story is that?"

"*C'est les Contes de ma mère l'Oye*," she told the children in French.

"Your mother is a goose?!" Mary Elizabeth asked, as much to tease her mother as to show she understood what she had said.

"*Ah, oui, ma petite fille!*" her mother replied. "*Ma mère, elle s'appelle 'Elizabeth Goose.' C'est vrai!*"

Standing, Elizabeth said, "*Et maintenant, mes cheris, il est temps de se coucher.* It is time to go to sleep."

A chorus of groans rose up, but Elizabeth would have none of it. She tucked them in tight, with Mary Elizabeth in the middle and Louisa and Peter on the outside. "Goodnight," she whispered, extinguishing the oil lamp on the bedside table and firmly closing the door behind her.

Late October and already so frightfully cold, Elizabeth thought as she made her way slowly into the front room. She dragged the Graces' chair closer to the fire and stood in front of it briefly, soothed by the hissing and popping, and feeling immediately warmer just from the sound. Their second Pennsylvania winter was bearing down, and the cold exacerbated the physical toll of another pregnancy. She ached in her bones, as if the marrow itself was being sucked out. Each laborious step made a brittle cracking sound in her back and knees, like dry rot under her weight.

Taking up the chair, she sat uncomfortably. She admitted to herself that she was tired of being pregnant; indeed, it was difficult to remember what it was like to not be pregnant, to walk unencumbered by a chronic ache at the base of her spine. Proper shoes were completely out of the realm of possibility. Her feet were too swollen, and even if they had not been, she would have needed one of the children to tie them. Although she rubbed pig lard on her belly daily, the skin continued to stretch to the point of rupture. Dark, lacy veins, like ragged incisions, threatened to crack her body open like an egg. *Just two more months*, Elizabeth consoled herself. Soon now, they would be blessed with another American baby, and she would once again be the only tenant inside her skin.

Settling into the chair, Elizabeth let her mind wander, thinking over the last twelve months since Philadelphia became home. The Franklins had celebrated the birth of their son, Francis Folger Franklin. Ben had dubbed the infant "Franky" almost immediately.

"Franky Franklin!" Elizabeth had jibed when she held the infant for the first time. "Frankly, Mr. Franklin, I wager a franc that Franky will grow up to be a frank young man!"

Ben was not the least bit offended, so full of pride was he with his little boy. Separately, to Louis, Elizabeth playfully suggested that perhaps their own next male offspring should be named Timmy Timothée.

She pulled a Pennsylvania Dutch quilt over her lap and moved the candle closer. Taking up her sewing basket, Elizabeth planned to use the time until Louis returned to catch up on her mending. Peter, growing in fits and spurts, needed his trouser buttons moved again to give the boy more room.

An abrupt rapping at the front door startled her so that she pricked her finger. *Who would be knocking at this late hour?* she wondered and set her sewing aside. Certainly everyone in town was aware the Grace family was abroad. No one would be calling this late to inquire about her husband's French lessons, and library hours had well passed. Every week she proofread ads in the *Pennsylvania Gazette* offering rewards for runaway servants, and Louis had cautioned her to keep the door locked.

"With the crowded conditions of the prison and workhouse ...," he'd start, but he didn't need to finish his sentence.

She knew about the deplorable conditions for vagrants, thieves, and the desperately poor, just a few blocks from Pewter Platter on

High and Third streets. Would someone knock that frantically if they were looking for food or a place to hide? She stood painfully, smoothing her hair and straightening out her apron, and made her way to the front door.

When she peered through the peephole, she saw a burly yeoman resting his right foot on a trunk. Immediately she flung the door open, which clapped the entry wall with a dead wood sound.

Johann, the sailor who had befriended them on the crossing, was on their step.

"Well, my sakes!" Elizabeth said, putting a hand to her cheek and embracing him warmly. "Have you sailed all the way to Philadelphia for another one of my home-cooked meals?" she teased.

Her oldest student from *Britannia* never missed a chance to eat with the Timothées when he was in port.

"Official business dis time, Frau Timothée! The captain sents hiss regards," the giant young yeoman bellowed, much too loud for the hour.

"I haff fer you a delivery," he announced, pointing to the ponderous wooden chest at his feet. "Cap'n Cornock said he vood be brinking you da packets himself, but I shoot deliver dis chest right away tonight."

His booming voice was thick with his German accent. The young sailor's big, toothy grin covered his entire face.

"It is pleasure to see you, Ma'am," he said.

Suddenly three small faces, at graduated levels, peeked out from the doorway, and Johann's warm smile was mirrored by each little Timothée. Louisa stepped forward and hugged one of the happy giant's legs. Peter, not to be outdone by his older sister, grabbed a leg also. Mary Elizabeth, not entirely sure she remembered the hulking young man, hid behind her mother's skirts. Johann acknowledged Peter with a tousle of his hair and Louisa with a bow. To Mary Elizabeth he gave a personal smile that sent her blushing.

"Now back to bed, children," Elizabeth said. "*Tout va bien!* Everything is fine." The children complied with reluctant obedience.

"Your English is improving every day," Elizabeth complimented, standing on tip toes to hug him again.

He was a comely boy, tall and burly, with blue eyes as big as pools and sea-bleached hair in sharp relief to his dark, suntanned skin. Even in October his face resembled one of her favorite leather volumes in the library.

"Do come in out of the cold," she insisted.

The mate bent down and hoisted the massive trunk above his chest, resting it on his right shoulder and steadying it with his left hand. The two stepped into the warmth of the entry hall.

"It is good to have you back, Johann," Madame Timothée said in German and closed the door behind him.

"*Dankeschön, Frau Timothée*," Johann answered and put the heavy chest down in the hallway.

Using the English she had helped him learn, he continued, "Mr. Peter Collinson put diss aboard himseff in London. He say, 'Johann, look out for dis chest on da ship all da way. I haff talked wid da captain,' he say, 'Und vin you arrive, as soon as *Britannia* dock, you yourseff take to Mr. Robert Grace house. First ting.' Iss he here?"

"No, I am sorry to say he is not," Elizabeth responded.

"What is in the chest?" she asked, but she hoped she already knew.

"'Tis books, forty-seven ov dim, fulfillment ov order placed by Mr. Benjamin Franklin," the young man replied.

"Mr. Timothée is handling Junto affairs in his absence; he was appointed librarian of the club," Elizabeth offered. "Might I accept it since he is away from the house? I could ask Mr. Franklin to authorize it if necessary."

Her student gave her a broad smile.

"Madame Timothée," he began, "I trust no one more than you."

A wordless look passed between them, an intense emotion that could be acknowledged for only the merest measurement of time. Johann reached out his weather-leathered right hand and engulfed her small, soft hand in his massive grip. Just the hint of a smile followed and, closely behind, a faint bow and a sharp click of his heels.

"I leaf it in your hands. I must go. Da captain say tell you more boxes vill be come-ink soon. 'Curiosities,' he call dem, or some word like dat," he said over his shoulder, his head grazing the bottom edge of the wooden sign that read, "French Taught Here—Louis Timothée, Master of the French tongue."

The impact set the sign swinging. Above it, the larger, fixed sign that read, "Philadelphia Library Company, Louis Timothée, Librarian," remained stalwart as if to imply it was an institution that would not be moved.

"Thank you," Elizabeth offered after him. "Stop 'round while you are in port, Johann! I will make *maultaschen*!"

Closing the door behind her, she turned her attention to the chest and bent down to read the writing:

The Library Company of Philadelphia
Pewter Platter Hall
Philadelphia, Pennsylvania
From Peter Collinson, Mercer, Gracious Street, London

She rubbed her hands over its fine woodwork.

"Ben and Louis will be so pleased," she said aloud, certain that her husband and Mr. Franklin would come as soon as they heard, heedless of the hour.

Ben might already know by now, perhaps from Captain Cornock himself, that the Collinson chest at long last had arrived and was at Pewter Platter Hall. She knew Franklin kept apprised of every ship coming and going in the Philadelphia harbor. Nothing escaped the notice of Philadelphia's newspaper publisher.

Elizabeth was not entirely confident, however, that she would have the patience to wait, even if Franklin was sprinting toward her home at this very minute. She knew what lay locked away, just a few inches away from her perspiring palms. She had helped prepare the booklist Collinson was asked to procure: eleven books on science, three on philosophy, nine on various literary and historical works, and several others on assorted topics. She yearned to touch the treasures that were contained inside. To smell the ink, paper, and leather—the combination was her favorite perfume. To lift them gently from their container, one at a time, and carefully turn each page. To absorb the intricacies of their etchings. To admire the printmanship of European craftsmen. And then to read the grand ideas of learned men.

Her curiosity of its contents had so consumed her that she forgot to ask Johann to move the chest into the Junto Room where it belonged. Elizabeth saw no purpose in calling for a servant when she could manage a job herself; snatching up her mending, she bit the thread off with her teeth and walked quickly to the children's room. Opening the door quietly, she realized her instructions had gone unheeded—all but Charles and Paul Lewis stared back at her. Elizabeth put a finger to her lips and motioned to the oldest three to follow her into the hallway.

"I have an errand for you, Peter," she whispered, handing her son his mended breeches. "Get dressed."

"What is it, Mother?" he asked, stuffing his nightshirt in bunches into the waistband and popping the button again.

"In a minute, son," his mother said. "First I need everyone's help moving the chest into the Junto room."

With the help of the children shoving hard, Elizabeth managed to push the exotic box down the hall to the Junto Room's locked door.

"Mother," Peter asked, "may I turn the key?"

But his mother shook her head. "Absolutely not," she told him, adding that he needed to stand aside.

Peter, sullen, hung his head. In his imagination, the Junto Room was a place of mystery and intrigue. It was strictly off limits, but that fact only heightened his curiosity. In the children's imaginations, behind that door lay such forbidden delights as pirate treasure and Solomon's gold, exotic embalmed animals that once roamed the earth on faraway continents, pharaohs' skulls, and scrolls from biblical patriarchs. None of them was allowed to touch the key that unlocked the room—an unbearable discipline to cultivate, particularly for Elizabeth's oldest son. With obedience, however reluctant, they watched in reticent silence as their mother turned the key in the lock.

The door creaked open to reveal a cavernous room paneled in dark wood. Light from a full moon filtered in through one window, casting dusty shadows on the room's contents as if, after centuries, an ancient tomb had been opened.

The children drank it in, as much as their senses could absorb, while they helped push the chest past the threshold. Book shelves covered three of the room's walls from floor to ceiling. The spines of the varyingly sized tomes created an irregular line around the room that looked like the spine of a mythical sea serpent. Hanging on the fourth papered wall were the fur robes and coronet of an Indian chief and an ancient cross-hilted sword.

Shelf space not filled with books was used to display navigational instruments and research projects with Latin names, telescopes, stuffed birds, dried plants, maps of far-flung places, bottles of wine, mirrors, and iron ore specimens. There were tables and cabinets full of jars and cases in varying sizes, collections of shells and rock specimens, handblown glass, assortments of skins and stuffed animals, arrowheads, deer antlers, and pressed flowers. Candle stands dotted the room at regular intervals. Furniture consisted of one large desk, two ladder backs, and a massive mahogany table guarded on all sides by a dozen high-backed chairs, perfectly spaced and eternally at attention like terra-cotta warriors. It all gave the room a museum look.

"Children, *out*," Elizabeth said, straightening her aching back and herding their retreat into the hall.

She closed the door firmly behind her and turned the key in the lock. More crates would be on their way, she knew, as well as a visit from *Britannia*'s captain. All the Junto members would be rushing in too, as word spread that the chest had arrived. There was much to do.

"Now, Peter," she said, placing her hands squarely on her seven-year-old's shoulders until he had heard all her instructions. "Run and tell Abraham the Junto is meeting tonight."

The boy lunged, but Elizabeth gripped tighter and said, "Make certain he understands he is to find Mr. Franklin and your father."

She could feel him flinch again, but she held him in place.

"Tell him to go to the printing house. If they are not there, he must look for them at the dock. Son, are you listening to me? Tell him the books have come from London. He will know what to do."

The African who worked for Louis would understand the weight of the matter, and he could be counted on to complete the task. Elizabeth let go of her son's shoulders. He was gone before she could turn around.

"Lou, go to Judith's quarters and tell her to bring wet and dry napkins straight away. And tell her I will need her in the kitchen tonight. Make sure she tells Martha to come along too. She can mind the babies while the Junto meets."

Both Abraham and his wife, Judith, belonged to Robert Grace, and the care of these family servants was part of the Timothées' rental agreement. Martha, however, belonged to the Timothées. Louis had answered an ad in the *Pennsylvania Gazette* to buy the young Irish girl's remaining time, owed for her passage to America.

Elizabeth felt physically sick, knowing the treatment of the Negro was as cruel, or worse, than the punishment for indentured White servants, both systems having sprung up from the same rank weed—the Dutch, alongside the Americans, could trace their dirty roots back to the same ugly need for forced manual labor.

But as much as it galled her, she could not deny she was deliciously glad to have help with the children and the housework. After John's death, and now so close to delivery again, it was hard to keep pace with all her responsibilities. Elizabeth and Louis had discussed it and decided they could buy Martha's time if the Library Company or perhaps Mr. Franklin himself would purchase some of the ancient manuscripts and books Louis had brought from Europe. Louis had offered Ben two old manuscripts in the Russian tongue, among other valuable printed items, and they had struck a bargain. Only then did Franklin, shrewd negotiator that he was, reveal that he was the actual owner of the girl's indentured time. Mr. Franklin had "bought" the contracts of several indentured servants until he could turn a profit on them.

The Timothées' decision to part with any volume in their collection was a mutually painful one.

But Elizabeth reassured herself that, as she often said out loud to herself, "Learning hath gained most by those books by which the printers have lost."

She took some comfort in knowing their titles had become part of the library's larger collection. And now, with the contents of the exotic chest here in front of her, she convinced herself it had been the right decision. The Timothée books, along with the treasures contained in the trunk at her feet, belonged to a greater audience.

At least two more trunks could be expected. These would contain an assortment of scientific and historic memorabilia and would need to be sorted and cataloged. She and Louis would also be responsible for other boxes from Mr. Collinson, the Quaker merchant from Philadelphia now living in London, which would be shipped to the Grace home for his many Philadelphia friends. Mr. Bartram, the naturalist, would be coming by to pick up a box of clothes for his son. There would be a microscope for John Logan, along with seed packages and other gifts for Collinson's friends.

With the chest's arrival, her help would be required more than ever. But for now, she had other priorities. In short order their home would be filled to capacity, and the Junto members expected their ale. She was glad about that; by staying around to keep the glasses filled, she would be able to eavesdrop on the men's discussions.

Chapter Seventeen

As dusk fell en route to the dock, Ben passed an exuberant yeoman striding along with a heavy chest on his shoulder as if it were a sack of feathers. Recognizing the big sailor as Johann, a friend of Louis and Elizabeth, the two exchanged hasty greetings.

"One more stop," Johann mentioned jovially.

"Come by and tell me about your trip as soon as you can," Benjamin had answered curtly, barely even turning around.

Seamen rarely realized the news value of what they had to tell, but Ben would listen as long as they would talk. He passed the Quaker Meeting House on Walnut Street where food and clean beds were being readied for immigrants with no place to stay. None of the passengers were leaving the ship just yet, though, and only the unloading of royal packets and boxes had begun.

Franklin had kept track of the incoming vessel since early yesterday morning when first sightings were reported. When the ship was close enough for the captain's wife to read the signals from her widow's walk, the town crier would be notified. Ben hoped the Collinson chest would be aboard this ship; he had been disappointed several times before.

When he had allowed enough time for the ship to make its way up the Delaware River and dock at the Philadelphia pier, Franklin left Louis and his apprentice at the *Gazette* and went to see what he could find out. If the chest was aboard, he might not see it for several more days; the ship would be heavily loaded, and royal packets for government officials would come off first. Passengers would claim their belongings: livestock, household furniture, plants, heirlooms, and the essentials for living. Besides, every merchant in town was looking for his own special cargo. Ben knew he would have a slim chance of talking with the captain, or even the first mate.

But his time at the pier would not be wasted. At the very least, he would glean news items, and perhaps even some advertising for his newspaper.

At the dock Ben surveyed the area, but it seemed his suppositions were confirmed. Then he considered the yeoman he had passed, carrying a chest toward Pewter Platter Alley. Could Collinson have arranged a special courier for their precious cargo? Robert Grace just might have pulled it off. In the time it took for Ben to reach *Britannia* and inquire about shipments, the chest was probably already being delivered to Pewter Platter Alley. He had just passed it.

Breaking into a trot, Ben circled back around the printing house and yelled for the professor to join him.

"I am not entirely sure, but the Collinson chest might already be at your house," Ben shouted excitedly, running on ahead.

Though still a young man, Franklin was puffing a bit. Between his rigorous work schedule and the toll his wife's cooking had taken on his waistline, he had not taken time for swimming or any other exercise. He had discovered that physical prowess was hard-earned and quickly lost if not tended to. But he had resolved to perform what he ought and perform without fail what he resolved. And at present he resolved to run a profitable printing house and keep a happy wife, who loved nothing better than to fill his requests for seconds of her fine cooking.

As he rounded the corner, he could see his destination, and getting his second wind, Ben raced down the dark, cobbled street as fast as the rough thoroughfare permitted. Louisa let him into the house and promptly called for her mother.

Ben went directly into the Junto Room. He stood for a moment, awestruck before the sealed chest, set like an offering at the altar of bookcases. Elizabeth was seated at the mahogany table, working on some papers. She looked up at him, but he made no greeting to her. The upper half of his body was bent forward at a precarious angle while his feet, dragging some unseen weight, moved haltingly but deliberately forward, like Lazarus commanded to come out from the tomb. There was only the chest—it held his complete attention—as Ben moved closer, mouth open, eyes transfixed. His arms hung flaccidly, palms out, a short distance from his body. She could hear the long breath of air he drew in.

When he reached the chest, Ben dropped to his knees, putting the sealed treasure on eye level. As though it were hot, he ran his hand gingerly over the chest's fine woodwork and read the address aloud. His big printer's hands were stained with black ink around the nails, but the touch of the fingertips was light, like that of a musician experimenting with a lullaby.

Likewise, when Louis received word of the trunk's arrival, he knew he could not go home looking as he did. Books like the volumes inside the Collinson chest must be handled with care; his long, leather apron was smeared with ink, and his hands were black from handling type. He paused long enough to grab a cotton cloth to wipe his hands and was out the door with unbridled excitement, fairly sprinting all the way to the Grace home.

When he arrived, Louis's explosive entry startled Ben and Elizabeth. The scholarly man came to an abrupt halt in the hallway, almost skidding past the library door. He stood there a moment, apologetically wiping the last traces of printer's ink from his fingers.

"The box is addressed to you, professor," Ben said, stepping away to give Louis the honor of breaking the chest's seals.

"The honor is yours, Ben," Louis said. "You worked hard for this, for a long time. There would never have been a Philadelphia Library Company if you had not resolved to make the idea work."

"But as official librarian you made it possible for the Junto Club to keep their books in one place," Ben said, still caressing the trunk.

"Your vision encouraged the fellows to see that a subscription library could work. We never would have collected all that money without you to give the project dignity and guarantee the books' safety."

Elizabeth saw that her husband was poised with a reply, but she could tolerate no more delays.

"He who hesitates is lost!" she said emphatically. "Gentlemen, you can stand at the precipice and argue protocol if you choose, but I, for one, would like to see what is in that chest."

Elizabeth's eldest daughter peeked out from behind the door casement in the hall, where Judith had placed clean napkins. She met her at the doorway.

"Thank you, my dear," Elizabeth said. "Now run and see if Judith needs help in the kitchen."

Elizabeth returned to the Junto Room and promptly handed her husband a wet cloth and a dry cloth for washing up before he touched the books.

"Here, Mr. Franklin," Elizabeth said, handing him cloths as well. "You talked the Junto boys into hiring Monsieur Timothée. You should open the chest."

With Louis and Ben both working eagerly at it, the cumbersome lid was off to a chorus of awed silence as palpable as any sweet note.

Inside, resting under wrapping paper, lay beautifully gilded volumes bound in dark leathers with tooling of the European masters. Just looking at them was enough for the moment. Some were small: little handheld prayer books no bigger than a cake of lye soap. Others were larger and thick with pages: words to be absorbed and lessons to be learned, along with rare and delicate woodcuts, engravings, and stipples to be examined. They smelled collectively of wisdom learned by men who had traveled the world, of lamplight and salt spray and animal hide—the masculine scent of education.

Benjamin, fastidiously wiping his hands as though he were Hamlet, reached in reverently to touch the aromatic treasures. Carefully lifting each leather-bound volume, he placed them one by one on the table. After the last book had been removed, Ben examined the chest one more time to make sure one or two had not gone overlooked under the lining.

Elizabeth watched him. His demeanor was that of a child on Christmas morning—delighted with all his gifts, but still hoping there was just one more that somehow had been missed.

Everyone set about indulging their individual literary appetites as the room fell silent, interrupted only by pages turning and audible sighs. Louis examined the ornate leather binding on an old favorite, lovingly caressing it with the respect of a scholar and skilled book binder. Elizabeth, not content with just looking at covers—beautiful though they were—had taken a seat in an armchair and was already engrossed in a new French novel entitled *Le Paysan parvenu*.

Ben was nose-deep in John Locke's *A Collection of Several Pieces*.

"I first read this in England," Franklin said. "Just about the time I met you and your lovely wife."

He glanced over at Elizabeth, but she was too intent on her own treasure. Each page she gingerly turned by touching only the top outside corner of each sheet. Ben watched her for some time, entranced with the respect she employed. He opened Locke's *Essays* again, this time emulating her technique and sighing with contentment as he did.

Still carefully holding the book in her left hand, Elizabeth reached for the tally sheet of books shipped and their costs.

"Mr. Collinson has spent our forty-five pounds well," Elizabeth reported with delight. "Just a minute, and I will tell you more."

She lay the book carefully and walked to the doorway where Martha held a tray of mugs.

"Place them on the sideboard, please," Elizabeth instructed the girl, "and bring chairs from the front room. Make sure Judith is at work on the pretzels. Louisa can help; tell her to braid them large and use extra salt. And tell Abraham to bring up a barrel of ale and have another at the ready should the Junto require it."

Back at the mahogany table, she took up her accounts book and reached for the tally sheet of books sent, and not sent, in the shipment, as well as their costs.

"He did not send all twelve of Rapin's *History of England*, but instead I see he substituted five of Alexander Pope's volumes of twenty shillings each. Evidently, that is how he was able to buy all these at less than ten shillings each," she said with admiration. "*The Faerie Queene* was only thirty shillings, and he bought Locke's essays too."

"But here is a copy of Sir Isaac Newton's *Philosophy* and Philip Miller's *Gardeners Dictionary*, unaccounted for," she continued. "Was there not a letter on top when we opened the chest?"

Amid a flurry of looking under wrapping paper, Elizabeth found an unsealed letter from Mr. Collinson, dated July 22, 1732, more than three months ago, in London. Elizabeth read it aloud:

> *Gentlemen, I am a Stranger to most of you, but not to your laudable Design to erect a public Library. I beg your Acceptance of my Mite—Sr. Isaac Newton's Philosophy and Philip Miller's Gardening Dictionary. It will be an instance of your Candour to accept the Intention of good Will of the Giver, and not regard the Meanness of the Gift. I wish you success and am with much Respect Yours—Peter Collinson.*

Benjamin was impressed that this young mother had arrived at the mathematical conclusion that, while not everything on their list had been purchased, many of their most desired volumes had been included. For those which Collinson could not find, he had substituted acceptable replacements. The answer to the equation, she had informed them both, was that they had come out in the plus column over all. Ben was impressed. She was a bright woman, without doubt, and Ben had observed that all her children, even the little girls, were being taught to read and write and do figures. He marveled at how she was able to speak and write in

German, English, and French, and perhaps other tongues he had yet to discover. She could quote from Alexander Pope eloquently. In London he had seen women like her, but never in America, especially not among the wives of his leather-apron tradesmen friends. His sister-in-law, John's wife, could set type and help print the paper, but not with Elizabeth's kind of scholarship.

From the corner of his eye, Ben noticed that two of the Timothée children—Mary Elizabeth and Peter—had quietly entered the room. The girl had retrieved a book from the library shelf, despite the strict rules of the Library Company. Ben could not help but be curious about the four-year-old's behavior. She had placed the book on the floor in front of her, not in her lap, and she lay down in front of it to look at the illustrations. A book about birds, Ben surmised. The child studied each page, left to right, as if she were memorizing every line in the engraving. She was careful not to touch the paper until she was ready to turn the page. This she accomplished exactly as her mother had done, by gently holding the corner of each right-hand page. Ben knew the child had been taught this reverence. He believed he would trust her above some adults with his special volumes.

Franklin turned his attention from the child to her mother, still seated at the library table. He allowed his gaze to follow hers, across the room to the doorway where her son Peter was standing. The boy had tied a shirt around his waist to imitate the leather work apron Ben usually wore. He took great care to stand in the exact posture of his idol: left foot under him pointing a little to Peter's left, right foot slightly in front of the left foot, pointing away from his body. The thumb of the boy's right hand was tucked inside an imaginary watch pocket; his left hand was on his left hip. From where Ben was sitting, the boy looked a human clock. *Ten till two*, Ben thought, and pulled out his own watch to check the time. *Big Ben, Little Peter*, he thought to himself.

"Good man, Peter," Ben said with a chuckle as he walked across the room to pat the boy on the head. "You shall make a fine printer one day. You certainly look the part, and under your father's tutelage you will become quite proficient, no doubt. And," he added, bending down to the boy's level, "you have excellent posture. Only thing missing is a gentleman's watch."

He said these words with a wink, and he produced his own watch from his vest pocket.

"One day you will have a fine timepiece of your own, perhaps your father's. Let it be a reminder to you that time is short, and you should always be employed in something useful. There is no finer craft than that of your father."

Peter, beaming with pride at receiving Franklin's praise, offered a serious nod of his head.

"Shall I put the children to bed now, ma'am?" Martha asked from the library door.

"Yes, please," Elizabeth answered. "Louisa is in the kitchen helping Judith. When the children are tucked in, please help her with preparations."

Although no child dared grumble, their mother could read the disappointment in their slumped shoulders and hung heads. Tomorrow would be a busy day though; she would require everyone's help, including the children. The pregnancy was slowing Elizabeth down more than she wished.

Louis had already begun to catalog the books for shelving.

"Well, we have quite the growing collection, do we not?" Ben announced rhetorically as he surveyed the shipment. "James Logan will be quite pleased."

"Godfrey told me that Logan was self-taught," Louis said. "I wonder how many of these books have already become a part of his intellect. Not to mention yours, Franklin."

Louis knew his friend had educated himself by reading everything he could get his hands on. He admired not only Ben's determination to learn, but also his ability, especially as a child.

"I was positively hungry for books," Franklin said, as he stood and walked over to the table to inspect the full order. "To cease to think is but little from ceasing to be. From now on these books will be available to young men in the colony who want to better themselves by learning. Along with the donations you gave us, Timothée—a copy of the *Torah* and of Melchior Adam's *Decades Duau* and my contribution of a black-letter reprint of the *Magna Carta*—we should create quite the intellectual conversation among club members."

A sharp knock at the front door caught them all off guard. Louis walked quickly to answer it. Elizabeth heard murmurings but could not decipher the words. When her husband returned, he had a packet in his hand.

To Franklin he said, "The ship's purser delivered this himself. He called 'round to the print shop, and Debby told him you were here."

Franklin accepted the packet from Timothée with a look of intense curiosity.

"Must be something important," he murmured, breaking the seal on the envelope.

Inside was a missive from Governor Robert Johnson, Charles Towne, dated September of that year.

"Oh my," Ben said, sitting down in the nearest chair. "My man Whitemarsh is dead."

Chapter Eighteen

Louis was livid because his wife had rebuffed his physical advances. "*Paranos*," he mumbled with a mixture of contempt and wounded pride and rolled over in bed with his back to her.

Elizabeth took offence at his accusation and would not be silent.

"No, monsieur," she said. "This is not the product of a disturbed mind."

She could feel him retreating, like a wave drawn back out to sea—the tension, the tug of a force much more powerful than she knew herself to be. She held her breath, waiting for the wave to inevitably come crashing back on her.

It was so late that it was almost early, and Elizabeth was weary from arguing. But she was angry too and would not ignore the remark.

"I *will* read the contract, and we *will* talk about it before you leave tomorrow morning," she said.

Neither one spoke for a long time. The air, thick and prickly, smelled of angry perspiration. She took shallow breaths in the weighted stillness, determined not to be the first one to stir the air with a conciliatory comment. Neither of them wanted to waste precious time arguing, but on this matter she would not relent.

At some length, Louis breathed in deeply and exhaled with a force that communicated his irritation. He rolled onto his back again, eyes fixed, unblinking, on some spot on the ceiling.

"You already know what it says," Louis said, so intractably patient as to seem impatient. "There is no need for you to read the document for yourself. It is the same contract, in writing, on which we have already verbally agreed."

He continued, "Elizabeth, we have so little time left to be together. Is this really how you want to spend it?"

Indeed, she had read the document Tom Whitemarsh signed before setting out to be Franklin's business partner in Charles Towne, South Carolina. Tom's story resembled their own too much to ignore. For Louis, there was comfort in that fact, but it was the similarities that frightened Elizabeth most.

When Whitemarsh arrived in Pennsylvania three years ago, it seemed the timing could not have been better. Franklin's partnership with Hugh Meredith had recently ended on bad footing. Elizabeth wagered a guess that it had something, or perhaps everything, to do with finances. Whatever the reason, Thomas Whitemarsh stepped off the boat and into an immediate apprenticeship under Franklin. Louis had done the same, becoming Ben's journeyman in Philadelphia.

Thomas had been a compositor, like Louis, and both men had known Ben in London. In both cases Franklin needed an apprentice, and in both cases that apprentice was sent to Charles Towne where the Commons House of Assembly was offering a bounty of one thousand pounds to any printer willing to move there. Three men had responded: Thomas, sent by Franklin, as well as a Massachusetts man named Eleazer Phillips, and George Webb, also of Pennsylvania.

Elizabeth remembered the rumpled man they called Webb, waving a broadside from Charles Towne's wharf to warn them away on the crossing. *Poor fellow*, she thought. He may have fallen to yellow fever himself. Whatever the reason for his death, he did not last long. And since he never officially printed for the colony, he did not receive the bounty.

South Carolina Governor Robert Johnson thought Whitemarsh was the better choice as official printer. It seemed Franklin's influence was not confined only to the Pennsylvania Colony. Ben had written up a contract, watertight, between him and his journeyman Thomas Whitemarsh. He had invested heavily in the man and was counting, no doubt, on receiving that bounty. Franklin now was on the hook for a printing press and types, in return for a third of Whitemarsh's yet-to-be-realized profit. Elizabeth felt sure it was a source of concern for Franklin, who knew the whereabouts of each and every farthing in his possession.

But the Assembly had preferred the Boston man, Eleazer Phillips, and he was awarded the money, much to Franklin's regret.

The advantage turned in Franklin's favor last year, however, when Phillips died. Suddenly Ben and his partner Whitemarsh were in the enviable position of sole printer to the government and editor of the *South-Carolina Gazette*. The bounty, to be sure, was considerably less now than what had been offered to Phillips, but Elizabeth suspected Franklin was only too happy to receive two hundred pounds as a bonus for his man to take over the *Gazette*. At least he finally had the opportunity to turn a profit.

And now Whitemarsh was dead of yellow fever. The black vomit, others called it.

Franklin had wasted no time in proposing Louis as replacement. Her husband had been offered the same contractual stipulations as Whitemarsh: surviving partner takes all, inheriting the full business and the option of printing for King George II of Britain and the Assembly.

To hear him tell it, Franklin had taken a great risk. After all, it was his printing press and shop that were sitting idle and collecting dust in the Carolina wilderness. Elizabeth had studied the contract, though, and the way it was written, Ben had risked nothing but capital. She understood that his priority now was to protect his investment and fulfill the contract to print the colony's business for the King of England, including printing the fledgling *Gazette* and all royal job work. But to do that, he would need another working partner, because Mr. Franklin would certainly not be going himself.

He needed someone who would travel to the colony immediately. Someone who was competent, of course, but also someone who was willing to do the heavy work of beginning to print again. Someone whose circumstances were such that the risk was worth the reward.

Elizabeth knew it was a great opportunity, and her husband was the ideal man to send. Louis was eager to go; he would sail tomorrow on a late-November tide and officially begin his new duties in Charles Towne in January. But the frightening thought kept intruding: what would become of them if he died? She knew she would have no recourse but to remarry. Perhaps it was wrong to let him go without her. The trip was only down the coast, two weeks at most—not nearly as far as they had come together already. She could help him more than he would ever admit.

But the point was moot; Louis would go first. She and the children would follow in the spring. Her husband needed to spend all his time in the shop Thomas Whitemarsh had set up, if indeed it was still there. It was imperative that he prove to the royal governor that he was capable of continuing the appointment as King's Printer. Before he left, however, Elizabeth was determined to make sure her husband's trusting, but naïve, nature was not a death knell for them all.

"Louis, ask yourself why Mr. Franklin, as sole owner, is willing to give up his best journeyman printer and send him on his way immediately as Tom's replacement," she implored.

"What accusations are you making, Elizabeth? Are you suggesting that Franklin, my *friend*, whom I have known for years and who has helped us in *every possible way* since we stepped off the boat, would be unfair?" he said, verbally punctuating the question as a statement.

His unblinking eyes were hot pokers that threatened to burn her, but Elizabeth returned his stare. She felt tears well up; her nose began to run with snot, but she wiped it hastily, refusing to cry. Right now, she wanted his respect more than his protection.

"No, Louis," she answered firmly, "Ben is not unfair, and neither is the agreement. But men are dead. Good men with families. What if Tom Whitemarsh had had a wife and five children with another on the way? What would happen to them? What would happen to us if you took the fever?" she asked pointedly.

The room was thick with viscous words hanging heavy, refusing to dissipate. Neither spoke; their exhales continuing to heat the suffocating air.

After some time, Elizabeth left their bed and put on her dressing robe and slippers. With her back to her husband, she walked to the bureau where the contract lay, written in Benjamin's fine hand. She could smell her husband's impatience, but unfazed, she picked up the document and read it again, not once but twice. When she had finished, she turned and shook it at him.

"Louis Timothée, how could you do this? Ben has looked after himself and his family, but who is looking after you and yours? Have you no concern for us?"

Louis sat up in bed, angry. "You are being ridiculous," he said. "You agreed that I should go. This is a fine time for you to be backing out."

"I am not backing out," Elizabeth said firmly, swallowing hard and forgetting to hide her nausea.

Perhaps a bit of vomit would help her case, she thought, putting a hand to her mouth.

"You just think about it," she said. "Just *think*."

She sat down heavily on the bed. Her black eyes softened as she looked at him. Anguish saturated her husband's slumped body. He was the one sailing into the unknown alone, not she. He looked so small, as if the small bones in his upper body had been winnowed like chaff. She could see the expression of abandonment in his slack shoulders, in the furrows and folds carved on his face. His hands— palms up, empty, and resting on his thighs—reminded her of a supplicant just realizing that God is a human invention, a figment. That there is no one to hear his lamentations and nowhere to turn.

She placed her hand in his and gripped it.

"I. Cannot. Lose. You," she managed to say, emphasizing each word. "Please. Think about how it would be for me and the children, including the one I carry now, if you came down with yellow fever and died."

Her words hung like a bad omen in the silence that followed. She regretted speaking them aloud. They both knew the dangers, which, like thoughts of home, were forbidden to be verbalized. Louis knew his strong wife would have to deliver their child without him. He knew she wanted desperately to have him with her, particularly after John's death. He knew the child she carried now would be several months old before he would even set eyes on him or her.

When Louis finally spoke, his voice sounded as if he was close to tears. "And what, my dear, could Franklin do, in Philadelphia, if I were to die? Do you think he wanted Tom to die so he could get his half of the partnership? Ben stands to lose everything unless another printer can look after his interests."

"That is true," she offered. "Certainly, Mr. Franklin did not intend Mr. Whitemarsh to die, and he would not wish it to happen to you."

Then, phrasing the words as gently as she could, she added, "But each must look after his own, my love. It is not Mr. Franklin's responsibility to look after you and your family. That duty falls squarely on your capable shoulders. That is why I am begging you, please, do not sign this paper as it is written."

She raised his hand to her lips and kissed it, then let it drop to his lap.

"What would you have me do, Elizabeth?" he asked. "Demand a magic potion for yellow fever?"

The beautiful enunciation she loved so much was edged with sarcasm, but she met his words calmly.

"Nothing but Providence can insure your health and safety. This is not the topic of debate, and you know it. It is precisely because there is no cure for yellow fever, or shipwreck, or Indian arrows, or hurricanes or—or anything else unforeseen that might take you from us that I am trying to get you to understand," she said. "This contract is not just a legally binding agreement to go to Charles Towne and open a print shop and begin publishing the newspaper. This contract is for the next six long years of your life. Men have died in this capacity already. That is a fact. Also indisputable is the fact that your oldest son is not yet eight years old. You need to make a provision for me to run the newspaper should anything happen to you in the next six years. Do it, if only for your son."

Louis turned toward her and sighed. He was listening, and Elizabeth seized the opportunity.

"Remember last August when Mr. Franklin traveled to Boston for an extended visit and left his wife in charge? We were the ones who put out seven issues of the *Pennsylvania Gazette* and ran his print shop for him."

"And all the time the masthead said, 'Printed by B. Franklin,'" Louis responded, "and you said one day we would have a paper that said, 'Printed by Louis Timothée, and that is what Ben is offering me now."

"Louis, Ben was away for *seven weeks*," she reminded him. "We did all the work and got the paper out, knowing full well that Debby would not recognize her own name in type if she saw it there."

"Ben took care of all that legally," Louis said with a bit of animation back in his posture. "He gave his wife power of attorney, but he willed the business to his son. If he had not come back, we could have gone on working for Debby until his son was old enough to take over."

"Exactly, exactly!" Elizabeth said. "And do you remember what happened when you hurt your hand while Mr. Franklin was gone and you were unable to set type? And what happened the week you were rushing to finish that book binding job and did not have time for the newspaper?"

"You did it for me, of course. But Elizabeth, you *said* you wanted to. You were happy enough to let Judith look after the children and the house for you."

"The point is," Elizabeth reminded him, "I *could* do the work. That is the difference. Three-year-old Will Franklin could not have put out the *Gazette* any more than Debby could have, if Mr. Franklin had not returned. My dear Monsieur, if you go to the Carolinas and die—I pray to God it will not happen—Peter could not run the business. But *I could*. And can you tell me please, what alternative you would offer me, as a widow, for raising our children?"

She could see in his eyes that he knew her only option would be to remarry. The thought of it galled him. But their young children would depend on her, and while the image of her lying with another man physically turned his stomach, he had personally seen what became of widows and orphans sent to the poor house. So many had so much in America, yet so often "the least of these" were ignored. All it would take is each willing man giving two bits a week to sustain a city's poor. Just two bits. But there were no provisions, and Louis could not bear to think of his family suffering from want. He had to acknowledge the sad fact: each must look after his own.

"All I am asking," Elizabeth said softly, "is that you not sign the contract as it is set up now. Just give me the power of attorney, as Mr. Franklin gave his wife, and let me negotiate with him after you sail for Charles Towne—some equitable method of protecting me and the children without harming Mr. Franklin's business interests. God willing, we will join you soon, and you can purchase the business from Mr. Franklin and write your own will as you wish."

She sat, quietly now, awaiting his reaction. Heavy syllables lingered, swirling around his ears while he evaluated each one. Elizabeth could taste a tinge of vomit staining the back of her throat, urging her to run for a cup of ginger tea. But she swallowed the acid and waited. When he turned toward her, his eyes were moist.

She had won.

He grabbed her and held her tightly. Business was not what was foremost on his mind now. Perhaps it never had been; perhaps he had let her win the point in order to move on to more pressing matters

She lay back, lifted her night gown, and let him win the next round.

Chapter Nineteen

"Elizabeth," her husband whispered. "Ship sails within the hour." She turned toward him, dark circles under her eyes. She felt like she had only just fallen asleep. The room was dark and freezing in the winter predawn. Louis was already dressed.

"I know," Elizabeth said, trying desperately not to sound like the helpless wife being left behind.

"My dear, we have been over this myriad times. Charles Towne is *settled*. There are people there from many different countries. It is the Europe of southern America; you yourself saw it from *Britannia*. And it is where the opportunities are taking us—not just opportunities for me, but also for Peter. I, for one, would not be surprised to find the Timothée family listed among aristocratic citizens within a decade. We will work hard. We are intelligent and capable. I have been trained well, and you are the best printer's wife one could imagine. Do not worry."

Elizabeth crawled heavily out of bed and removed a waistcoat from his trunk, mindlessly refolding it and placing it neatly on top of his breeches.

"I have read reports of settlers reduced to eating each other rather than starve."

Louis turned to face her. "Elizabeth," he said, taking her hands in his, "let us leave cannibalism to the cannibals, shall we? And most of the natives have left Carolina for more remote wilderness. Those who have remained are friendly."

"These were not cannibals, Louis. They were Frenchmen who sailed under Jean Ribault to the colony first. When they were left alone longer than expected without enough provisions and in the company of hostile natives, they attempted to return to Europe under sails made from their own garments. They did not have enough food to make the trip and were reduced to eating their leather shoes and, ultimately, the corpse of a friend to stay alive," she said.

The corners of Louis's mouth rose into a cautious smile. She could tell he had stopped listening and was instead thinking about his response.

"Elizabeth," he said, unable to contain a complete grin, "surely after these many years of marriage, you realize ... we French will eat anything."

She tried not to laugh but could not.

"I will start a fire. At least, with a hearty breakfast in your stomach, the other passengers will have a fighting chance," she mumbled. She knew he would need a good hot meal before boarding the sloop *Lydia*.

Wordlessly, they walked together, arm in arm, to the kitchen where Abraham had already laid down firewood for the kettle. Elizabeth sent the Negro to the pump for water and told him to check the chicken coops on the way back.

"The Barred Rocks should have laid early today," she told him. "If there are two nice brown eggs in the nest, bring them to me."

Wrapping an apron around her huge belly, she carved sourdough bread from the sideboard platter for Louis but snuck a piece for herself too, chewing it slowly. In a few minutes, it was working; the ever-present nausea was letting up.

As nervous as she felt about being left alone to deliver their baby, she admitted to herself that she was even more nervous about negotiating directly with Mr. Franklin on the terms of her husband's six-year printing partnership.

"Were you able to sleep?" she asked Louis, knowing it had been a short night for both of them.

"Briefly," he said. "I finally just got up and went to the print shop. You know Ben; he is an early riser and was hard at work already. I asked to look at the power of attorney he had drawn up for his wife."

"What did he say?" Elizabeth wanted to know.

"He looked puzzled and asked me why I wanted to see it. He reminded me that he had blanks, but I told him I preferred to use his own document as my template in case there were specific changes he had made for his wife from which you might benefit."

"And what was his response?" Elizabeth asked.

"Without looking up from his ledger books, he said, 'My good man, whyever would you want a power of attorney document?' And I told him I wanted it for my wife so the two of you can work up our contract after I am gone."

Elizabeth tried to steel herself against panic. *Ridiculous*, she told herself, rubbing her palms on her apron. She thought about the expression Ben must have had on his face when Louis told him he would not be signing the Charles Towne contract as written. By now she was used to that somewhat startled look of disbelief any time things did not go entirely Franklin's way.

Louis said Ben had played his cards close to the vest.

"He asked me, 'Do we not have an accord?' and I assured him we most certainly do. I told him I merely preferred not to sign it until you had an opportunity to study it in greater detail. With power of attorney, you can sign the contract for me," Louis said.

Ben offered the document he had drawn up for Debby, dated August 30, 1733. Louis typeset the exact wording, substituting the correct names and making only one change in Franklin's original document: on the line where Ben referred to Deborah Franklin as his "trusty and loving Friend," Louis had struck out "Friend" and wrote in "Wife."

Louis said Ben was somewhat uncomfortable about sending him without a signed contract. Elizabeth reckoned that, although the two men had enjoyed a mutually beneficial working relationship without even the first misunderstanding or disagreement, business and profit had a way of separating the best of friends from their common sense.

"To satisfy Ben, I said I would sign the contract as it is written with the caveat that he would write in the changes you want," Louis told Elizabeth. "Ben knows our concern is over an inheritance clause, and he is agreeable to the revision. He said, 'I have your word that there will be no other substantial changes?' and I assured him there were none. I told him I was only asking for a few minor changes to satisfy my pregnant wife and that you had some ideas about being the King's Printer yourself in case a Carolina crocodile eats me."

Louis said when Franklin heard that, he was immediately satisfied. Ben knew, from what he had observed at the Philadelphia Library Company and at his print shop, that the woman was quite competent.

Suddenly there were two arms wrapped around Elizabeth's belly.

"When will breakfast be ready?" Louis asked, turning her around to face him. "I hope, if you are planning to serve one of the neighbors, it is that man next door who empties his privy in our yard. Just make sure you serve him with plenty of honey."

"Stop it, Louis," Elizabeth said, rapping his knuckles with a wooden spoon. "You will have to indulge your taste for human flesh some other time."

She placed two boiled eggs in front of him with a thick buttered slice of sourdough bread, hot from the fire. In his mug she poured a stout cup of tea and offered him cream.

"The children are still sleeping," she said as she took a seat beside him at the long wooden table near the fire. "I think it is best to let them."

Louis agreed.

"It is so early, and we have already said our goodbyes. Besides, I have very little time to get to the dock," he said, wiping his mouth and standing to leave. "I will have Amsterdam carry my trunk. No need for you to follow, Elizabeth."

He took her hands in his. She looked into his eyes and held his gaze. It was a soulful exchange; his eyes said everything he could not say: that the separation would not be long, that he would arrive safely and would be fit as a fiddle when she saw him again, that he would restart the newspaper and print shop, build the business, and be ready for her capable assistance when she and the children arrived in just a few months. She heard all his unspoken words, and her eyes answered with her own unspeakable thoughts: *do not worry about me, or the children, or the baby; you can trust me to discuss the contract with Ben to our mutual satisfaction; I will pack our family and meet you at the dock in Charles Towne in the spring.*

And then, in a kiss that was meant to be remembered hungrily until they were together again, their tongues found the soft, warm places in each other's mouths. She felt herself flush as if for the first time. When their lips parted, her eyes fluttered open. He kissed her tear-dampened cheek and squeezed her hands before letting them drop. She turned toward the hearth, only for a moment, to collect herself. When she turned back around, he was gone.

Chapter Twenty

Early the next morning, Elizabeth rolled laterally to the edge of the bed, seeing no reason to continue lying there alone when sleep refused to come. The fire had all but gone out, and her fingers were stiff from that kind of bone-gnawing cold. Pins and needles sparked in her numb, icy feet, so cold they felt hot. She stood up and stamped them, tingling. She bent over awkwardly—just enough to stoke the fire—and the child within her stirred, catching her off guard. Elizabeth grabbed her womb as a wash of memories suddenly flooded her. Coarse emotions, like the groans spoken of in Romans, welled up. Tears boiled over, running down her cheeks and into her mouth, leaving their white scars. She shook under a raw injury that would not close, remembering their newborn buried at Christ Church.

John had been born in the arms of Debby Franklin's mother on a cold Philadelphia day in March. He died three weeks later on an even colder day. The frozen ground refused his small coffin, turning the spade away. Men used axes to force the earth to take him, digging in teams to reach a depth below the frost line.

What was it the clergyman said? Some quotation from William Penn, founding father of the Pennsylvania province. She knew it from the *Oxford Book of Prayer*. Elizabeth cleared her mind and saw the words: "We give back to you, O God, those whom you gave to us. You did not lose them when you gave them to us, and we do not lose them by their return to you. Your dear Son has taught us that life is eternal and love cannot die. So death is only an horizon and an horizon is only the limit of our sight."

"Let me just keep him," Elizabeth had begged her husband, choking on her own sobs and cradling the corpse that was no bigger nor heavier than a cornhusk doll in her arms. "*Please*, Louis."

The words echoed like lunacy in her memory now. She knew in her heart he could not allow it, but she could still feel the tiny bundle in her arms. *He just needs to be warmed*, she remembered thinking as she paced across the kitchen floor, shouting at Peter to stoke more wood on the fire.

"Hurry up!" she had yelled angrily. "Can you not see your baby brother is cold?"

Whispering to the dead child, she held him tightly against her breast and reached for another blanket to wrap around him.

"John, more wood is coming. Mama is here."

Elizabeth clutched her chest now as buried bruises continued to push their way to the surface. The weight of it kept her from breathing.

Louis had tried to comfort her. When she finally relinquished the body to him, he was so gentle. She knew her husband to be a sensitive man, but this gentleness, on this occasion, he performed purely for her.

"Sweet child," he whispered, rocking the bundle. "Sweet, sweet baby boy of mine. Too soon for this world. We shall see you again, one day."

Louis gave the body to Debby as tenderly as if he were handing her a butterfly with a broken wing, then quickly turned to his wife and embraced her. He hoped to spare Elizabeth the indelible image of Debby walking away with John, their embodiment of all New World possibilities. In her husband's arms Elizabeth had dissolved into weeping convulsions: angry, soul-piercing cries that begged for answers.

But receiving none, Elizabeth backed away from Louis and drew herself up to her full height. She wiped away the tears, blotted her nose, and smoothed her skirt.

Let it go, she had told herself. *Let him go. There are living children who need your attention now. There will be more babies, God willing.*

The fire crackled, distracting her. Pennsylvania weather was brutal on a pregnant woman's extremities, but it was her aching back that continued to suffer most.

Nothing was more uncomfortable than the lower back pain toward the end of a pregnancy, she thought.

Best to keep off her feet and as warm as possible, wrapping one of Debby Franklin's beautiful knitted shawls tighter around her shoulders. Her gray flannel maternity frock was a bit scratchy but warm, and it helped insulate her from the bitter wind whistling through narrow openings around the drawing room window.

Winter was such an unkind season to bear a baby, she thought, absently staring out the window.

She could see billows of snowdrifts leading down to city streets, where muddy ruts were glazed over with thin orange sheets of ice. Wagon wheels and horse hooves carved bleeding wounds that puddled in the battered ground. The deep cuts almost immediately froze over again: scabs waiting to be reopened by the next passerby.

From the side table, Elizabeth picked up the contract and read it again. It was five and a half pages of carefully chosen words. She had put a mark near each change she wished to make, corresponding to a long sheet of paper where she had written out her corrections. Each item was identified for quick location on the original: page, paragraph, line.

Before he left, Louis had signed the original. His lovely signature practically leaped off the page at her, some familiar remnant of himself left behind to give her courage. *The joined-up cursive writing of a person bears so much of their essence*, she thought, *each so unique, so descriptive of an individual's attributes.* In her husband's hand she could see the creative side of him: large loopy letters, beginning with the *L*, like waves across a pond; the *o*, a pebble, tossed in, sending undulations from the *u* to the *i* and finally, the *s*, where the finishing stroke to the right suggested all would soon return to glassiness in this scripted body of water.

Optimistic, she thought.

But it was in the *Timothée* part where he got serious and buckled down to business: a strong *T*, as if he meant to tear the page with the stroke, followed by dark and unintelligible letters atop each other, until the final *e*, which was drawn out in a jagged straight line. It left her feeling that something was being continued, perhaps on the next page. She held the paper close to her heart and breathed in the ink. In her imagination, she could smell him there.

But Louis had already sailed for Charles Towne, of course, leaving the final details to his capable wife. Girding herself for the meeting with Mr. Franklin, Elizabeth wondered what Ben's response would be when she informed him that she had more than just a few changes to make.

Mary interrupted her mother's thoughts when she brought in another load of cataloged books.

"More volumes from the Broughton donation," the child said with pride.

"M.E., you are a big help. Monsieur Papa would be so proud of you," Elizabeth said, laying the contract aside. "Here, give me your hands, and let me warm them."

"I am not cold," Mary Elizabeth insisted, but she was happy to let her mother rub them together in her own larger hands. "I like helping you, Mama. Is Mr. Franklin coming to learn French today? Papa said he is certainly having trouble with it."

"I hope he does come," Elizabeth said. "I need to talk to him."

All morning she had thought of nothing but the contract. She was not entirely sure she could summon the courage again if Franklin were to postpone.

"En français, *Maman*?" the little girl asked.

"*Non*, ma petite fille," Elizabeth responded, pulling her daughter close. "It will be in the King's English today. This conversation requires a thorough understanding of our discussion. But yours is an excellent observation. Perhaps we might have a conversation in French with Monsieur Franklin someday soon."

If he did not come, Elizabeth knew she would have to go to the shop to see him. Talking here would be easier on her physically, but also because she felt so much more confident here. She knew she could better present her case in familiar surroundings, and that would translate into his seeing things her way. Everything depended on it.

Complicating matters, too, would be Debby Franklin's presence at the print shop. She would not understand their discussion and might ask questions. Debby was a dear, but she had not a head for business. Earlier in the year when Ben left to visit relatives for two months, he had given Debby power of attorney, but it was clear his "friend" of a wife had no idea what that meant. Debbie was not ignorant; she seemed to want to learn, but Elizabeth feared her questions could risk the discussion becoming a lesson in parliamentary law rather than the resolution of personal business Elizabeth intended it to be. It would be easier to accomplish her goal in the atmosphere of the library. Surely, he would come.

"Mr. Franklin will be here," she assured her daughter. "He has not missed a day since the books first were delivered. And you are right, he is having a bash of a time trying to learn French, n'est pas?" she said with a wink to her bright young daughter who had a bent for languages, just like her father. "But today I must talk with him about other business besides French and his studying."

"Will I have to leave when he comes, Mama? I can be quiet," Mary asked, her eyes wide with pleading.

"Yes, M.E., all of you must go. The matter is strictly between Mr. Franklin and me."

Elizabeth saw the shadow of disappointment creep across the child's face.

"But do please serve the cider before you leave. We shall require your considerable hostess skills this morning," she offered.

The child's face brightened; Elizabeth could see how happy that made her daughter.

"And I shall require one more thing of you, dear," Elizabeth added. "Please say a prayer that I can make Mr. Franklin understand what I want him to do, and why."

Her namesake smiled and nodded agreeably.

"Mama, are you afraid to talk business with Mr. Franklin?"

Elizabeth was not afraid of Mr. Franklin. She was afraid of her temper and lack of patience and self-restraint if she could not make him understand.

"No, M.E., I am not afraid. Mr. Franklin is just not accustomed to talking over business matters with a woman."

To that end, she was prepared for a fight; she would call in the scrivener if necessary and let him speak for her, but on this matter, she would not yield. Franklin would discover that she was not cut from the same cloth as most American women, nor even some men—including her husband—when it came to business matters. When Ben arrived, she would be casual and work up gradually to the subject of her husband's contract. She would be cordial; he was a friend, after all, in addition to Louis's employer. Good God, if she could not talk to the man in a civil manner ...

Elizabeth stood quickly when she heard the front door open. Muffled male voices. Exchanged garbled pleasantries. His hat was taken. Hung on the hall tree. His coat, scarf, walking stick. "Please come in." Heavy footfall down the hallway.

Her heart was beating faster, and her hands, so unbearably cold just a few minutes earlier, now began to sweat.

"Mr. Franklin, please come in!" she managed to say, a bit too flustered-sounding. "How good of you to come. Warm yourself by the fire. Difficult weather, would you not say, Mr. Franklin?"

Elizabeth felt herself prattling on, filling the silence with unrelated topics as if to talk about anything but the matter at hand. By the time the firewood was laid and stoked to a crackling roar, Ben had already taken up his place at the big work table.

She blurted out her problem.

"Mr. Franklin," she said, coming across more defiantly than she would have wished, "you and I need to change some items in the contract between you and Louis. As you are aware, he has given me the power of attorney in his absence to negotiate with you."

She studied his face for his reaction. Franklin always had a look of someone biting down on a bitter pill and discovering a honey taste when he talked with her. His brow furrowed and his mouth pursed into a frown momentarily but quickly melted into a half smile, as if he were suddenly surprised and pleased with the interchange.

He ignored the gauntlet, however, and turned to face Mary Elizabeth, who was just entering the room with a silver tray containing a steaming kettle and two mugs. She hung the kettle on the firebox hook and turned toward Franklin to set down the tray. Engaging the child with his solemn gray-blue eyes and good-humored twist to the corner of his mouth, he made a formal bow to her, which brought out the little girl's dimples, and cleared a spot for the refreshments amid his papers on the library table.

"I still cannot get over your mother's considerable talents," he told the girl as much for Elizabeth's ears as for anyone else's. "She continues to surprise me. She has proven herself to be a master typesetter, and now, it seems, she is also a shrewd negotiator."

With a wink to the young girl, he turned his back on them both and made a big business of jogging his papers together in precise order.

When he had seated himself again, he smiled at Mary and made a mock gesture of wiping the smile off his face. M.E. giggled as she left the room.

Looking his sternest possible, Ben said in the voice of old James Logan, "The defense rests, Madame. And what is the pleasure of the plaintiff?"

He is not taking me seriously, Elizabeth thought. His attempt at levity made her more determined that he would hear her out. But before she could say or do anything further, Franklin handed her a manuscript in his fine handwriting. Stunned, she recognized it as a fresh copy of the contract titled, "Articles of Agreement with Louis

Timothée." She turned to the final page. Her husband had already signed it, dated two days ago.

"Louis told me you were unhappy with the agreement and wanted to talk with me about it," Franklin said casually.

"I can tell you right now what I want," Elizabeth said firmly.

She knew Mr. Franklin had acquired some of his interest in the Carolina paper because his first partner there had died and left it to him. Perhaps their predecessor Mr. Whitemarsh had accepted the survivor-takes-all contract because he had no surviving family members. Louis, however, had a wife and children to consider, an argument a fortiori for stipulating survivorship. With her husband already on his way to Charles Towne and the contract negotiations still unsettled, she was determined to insist that an inheritance clause be inserted. If Louis were to be incapacitated or die before Peter could assume responsibility, Elizabeth would run the paper in his name.

"I know a bit already," Benjamin replied. "Your husband told me you want the contract to say your young Peter can take over the business should Louis die within the term of the agreement. Will you do me the honor of reading the changes I have made, and afterward, tell me if you wish anything to be different?"

Elizabeth looked up from the document in disbelief. Mr. Franklin was dead serious.

"After that," Ben said, "if necessary, we will have the scrivener in to make sure the contract is as right for you as it is for me. It is better to have these things understood in the beginning."

Franklin, pleased with himself for having already given considerable thought to how he could word the thing to her advantage, was eager to hear her assessment of his efforts.

Elizabeth sat down abruptly.

Mary Elizabeth, who knew she should not be present, had been watching solemn-eyed from the fireside and giggled at the suddenness of her mother's movement.

By now Elizabeth was dimpling as much as her daughter.

"What I want to know," Elizabeth laughed, "is how are you going to let your Poor Richard explain the business principle you are using here?"

"I have already written it," he said, "but not for Poor Richard's *Almanack*. This is for Poor Benjamin. Shall I quote it for you?"

Mother and daughter nodded simultaneously.

"I knew a miser," Ben began, "who gave up every kind of comfortable living, all the pleasure of doing good to others, all the esteem of his fellow citizens, and the joys of benevolent friendship, for the sake of accumulating wealth. Poor man, said I, you pay too much for your whistle."

For a moment, the words hung in the air. Benjamin seemed to lapse into awkwardness, as though he regretted his audacity in quoting his own work to this scholarly woman whom he so openly admired. He looked at her, ripe with another pregnancy. She had borne her husband seven children and raised four of them, soon to be five, past teething. This woman had given him a glimpse of what marriage could be, with a woman who was not only a bed partner and a keeper of a man's house and effects, but also someone who could understand the yearnings of his heart and mind and work alongside him to create a prosperous future. Good and faithful Debby, with her childlike devotion, her continual war on dirt and gift for thrift, was a fine woman, but she could not be compared with someone like Elizabeth. Debby was dependable, hard-working, and anxious to please, a good companion rather like a dog with whom one might enjoy passing the time of day. But Louis Timothée's wife was far and away more capable of carrying on an intellectual conversation than his own good helpmate. Madame Timothée was just as competent as her husband in doing the work of librarian for the Philadelphia Library Company. She was more familiar with the writings of the books in the Philadelphia Library Company perhaps even than Ben himself, and he was the one person most responsible for bringing the company into being. This woman could set type and read proofs faster and more accurately than he. But most astounding of all, she had put the accounts of his shop in good order, sent bills for overdue payments, and collected on them. This woman could foresee accounting problems and ward them off. She had made it easier for him to pay off his debts. How could Louis Timothée fail at anything with a wife like that? Here was the Greek archetype of a woman: mentally stimulating, a true partner in life, and all the more physically alluring because of it. He had no reason to doubt her competency in the area of discourse, or intercourse for that matter.

Franklin, ashamed of his thoughts and glad she could not read them, returned to a feigned absorption in his papers. He hoped she would break the silence. The kettle over the fire began to whistle.

Smiling, Elizabeth nodded to her daughter to begin pouring. She jogged the papers on her desk, as Benjamin had done, for their most precise order. This Benjamin Franklin, so young and so serious and so in need of someone to smooth out his edges, was not the shrewd ambitious young tradesman she had thought him to be. Ambitious he was, and cleverly shrewd, but there was a benevolence about him and an exposed rawness, almost tenderness, she had not seen before.

Finally, Ben spoke.

"Do not do anything at all with the contract now, Elizabeth," he said. "When I am gone, write in the changes you want. I will read them, and we shall talk about them."

Elizabeth studied his face. Was he, after all, only humoring her about the changes in the contract? Their eyes locked in a gaze of mutual questioning.

"My dear Madame Timothée," Ben continued, choosing his words carefully, "Peter is not yet eight years old. In six years, he will be only fourteen."

He paused, allowing her time to follow his words to their logical conclusion.

"Are you certain you could be the King's Printer and put out a weekly newspaper in the semitropics of Carolina?"

He looked at her shivering over the contract and wondered if it was the temperature or nerves that caused her to shake. She could not be more than a year or two older than he. He felt a sudden urge and would have embraced her in an effort to warm and comfort her, had it not been inappropriate.

"I certainly hope to never find out, Mr. Franklin," Elizabeth answered. "But I should not want my husband's heir to suffer, should we lose our head of household prematurely. For his sake, I can assure you I would endeavor to be a suitable substitute as King's Printer until my son reaches majority."

Ben stood and met her gaze briefly, then focused on his shoes as if they were the most curious things he had ever seen. Finally, he spoke.

"An admirable parry. But you should know that, in this, I am not your opponent. I should have no trouble believing you would be able to handle some of this Carolina outpost work," he said confidently.

Elizabeth called for Franklin's coat and hat. Together, they walked to the door, footfall and folds of fabric the only sounds echoing in the hallway.

As Franklin was backing out the door, he bowed low to her and repeated, "No trouble at all, Madame Timothée."

Chapter Twenty-One

Elizabeth's mouth flushed with saliva, the way one does just before vomiting. The pain of her tender breasts made her cringe as she rolled over in the big four-poster bed. With Monsieur Timothée gone, their bed no longer seemed nearly as big as she had dreaded. For just this minute she was glad to be alone. She was free to give in to the nausea without having to hide it from her husband.

If she were back in Holland, she would be sipping kinder draught, the bitter brew for female complaint that had united and strengthened all the women of her family: strong women who did all their work and half of their husbands' while carrying their babies. She reached behind the nightstand curtain where she had put some pumpernickel the night before. The bread, swallowed slowly before she got out of bed, usually helped.

"You, of all people, Elizabeth," she chided, "still in bed when there is work to be done."

The headache—the whole top of her head was pounding—was never like this with the other children.

The contract sat on her bedside table. She reached over, picked it up, and read it again.

With satisfaction, she read the parenthetical phrase in Ben's handwriting: "now bound on a Voyage to Charles Towne in South

Carolina," after her husband's name. While the document did not name her specifically, she was there, between those parentheses.

Further down, she noted the lengthy addendum Ben had written in, taking satisfaction in knowing the words were hers. She had no need for mere recognition of authorship.

She held the paper to her heart and closed her eyes. Peter was protected.

The child inside her kicked, visibly moving her gown. Elizabeth wished she could tell her mother about her grandsons: the one she lost, and the one who survived. She wished she could place her mother's hand on her belly and ask her if she thought this child would be a boy or a girl. She wanted to watch her mother's face, trying to discern if she thought the newest Timothée would be strong, a survivor. Elizabeth would not tell her mother she was afraid of losing another baby. She would not have to. Her mother would know what to say to ease her apprehension. She would know what to do to get her mind off the unanswerable questions.

But, of course, her mother was not here. And she never would be.

Elizabeth let herself feel that awful fact for a moment. Her face warmed as tears ran down her cheek in stinging, salty rills at the thought of never being hugged again by her mother, never smelling the vanilla scent of her hair, never hearing her sweet voice reassuring her that she was a strong woman: capable, intelligent, and kind. Words every girl, no matter how old, longs to hear from her mother. She could almost feel her mother's arms around her, rocking her slowly, her warm breath gently lifting Elizabeth's hair with each rhythmic exhale. Emotions got the better of her, and Elizabeth allowed it, burying her head in her pillow until it was hot and wet with tears and sorrowful words spoken into it as secrets.

When the well was dry, she rolled over onto her back and wiped her eyes and nose with her sleeve. She took a deep breath, in, in, in, until she crested the rise luxuriously, and exhaled a calm, clear sigh. Her mother would tell her: sometimes there is no other way to release emotion except to submit to it.

"Bottled up does not help mother or child," she could hear her say. Elizabeth smiled at the thought. *Sours the milk.*

The door opened behind her, and Deborah Franklin's rotund frame backed in with a tray.

"How does biscuits and gravy sound on this frightfully cold morning?" Debby was saying in a singsong voice as she made her way heavily around the bed.

Elizabeth endeavored to raise herself to a sitting position. Once the tray was set down in front of her, Debby went to work plumping Elizabeth's pillows and adjusting the quilts to her own satisfaction. When she was done, she dragged a chair up beside the bed and sat down with an audible thud, letting her feet kick up a bit in front of her.

"Whew!" she exclaimed, fanning her red face with her apron. "Mind if I take a load off fer a spell?"

Elizabeth could not help but love the simple, burly woman. She was so full of life, with not one unkind bone in her body.

"I *insist* you keep me company," she said. "Fer a spell," Elizabeth added with a wink and a smile.

"Here, here now," Debby countered, "if it is thoughts of making fun of me accent you have in mind, perhaps I am needed back in me own kitchen." The jolly woman winked back at her friend playfully.

"Now, Deborah," Elizabeth offered, "you know I love the way you Yankees talk."

The term was not appropriate for Americans, of course, and in point of fact was more a slur against her own heritage than Debby's. The Flemish and Germans called Dutchmen *Jan Kees*, and the English picked it up in the New World as a slur against the Dutch. But sometimes it was diverting to talk with someone with very little learning at all.

Suddenly finding her appetite, Elizabeth hungrily devoured the food in front of her. She could see Debby's pleasure in the way she gobbled up every bite, using the last scrap of biscuit to mop the remaining gravy.

"More?" Debby asked.

"It was delicious, Debby, thank you," Elizabeth replied. "But I have work to do this morning, and I fear if I have another helping, I would be tempted to lie in bed all day."

She shifted toward Debby to hand her the tray, but a spasm of searing pain caused her to dump it over the bedside before her friend could catch it. Dishes clattered to the floor. Debby was on her feet in an instant, yelling for Peter to fetch the doctor.

The boy was already running toward the door when Debby called out, "Tell him her water broke!"

Peter was halfway down the street when she added, "Tell him the baby is coming early!"

Chapter Twenty-Two

As she finished packing what few household goods and clothing remained, Elizabeth paused over the books Louis had left behind: precious volumes brought with them from Holland. She opened their Bible to the page where family members' names were inscribed. The last entry was Michael Timothée. To her eye, the ink was still wet; a salty tear ran down her cheek.

This is silly, she chided herself. *Our future is in Charles Towne now.*

But after almost three years in Philadelphia, it was difficult to be enthusiastic about moving again. She knew she should be excited about the reunion with her husband, but she dreaded the news that must be shared. He would be expecting to hold his newborn son or daughter; the thought of reliving the loss of John with Louis made her weary.

"Is everything all right?" M.E. asked as if she were the mother and Elizabeth the child.

Elizabeth smiled at the girl's concern.

"Everything is fine," she reassured her.

It was a lie, of course. The truth was she was tired. Tired of leaving friends. Tired of making new ones. Tired of leaving a breadcrumb trail of her life around the globe.

Yesterday, she had gone alone to Christ Church. She had stolen out of the house when no one was looking, leaving the children in the servants' care. She wanted to say a final goodbye to her baby boys. It was quite a walk from the Grace home to the burial grounds at Mulberry and Fifth on the outskirts of town, but Elizabeth rather welcomed the pain in her feet and the labored breathing; it was a reasonable and just sacrifice. With a handful of tulips, she knelt by the little headstones and placed her offering.

She stayed there for an unknown length of time, thinking about the day aboard *Britannia* when she knew she was pregnant. Suddenly every other concern had passed away, supplanted by the happy thought that a spring baby would be born in the New World. The fetus she carried had been her secret strength, even while it sapped it. He became the personification of their new beginning—the first American Timothée. For Elizabeth, this baby had been a barometer, used to measure the decision to come to America. And while he was a physical drain on her body, he was also her bolster of hope, and the single most important reason for keeping spirits up on the long voyage when the nausea of seasickness blended with the nausea of pregnancy and physical weakness tried to steal her resolve.

She fingered the headstone's markings. John's little plot of land in the churchyard was a cruel reminder of the new country's opportunities that would never be his for the taking. She had been so sure when he died that her capacity for grief had reached its saturation point. Nothing could possibly hurt her that much again, because nothing could be as horrific as losing a flesh-and-blood dream.

So when Ben offered her husband the job of King's Printer in Charles Towne last November, Elizabeth, almost full-term again, gave Louis her blessing. After all, she was born to be a mother of men, one whose babies came easily. Ben and Debby promised to take care of her, and Debby's mother was the most competent midwife in Philadelphia. She and the children, all six of them, including the one she had been carrying, would join him in the spring. She could manage without him.

But there, at her babies' graves, she silently admitted that she had lied to her husband. She could manage to survive without him; that much was true. She could manage to keep the household running. She could even manage to fill his large shoes at the print shop and the library.

But she could not manage the loss of another child, Michael. Not without him.

She understood now her mother's restraint at saying good-bye. Mama could let her go because Mama had never grasped her too tightly.

She and the children stepped outside to a predawn Pennsylvania spring morning and closed up the house at Pewter Platter Alley. Martha stayed behind with Debby Franklin; her indenture was very near completion, and Elizabeth could not ask the young girl to travel to South Carolina when her family was here in Pennsylvania.

Turning right onto Front Street, the only people they met were men extinguishing lamps or delivering fish from the docks to taverns. It was a reverent time, this hour before the city came to life, permeated by the spiritual hope of a fresh new day. The few silent souls they passed only nodded respectfully; footsteps echoed softly off brick and wood buildings as they made their way to the sloop.

Their little brigade turned left onto Market; Elizabeth could see the hulking three-masted merchant ships tied up to the docks with ropes as big as young trees. Smaller, two-masted cutters and jolly boats, rigged for rowing, dotted the in-between spaces like elliptical marks connecting one large thought to another. As the sun rose higher, the mackerel scales of the early morning sky burned away, and the air began to warm to the salty smell of the morning catch. Elizabeth breathed in the last dram of cool Philadelphia air as if to take it with her.

Their belongings had already been loaded when the Franklins and Debby's mother arrived at the docks to say their goodbyes. Conversation was awkward, and Elizabeth found herself wishing Captain Goodwin would just tell them it was time to board. Ever-genial Ben Franklin offered few words, but he did not have to;

she knew. To see them safely off, Ben was missing a meeting of the Philadelphia Masonic Lodge. He had never missed a Masonic meeting before, and probably never would again. It was certain that his own wife's problems had never stopped him. But Debby had told her that he informed his Mason brothers that he had lost one journeyman in the Carolinas; this time he was responsible for a family, including one of the most remarkable, learned women he had ever known. Elizabeth flushed, remembering the secondhand compliment.

Dry-eyed, Elizabeth tried to thank the Franklins for all their help.

"Debby," she began, taking her friend's hand.

Debby squeezed Elizabeth's palm and responded kindly but curtly, "Now, now, none of that."

She patted Elizabeth's hand before letting it go and turned her full attention to rummaging through the bag she had brought with her. When her hand emerged with a wooden spoon, Debbie bent over to look the toddler in the eyes and offered it to him. The two-year-old smiled and reached out to grab it.

"Deborah," Ben began, "'tis an odd gift for a small boy."

Debby ignored his comment.

"Paul Lewis," she said, pointing a mock disciplinary finger at the boy, "you take good care of this spoon for Mister Franklin. Perhaps you will learn to use it with more skill than he, whilst eating your soup."

Elizabeth started to protest. "Debby, I have nothing to give you—" but her friend interrupted.

"Pish posh, my dear," Mrs. Franklin replied. "'Tis a going-away gift for the boy, not for you. It will amuse him on the voyage."

"And besides," she continued, looking directly into Elizabeth's eyes, "you have already given me the best gift of all: your friendship."

Turning back to Paul Lewis, she said, "Besides, Master Paul, Mr. Franklin will have another spoon soon enough."

The boy toddled on tiptoes to his mother and held up his prize.

"And for you, young lady," Debby said, turning to the Timothées' eldest child, "Louisa, will you look after this for me?"

The girl accepted the crockery bowl she had often seen Mr. Franklin use for porridge.

"I thank you, ma'am," Louisa said with a curtsy.

"I expect you to work on your cooking skills, my dear," Mrs. Franklin said, putting her hands on her ample hips. "Many's a fine meal I have served Mr. Franklin in this very bowl. I am certain it will serve you just as well. You must learn to cook American food for all your suitors!"

"I will, ma'am. It is quite lovely," Louisa said demurely.

This time Ben was a bit more pointed in his comments.

"Look here, woman," he said, "what other belongings of mine do you have in your sack? And what do you propose I should use now at mealtime?"

"Never you mind, Mr. Franklin," Debby said, digging in her sack.

"Master Charles," she announced, but the boy was already queued up and waiting, with his hands clasped behind his back and his body twirling left to right in anticipation. "Will wanted you to have this."

The boy held out his hands to accept the gift. It was a carved wooden top.

"Something to play with on the boat," she said.

Charles hugged her knees and ran to the edge of the wharf to try it out.

"And Mary Elizabeth,"—the girl had been waiting her turn patiently—"I want you to have this."

Debby again reached down deep in her bag, thrusting her tongue in the corner of her mouth as if to help her find what she was looking for. Locating it, Ben's wife presented M.E. with a Bible.

"Your sister will receive your family's Bible. But I wanted you to have one of your very own."

She showed the child the pages at the front where she could write in her family heritage.

"See, I have already written the year of your birth. Here is where you will record the name of your husband. And here," she pointed a little farther down the page, "is where you will write the names of *your* children."

Six-year-old Mary Elizabeth looked up into the kind face of the woman she had come to regard as a grandmother. M.E.'s eyes were wide as she drew in a breath. The idea that she would be a mother herself one day was all the child wished for.

"You are already such a fine little mother with your dollies," Mrs. Franklin offered. "In no time at all you will be filling in these pages."

The child curtsied and took her treasure to her mother.

"Deborah," Elizabeth began, "you really should not—" but her friend would have none of it.

"You and your children are part of our family," Debby said. "And now, young master Peter."

Peter had been fidgeting like a child with pox, twitching and itching and barely managing to control the desire to leap ahead to the front of the line.

"For you, young man, I have a man's gift."

The eldest Timothée boy stood up straight and walked forward to stand in front of the Franklins. Her bag was empty now, except for one large square linen handkerchief, skillfully hemmed and embellished along each edge with an intricate scalloped embroidery. In the upper right-hand corner, Debby had satin-stitched the initials, *p* and *t* in a scripted font. She presented her gift to him.

When Peter failed to make an acknowledgment, Debby began to chatter uncomfortably.

To Elizabeth she said, "I felt your oldest son and heir should have a man's accessory." And then, turning back to the boy, she said, "Peter, this is just like the handkerchiefs I make for Mr. Franklin."

"And look here," she continued, borrowing it back from him temporarily, "if you turn it over, your initials are the reverse image of Mr. Franklin's."

She flipped the top corner of the hanky over to display that the *p* and *t* of his initials became a *b* and *f* when viewed from the back side. "Big Ben, Little Peter," she offered awkwardly.

"Just like setting type," the boy finally managed to say.

"Exactly, that!" Mrs. Franklin agreed. "It is a small gift, but one fit for a printer."

Peter studied the cambric handkerchief for what seemed to be a very long time before speaking.

"Mrs. Franklin," he said, choosing his words deliberately, "this is the best present I have ever received."

Debby let go of the breath she was holding and hugged the boy unmercifully. Peter's feet left the ground, and his mouth and nose plunged into the woman's ample bosom for the duration of the embrace.

When she set him down again, he said, "Next to my father, Mr. Franklin is my idol. I will take excellent care of this hankie and think of you and Mr. Franklin every time I use it."

Ben could not contain a chuckle.

"It is snot the best compliment I have received. But certainly it is snot the worst. And coming from a young man I so highly revere, I say, 'God bless you,' Peter."

Franklin extended his right hand, and the eldest male Timothée shook it soundly, as he presumed his father would do.

Elizabeth gathered up her children and announced that it was time to board the sloop. The children said their final goodbyes and stepped aside for their mother to bid the Franklins farewell.

Even more than Louis, the Franklins could understand her grief at leaving. Ben, his wife and children, and Mrs. Read were like family to her now. To make matters worse, she was turning her back on two little graves. With a melancholy she could not express, Elizabeth admitted to herself that she had set her heart on staying in the Pennsylvania Dutch country where her native tongue was spoken. She gave Debby a long, warm embrace, and then turned toward Ben. Taking his hands in hers, Elizabeth looked at the rough, stained skin of the printer before meeting his gaze. Those blue-gray eyes, too deep to plumb, looked as if she could drown there if she allowed herself to be pulled in. Wordlessly she let go of his hands and stepped aboard the *Carolina*.

Debby was inconsolable as the crew hoisted sail and pushed off from the dock. She waved a tear-soaked handkerchief as if she were surrendering to the grief of losing her best friend and confidante. Mrs. Read wrapped two arms around her daughter and led her from the dock with Will and Franky. Ben remained, with one hand held up. When they were almost out of sight, he closed his fist, bowed his head, and turned toward the city.

Chapter Twenty-Three

In his Charles Towne print shop on Church Street, Lewis Timothy smiled broadly despite all the difficulties of restarting the printing business.

"It will not be long now!" he gleefully announced, again, to his apprentice Jonathan. The boy inconspicuously rolled his eyes, but the audible sigh did not escape Timothy's notice.

"Look here, boy," Lewis began to reprimand the lad, but stopped himself. He was in too fine a humor to punish him today. Instead, he gave him an errand.

"Run to the waterfront and return immediately with news of her ship's sighting."

"But sir," Jonathan protested, "if we are to complete the *Essay on Currency* I shall—"

Timothy interrupted him. "My dear fellow, nothing supersedes my family's arrival. If I have to work day and night to meet the April 13 deadline, I shall gladly do it. Now off with you!"

Lewis could not keep from whistling. He was bone-tired, but today he felt new vigor: Elizabeth was on her way. He ached to embrace his wife and children again. And he was particularly anxious to hold his newest child. *A boy or a girl?* he wondered. *No matter. As long as he or she is healthy.*

Elizabeth is going to love it here, he thought to himself.

He could see a good life ahead for them and had already found a significant source of income in government printing. The Common House paid him ninety-six pounds in February for printing several laws, and with Elizabeth's help, he would have no trouble completing the *Essay on Currency* pamphlet. This would free him to begin work on Judge Trott's laws, for which he had been awarded four hundred pounds. They might not be as wealthy as some of Charles Towne's first citizens, but Lewis was certain the Timothy family would prosper. He had given up so much for their dream, and he knew his wife had worried that he would die in the Carolina wilderness.

He chuckled to himself; in point of fact, Louis Timothée was dead. Standing in his place now was Lewis Timothy, an American colonist, printer by trade and making his mark in South Carolina.

The door swung open again, much too soon for the boy to be back with news of Elizabeth's arrival. Lewis turned to reprimand Jonathan, but he smiled when he saw it was Judge Trott.

"Ah, Judge," Timothy said, shaking his friend's hand, "I have some galley sheets for your perusal."

Nicholas Trott, a portly, older man with dark, deep-set eyes of ponderous pools from which no wisdom could escape, nodded his approval and walked over to a tall table set at a 45-degree angle. There, the first sheets of one hundred fifty provincial laws, deemed relevant to South Carolina by the good judge himself, were almost dry.

"After ten years of writing everything by hand, the Assembly was desperate enough to try out my idea," he said, taking a page and dragging up a stool.

"We would still be working in the Dark Ages without the likes of you," Judge Trott continued, "if I had not persuaded the Assembly to forget about petitioning the king and start posting broadsides in print shops for printers already on *this* side of the Atlantic— in Philadelphia and Boston and New York and even down in the Sugar Islands."

Trott shifted his weight on the tall stool and held the galley sheet high over his head, like a Roman general in triumph.

"I have been editing these things for years, just waiting for someone to print them," the old man said as he patted the galley sheets.

"Yea yea. Hear Hear!," Lewis chuckled, clapping his hands over his head.

"And the sooner you proof each page, the sooner I can move forward with binding. Jonathan will handle the beating work, so the book will lie flat. And when my Elizabeth arrives," the giddy man said, making no attempt to conceal his excitement, "she will stitch it together. From there it will simply be a matter of trimming out the edges on the ploughing press and pressing the bound books on the standing press."

Judge Trott smiled admiringly at his friend. "Even with all your skills, I had never dared hope to find a man of your scholarship to help me."

The judge sighed approvingly as he proofed the first printed impression of his work.

"Excellent craftsmanship, my good man," he said.

It seemed Judge Trott, now Timothy's closest friend and colleague in the New World, thanked him a hundred times each visit for Lewis's work, and was always apologetic to suggest a correction. It did not deter the old man, however, from ferreting out each and every error and marking the proof with a hairsplitter. Lewis was as much of a perfectionist as the old man, though, and never accepted his apologies.

"I have learned more from reading your erudite work than from many great scholarly books," Timothy offered.

"That is indeed a high compliment, coming from you," Trott responded. "You have quite the collection of volumes in your possession. Perhaps one day they will become part of the scholarly library you envision."

Trott knew his young friend had not given up the idea of starting a university on the order of Cambridge in the New World. But this job of King's Printer was a bird in his hand. *A shame*, Trott thought; *the idea was most intriguing.*

"Most of my books traveled with me, at great peril I might add, on the crossing. But if we were to pursue my goal, these precious volumes would be required for the university library," Lewis said dreamily. "My books are my second love."

"Does your good wife know of this?" Trott jibed. "Is she aware that you sneak away in the night to hold your paramour, probe the secret places—"

Lewis interrupted him with a wagging finger. "You jest, my friend, but I will do you one better."

Locking Trott's gaze with exaggerated theatrics, he said, "My wife is as much in love with this 'paramour' as I am."

"There is the Frenchman in you!" the older man laughed. "Menage á trois! I knew there was more to you than bookishness and lampblack."

Timothy smiled at the joke. "Actually, my love affair with books, as you so aptly put, is a calling card that has opened many doors here. Of course, I knew Ben Franklin in London, and that relationship has been of incalculable value. It was Ben who suggested to the Junto members that I be installed as librarian for the Philadelphia Library Company. Besides knowing the Cambridge University plan for cataloging books, I also owned books, which I was prepared to share—very advantageous to the Club."

Trott nodded in agreement. "An excellent idea for men of good breeding here as well. I should like to see a similar group organized in Charles Towne. But how is it that you were able to bring so many rare volumes? I believe you mentioned an old copy of the Talmud in your possession."

Lewis winced.

"No longer," he said, shaking his head. "My father, a Swiss native, had kept it in his collection. I gave it gratis to the Junto, despite the fact that I could have profited by it. Benjamin actually argued with me about that one."

Timothy said the words out loud as if he could see the memory playing out in his mind.

"He said I was already on record for donating several rare copies and suggested I sell one of my books to the new library."

"So you took great care to bring them to America," Trott said, "and then left most of your precious collection in Philadelphia? I cannot fathom that you would not keep one or two. Within every harem, my young friend, there are some favorites of the sheikh."

"Ah, now you speak of the greatest masterpiece of all," Lewis countered. "And there is but one volume in that collection for me."

"I hope to meet your Elizabeth soon," Trott said with a grin, clapping Lewis on the back. "I am certain she is everything you describe, and more."

Chapter Twenty-Four

When they arrived in Charles Towne, Elizabeth could barely take in every detail. Walking the cobbled streets from Bay Street to Broad, then turning onto Church Street, she no longer had to imagine the smells and sounds of the city. It was as real as the bickering of a shop owner with a customer, as reassuring as a neighbor greeting a friend. A constant breeze circulated through the peninsula streets, fresh and mild with a scent less of sea and more of the fresh water that cradled Charles Towne on two sides. The hem of her dress swished softly in the spring air, mimicking the pulse of the ocean. Her bonnet lifted slightly; she raised her hand to the top of her head to keep it in place. Suddenly a familiar scent brushed by: magnolia, the smell of Holland, and of home. In it she realized she had not traded one for the other. Home was bound up here.

Lewis had been there, at the very edge of the pier, as the sloop *Lydia* made her way up the Cooper River. Even from a furlong out, he had the appearance of a man willing to throw himself into the water if necessary, to drag his family's sloop to its mooring. His stance was expectant to the point of agitation; as they drew closer, she could see that he was shifting his weight from one foot to the other and twirling his hat brim in his hands. The ship neared the quay by inches it seemed, as Lewis and Elizabeth held each other's gaze. A partial smile lay heavily on his mouth, mimicking the furrows in his brows. It was the sort of smile a person offers when a long sadness is over, and the thought of so much happiness overwhelms them with the longing they have carried too long.

When the sloop was secured, the children took their respective courteous and proper turns greeting their father. The girls, emotional, offered curtsies that melted into tight hugs and tears. The boys, trying so hard to be men, shook their father's hand and quickly turned away from their sisters so as not to give them any ammunition to tease them.

The children stepped aside, and their parents exchanged their own greetings. Lewis took Elizabeth's hands in his. His eyes held hers captive with his knowing—longing to say or do anything that would alleviate her pain of losing their latest baby. He held her, kissed her hair, and reverently said nothing at all. For two people who admired words so greatly, they silently agreed that sometimes words obstruct what needs to be said.

It was a short walk from the wharves to their home and business. Lewis opened the door and lit a lamp, then stepped aside to let Elizabeth walk into the front room facing the street. He had done an excellent job putting the street-level floor, where the print shop was located, in working order. The little two-story wood frame house was one room wide and two rooms deep, connected by a door in the center wall. A stair rose from the back room to second-floor living quarters; another door in the middle of the back exterior wall led to dependencies at the rear of the lot.

Elizabeth removed her bonnet. On a table to her left sat the next *South-Carolina Gazette* in its hard metallic reverse image, ready for the press. She could read it backward: "Whitemarsh estate settled. Small debts payable to printer of *Gazette*, Lewis Timothy. Robert Pringle, Administrator." The whole page had been tied off with string and secured inside an iron chase, then locked into place with printer's furniture and quoins.

When it was time to print, Lewis or his apprentice would lock the chase on the bed of the printing press, which sat like a wooden sphinx in the right-hand corner of the room. The press was a large structure made up of two components: a thigh-high horizontal frame—a low table, of sorts—and a bookcase-looking apparatus, about six feet high from top to bottom, which sat perpendicularly over the horizontal table. When not in motion the apparatus looked harmless enough. But with pressmen working at full speed, Elizabeth imagined it to be an ominous beast that could not be fed fast enough. It was hungry—insatiably so—for one thing only: it was hungry for the chase.

This was Elizabeth's favorite point in the publishing process. The paper, locked in place over a chase full of backward words and ready to be fed into the press, reminded her of a tabula rasa. Soon the beast would ingest the blank slate and spit out the most dangerous of all things: ideas.

To make the impression, the puller rolled the chase over the bed of the press until it was directly under the platen, which was nothing more than a flat wooden block. Using a large screw, he applied pressure evenly with the platen, and then rolled the chase back to inspect his work. If satisfactory, the page was hung up to dry. Producing one sheet at a time, a good beater and puller working together could print two hundred sheets an hour.

Elizabeth glanced up at the ceiling. The lamplight revealed long poles, running the length of the rafters, draped with sheets of freshly imprinted paper, hung to dry. The paper sheets looked like so much shadowy laundry.

Shelves lined the perimeter of the room: rows and rows full of wooden boxes containing newly made paper awaiting its turn on the press. A ladder leaned to the left of the fireplace. Reticent, Elizabeth walked through the rear door to the back room.

Shelves of wooden trays, partitioned to hold each character and sort, greeted her to the left of the door. Her prudent husband had put the composing room at the back of the house, making it easier to protect the bulk of their investment. The printing press, of course, was the most valuable asset, but it was also the most difficult to steal. But their second most expensive commodity—movable metal type—was more difficult for thieves to access through the rear of the building. She walked over for a closer look at the letters, numbers, ligatures, and ornaments. The small letters and numbers were kept in the two lower cases. Elizabeth randomly picked up an "A" from one of the two upper cases containing all the Roman and italic capital characters. She fingered the raised, reversed portion of the cool metal block, stained black from use, then returned it to its case. Around the room, high wooden stools perched under tall easels; nearby, composing sticks stood at the ready to be loaded and then transferred to galleys. An imposing stone—a flat marble working surface about waist height—sat very near the galley easels.

Salt glaze jugs filled with lampblack—the pigment of printer's ink made from the soot of burning oils—as well as jars of pine resin and linseed oil lined the floor around the room's periphery. The pine resin would be boiled in the linseed oil until it was clear, resulting in varnish. Ink, the product of mixing varnish and lampblack on a block with a wooden brayer, was the dense and pungent "blood" that gave life to words when brushed across type and pressed onto paper.

On the far-right wall stood more of Mr. Franklin's equipment shipped down for Whitemarsh: a large wooden bucket contained cloth rags that were soaking in water. These would be pounded into pulp. It would be the children's job to gather rags, preferably linen, as the raw material of their business.

Next to the bucket was a larger vat with a deckle and screen, where the mushy mixture would be strained evenly to make single sheets of paper. When a nice, even distribution of pulp had been achieved, the deckle was removed, and the water would be pressed out of the paper onto a piece of felt. This process would be repeated, alternating paper and felt, until there was a good-sized stack of about 144 sheets, called a post.

For final drying, the sheets would be laid out on a rack in front of the home's second fireplace, located in the center of the outside wall of the room. The finished paper was then stacked in large bundles and placed on the paper press where a massive wooden screw was turned to apply pressure. The process was complete when the paper was stacked in boxes on the shelves in the front room, ready for printing.

These last steps in the paper-making process were the coucher's responsibility. The French term *coucher*, meaning "to put to bed," was beautifully appropriate to Elizabeth's way of thinking.

A back doorway led outside to a small brick dependency. Before leaving the main portion of the house, though, she turned around to survey the organization of the rooms. From the rear she could see through to the front room, with windows framing the street just beyond. Everything looked well-organized and in good working order, from the printing press to the vat, poles and racks and storage boxes, down to the planes, tympans and friskets, the mallets, chase, and type cases.

Just a few steps from the back door of the main house, there was a small but agreeable kitchen dependency with a fireplace and bake oven. Eight chairs sat around a sturdy wooden table. Quite satisfactory, she decided, looking beyond the kitchen to the privy and servants' quarters in the back lot.

Elizabeth went back inside the house and took the stairs to the second floor, with her mute husband, itching to receive her final assessment, a few steps behind.

Two rooms upstairs mimicked the downstairs layout. There were two brass beds in the back bedroom with a window overlooking the rear of the property. Elizabeth surveyed the area; from this height she could see the other houses behind and to the side of theirs. In the full moon, little patches of garden just beginning to sprout dotted the evening landscape indiscriminately. A short distance back and to the right, an apron-clad woman emptied a chamber pot onto Carolina's sandy soil.

Opening the door between the two bedrooms, Elizabeth walked to the window in the front room. This bedroom, with a high bed and bureau, looked out onto Church Street where small single houses turned their profiles to the street, revealing bright little piazza necklaces at their throats. Smaller houses, and the wooden tenements interspersed among them, sank into the shadows of large family dwellings rivaling any in Europe. These stately homes—some made with Flemish bond brickwork and brick jack arches and others with exotic imported Bermuda stone—rose regally behind secure iron gates.

Charles Towne was indeed a curious mixture of need and greed, she thought. Down the street on the broad path sat palatial homes where women and their young sons awaited carriages on upping stones. Inside these mansions, Elizabeth imagined Black slaves offering silver services to the colony's elite. Parties would be gentile, powdered clean and fresh, where imported lace gowns and formal manners were de rigueur. Even the requisite gossip, whispered behind closed doors, was likely spoken with the best grammar and a continental accent.

Elizabeth wondered if her family had been a subject of polite conversation, and if they were, whether they would be difficult to classify in the rank-conscious, rough and rowdy town.

The tenements, she was certain, were owned by wealthy families who received tidy rental incomes from the struggling working class. Most of these dwellings were built property line-to-property line and abutted the edge of the street—crowded together like crickets in a bucket, practically climbing on top of each other to be free of their cage. Brick borders defined the delineation between pariah and patriarch.

"I am aware the accommodations are tight," Lewis offered, hoping to coax some hint of approval from his reticent wife. "And you are correct in assuming that at night, with regularity, the raucous discord emanating from those bawdry dwellings is punctuated with gunshots and fisticuffs well into the wee hours," he admitted.

"But," he said, hoping to dissuade her criticisms, "the wooden tenement houses, liveries, and mercantiles sit shoulder-to-shoulder with the aristocratic homes laid out on the Grand Modell.

"And our profession," he said in a tone that conveyed even his own skepticism, "will open doors to the town's social circles."

Elizabeth, to her husband's relief, finally said, "We shall require book binding equipment."

"Yes, there is significant work here for binding," Lewis said, breathing easier, and glad she had agreed. "I shall introduce you to an influential gentleman tomorrow who is anxious to produce several volumes."

His wife nodded without looking at him, still preoccupied with inspecting their new home.

Lewis continued filling the verbal void. "This is only temporary. We can continue renting this space exclusively for the business when we have moved to a larger house."

His wife turned to face him.

"Lewis," Elizabeth said, "I have missed you so terribly."

Her husband smiled, at last able to let go of the sigh he had been holding on to, and closed the distance between them with a warm embrace.

"And I you, my dear," he said with relief.

* ★ *

After a meal of beef stew and biscuits generously provided by a neighbor, the children could not wait to show their father the Franklins' gifts.

"Mrs. Franklin gave us each a keepsake!" Mary Elizabeth announced.

She showed him her Bible. Lewis studied it intently while the child explained where Mrs. Franklin had told her to write her own children's names.

"And what will you name your first baby?" her father asked her.

"I shall name her Elizabeth!" the girl responded.

Her father agreed it was a very good name, and squeezed his wife's hand as he said it.

Charles had been playing with his top since they left Philadelphia, trying it out on every surface he could find. Paul Lewis had long since abandoned his spoon, but Elizabeth had retrieved it and put it away for safekeeping. Louisa showed her father the pottery bowl she had been given and announced that the first dish she would cook would be a warm Carolina rice pudding.

"And you, Peter?" his father asked. "What did Mrs. Franklin give you?"

"A handkerchief, Father," the boy replied, and retrieved it from his trousers. "A man's accessory," he announced proudly.

"True indeed," Lewis responded. He fingered the embroidery at the bottom. "Your initials?"

"Yes, Father," Peter said. The boy demonstrated how Mrs. Franklin had turned over the corner to reveal Mr. Franklin's initials as the mirror opposite of his.

"I should expect you to take very good care of such fine craftsmanship. Mrs. Franklin no doubt put much time and effort into the needlework," he said, examining the delicate lace edging.

"You know what Poor Richard says happens after losses," Lewis said, handing the handkerchief back to his son.

"Men grow humbler and wiser," the boy responded, carefully folding the gift and replacing it in his pocket.

That night, Elizabeth put on her nightgown and brushed out her long brown hair before climbing into bed with her husband. It had been an exhausting day for them all.

"Lewis," she whispered as she nestled under the blanket with him and rested her head on his chest. "I have a confession to make."

Lewis's pulse quickened when he heard the words; they had been apart four long months. "What is it, Elizabeth?" he said at last, finding the courage to ask.

"I confess that I am about to be unfaithful to my husband," she answered.

"I do not understand. What do you mean?" he asked.

She turned to look at him and smiled. "I saw the name of the printer of the *South-Carolina Gazette* today, set in type for the next edition. This printer is the same man I lie with now. And it is not the Louis Timothée I married."

He smiled, realizing his clever wife had seen his Anglicized name, Lewis Timothy, slugged on the galley and ready to print.

"A rose by any other name, my love ...," he offered.

"Would swell as sweet," she replied.

Chapter Twenty-Five

Elizabeth and the children had begun helping in the business immediately after arriving in April. By June, they had outgrown their accommodations and moved to Union Street. The new location next to Charles Pinckney's offered more room for the business and for their expanding family of seven, now soon to be eight.

Elizabeth required the children to keep their own handmade paper tablets in the print shop, for lessons when there was time. Each little Timothy had hand-pressed the uppercase and lowercase alphabet letters neatly on the first page. When Elizabeth was instructing only the oldest three, she would include ligatures and the italic and bold fonts of the twenty-four letters that form all English words. But today, with all the Timothy children in the classroom, she worked only with the regular font letters and numerals.

"Open your tablets to your alphabet please," Elizabeth said. "Peter, can you tell me which lowercase letters are reverse images of each other?"

Six children, even two-and-a-half-year-old Paul Lewis, raised their hands. Peter, however, was busy rolling a wooden bird around the room—a gift he had received for Christmas. John Neufville, Lewis's friend and fellow Huguenot, had made it for him.

The boy was completely absorbed in the distraction. Elizabeth walked with purpose and snatched Peter up by his ear.

"Young man," she said sharply, "this is not merely an alphabet lesson. This is your *livelihood*."

Dragging him to her contrived dunce table, she forcibly sat him down. The toy was deposited on the highest shelf she could reach. The other children kept very still lest they be disciplined alongside their brother.

"Now children," she said to everyone but Peter, "can anyone tell me the lowercase letters that are reverse images of each other?"

Louisa raised her hand. Elizabeth knew how much Peter disliked being outdone by his older sister.

"Yes, Louisa, will you answer my question please?"

Louisa was all too happy to do so. "There are none, Mother."

"Are you certain? What about lower case *b* and *d*, and *p* and *q*?" her mother asked dramatically, handing out examples from the old Dutch type they no longer used.

Everyone, including Elizabeth, noticed Peter's suddenly raised hand.

"To the untrained eye," Louisa was having fun now, "reversing a *b* for a *d* would probably go unnoticed on a printed page. The difference is very slight, but a good printer would never make such a mistake. The ascenders and counters are slightly different."

She continued, "The *p* and the *q* are more dissimilar. In addition to a variation in the ascenders, the descender of the *q* is longer. Even the letter *o* should be set in one way only, because of the bowl configuration."

Louisa gave a sideways glance to Peter in that deprecating way young girls can be with their brothers. Accompanying it was the smallest evidence of tongue, coyly placed in the corner of her mouth.

"Excellent," Elizabeth said, praising her daughter more than she normally would have while still keeping her back to Peter. "Louisa, please go to my bookshelf upstairs and bring down the Catesby volume."

Elizabeth turned to her eldest son.

"And now, Peter," she said, "perhaps you would do us all the favor of listing the Caslon blocks that can be interchanged."

The Timothys used William Caslon's fonts to set the *South-Carolina Gazette*. It would be most beneficial if Peter became familiar with the type he would be using in later years.

"Yes, ma'am," Peter responded, with a sideways glance to his nemesis Louisa who was already returning with the book.

"The only Caslon blocks that can be interchanged without error are the 6 and the 9," he said with little hesitation.

Elizabeth nodded without comment and turned her attention back to her daughter.

"Louisa, please put the book on my desk. And now, Peter, let us see if you can handle another puzzle. I want you to list all the Caslon letters that are often misused because they appear to be both reverse and/or mirror images of another letter."

This was a more difficult question, one she had purposefully saved for him. In the letter box, Peter would need to quickly select the correct letters from their reverse images. He would also need the skill to recognize letters that may have been stored in the wrong location, a lazy error that Elizabeth intensely disliked when she was setting type. A lower case *b* could be confused for a *q* if it was slugged upside down. Slugging a *t* for an *f*, an upside-down *b* for a *q*, or *n* for a *u* was inattention to detail that Elizabeth would not tolerate in her husband's successor. She saw that tendency in her eldest son and intended to rid him of it, forcefully if necessary. Readers of the *Gazette* might overlook such errors, but the print jobs done for Judge Trott and others on Council must be accurate in every detail.

Peter sat with his arms crossed, a look of disdain seething on his face. He was angry, but he dared not speak or act on it. He knew his mother's temper.

"Peter?"

"No, Mother, I cannot write the letters that are upside down and reverse images of each other."

It was his mother's turn to cross her arms and return his look, reflecting less disdain and more disgust.

"Oh, what a pity. Some students are better at puzzles than others. It does take a skilled mind to think in different ways than those to which we are accustomed. But it can be learned, for anyone willing to try," Elizabeth said.

Taking up the Catesby volume, she asked, "Who will do us all the favor of listing the Caslon blocks that can be interchanged?"

Louisa raised her hand.

"Yes, Louisa? Care to venture an answer?"

Though Louisa did not name all the letters, Elizabeth was pleased at her daughter's attempt. She knew her oldest was in many ways more skilled than her brother, but that would not help her any more than it had helped Elizabeth. Louisa could not inherit the business. Her daughter's dower and marriage to a man of sound financial standing would be her only hope of solvency as an adult.

Elizabeth wrote all the letters on the blackboard and turned her attention to the younger children. She told them to make three horizontal lines, spaced evenly, on their tablets.

"And now Mary Elizabeth, please make a three-letter word with any combination of letters, using each letter only once."

After several minutes the precocious six-year-old rose to her feet to present her word to the class. This was a game she loved to play, and her mother knew it. In the first blank, the child had written the letter *l*. In the middle blank she had written *o*, and in the last blank a *t*. Triumphantly she turned her tablet to show her brothers and sisters and announced the word: "L-O-T, lot, as in the sentence, 'His lot in life was to be a printer.'" Rocking up and down from the heel to the ball of her feet and back, she awaited her mother's praise.

"Excellent, M.E.!" Elizabeth said without hesitation. "Now please sit down, and we shall let your older brother take a turn."

This time Elizabeth told the children to draw three horizontal blanks resembling ladder rungs underneath Mary Elizabeth's *t*.

"Peter," she said, "would you please give us a four-letter word, beginning with the letter *t*."

Peter bit his lip. Clearly, this was giving him difficulty, but he would never admit it to his mother.

"Can anyone give Peter a clue that might help him?" Elizabeth asked.

Mary Elizabeth raised her hand. "Peter," she said, "you may want to think of a synonym for your *work*."

"Excellent clue, Mary Elizabeth! Does that help with your double trouble, Peter?"

With a self-satisfied triumph, Peter turned to the board and wrote T-O-I-L.

"A passable answer, Peter, considering the help you received. Now, Charles," his mother said, "it is your turn."

No longer the youngest of the group, four-year-old Charles stepped over his little brother, Paul Lewis, to stand beside his mother at the front of the room.

"Please make a two-letter word using the letter "o," Elizabeth told him.

Charles, building from the word "TOIL," wrote a "t" below the "o," spun his tablet around with pride, and announced, "Ot—I ought to study my letters so I might learn to be a printer!"

Elizabeth concealed a smirk and quickly eyed the other children, silently warning them against even a single giggle. Before anyone could say a word, she took control with loud applause.

"What a bright child you are, to think of the word 'O-U-G-H-T,'" she said as she spelled it out loud and wrote it on his tablet for him. "That is a word older students learn, and you already know its definition."

Elizabeth walked over to a wooden box on the table. Opening it, she took out a small pinwheel made from newsprint and fastened loosely with a button in the center. It was held to the top of a small stick with tightly wound thread.

"I *ought* to give my Star Student a prize!" she announced and handed it to Charles. "Everyone, please write the word *ought* in your tablets."

She paused a moment before continuing: "The word 'ought' makes the short *o* vowel sound, but it utilizes the letters *o-u-g-h* to accomplish this. For homework, I would like each of you to write the word 'ought' twenty times in your tablets. In a separate column, write two other words that use the *O-U-G-H* letter combination but make a *different* sound. Your assignment for tomorrow is to write the definition of these words and their part of speech. Finally, copy down the puzzle we have begun on the blackboard, and complete it with as many words as possible from the letters already filled in. Peter, you will present your findings to the other children when school reconvenes in the morning."

"But I already took a turn, Mother," came the whining immediately. "That is not fair!"

Elizabeth began ushering the children out the door like she was shooing chickens into the yard, waving her apron at them to encourage forward movement.

"Fair, my son, is what we call a comely young lady and a country festival. The word has no application here. The woodpecker is mine until such time as I am convinced it is no longer a distraction. Before our next lesson you will identify all the letters and all the numbers which are upside down and reversed images of each other, or of close enough resemblance to confuse a reader if set incorrectly," she said as her son scuffed the floor with his boot.

"Your assignment includes upper- and lowercase, as well as the italic font," she added emphatically.

Peter began to object, but Elizabeth grabbed him sharply by the shoulders. Her dark-gray gown bumped him just under his chin; her belly preceded her everywhere these days.

"Listen to me, young man," she said roughly. "Do not make me tell you twice. I will tolerate no laziness from you. This business will be yours one day. Show me you have the aptitude and inclination to succeed, in every definition of the word. Show me something of your father. Show me something of Mr. Franklin."

Elizabeth would never tell Lewis, but Ben was probably the man most responsible for Peter's desire to become a printer and publisher.

After all, Lewis was also a protégé of Franklin. Father and son both had learned much of the newspaper and printing business under Ben's tutelage. But though Lewis had become a printer and an editor by trade, the ugly business of survival—feeding a family, providing shelter, clothing, and education, and leaving a legacy for their eldest son—inevitably supplanted his true dream. Lewis never complained. She would not allow his beneficiary to either.

Elizabeth let go of her grip, stood up straight and smoothed the folds of fabric around her ripe womb. A forced smile spread across her face as she spoke loudly enough for the apprentices to hear.

"For your insolence, you will take the Catesby volume, and mind you treat it carefully. There is a printing error," she said.

"Find it," she added, to punctuate her authority in this matter. "Now run along."

Her son kept his head low as he retrieved the massive book.

"Yes, ma'am," he muttered grudgingly, under his breath.

Chapter Twenty-Six

"Well, how was it?" Esther Crokatt asked, poking her head in the print shop door very early one morning.

"How was what?" Elizabeth answered without looking up from her proofing copy. She knew exactly what her friend meant, but she rather enjoyed keeping the busybody guessing for a few minutes longer.

Esther closed the door behind her and walked quickly to the tall, slanted table where Elizabeth was sitting on a high stool. She could feel Esther reading over her shoulder. The woman's exhalations—hot breath laced with a disagreeable onion scent—were close enough to stir the hairs on Elizabeth's neck. Esther would never admit it, but Elizabeth knew she enjoyed reading the newspaper before it came out on Saturday. She had witnessed, on too many occasions to count, how masterfully Esther could drop a comment in casual conversation about something in the upcoming *Gazette* as if it was yesterday's news.

"The play, you silly goose!" she said glibly, putting her hands on her friend's shoulders and physically turning Elizabeth around to face her. "Of course, *I* was in attendance for the inaugural performance, but I have been dying to hear your review of the endeavor. What say you? You have my assurance I will share the information with no one."

She put a finger to her lips and glanced toward the coucher, who could not have cared less about the ladies' conversation.

After the birth of their daughter Catherine, Lewis had surprised Elizabeth with an evening of theater. Charles Shepheard had placed an advertisement for the speculative venture, although the tavern owner was less than enthusiastic about it.

"We shall call this 'an experiment,'" he told Lewis. "If we are successful in selling even a dozen tickets at forty shillings each, I shall consider it worth the effort."

Shepheard's establishment on Broad Street also held the courtroom where most civic functions took place. Even more influential was its function as a meeting place where men of all trades discussed news and ideas over a pint. Elizabeth had suggested more than once that it would be far more expedient to locate the *Gazette* inside the tavern. So much of the newspaper's information came from there anyway.

Lewis had asked Charles what sort of play would be performed. Shepheard chuckled.

"A tragedy will be attempted, the title of which is *The Orphan*, or *The Unhappy Marriage*, by Thomas Otway," he said.

Lewis had responded that it sounded like a pleasant fiction and bartered newspaper space for two tickets.

"Well?" Esther asked again, as if she was positively itching to hear Elizabeth's assessment of the play.

"Oh, but have you not heard?" Elizabeth said with a straight face.

"The performance I attended featured an extraordinary new pantomime. It was titled *The Adventures of Harlequin and Scaramouch*. It is all the talk," she continued, baiting her friend to the trap. "It was billed as an entertainment in grotesque, and it certainly did not disappoint. Harlequin hit Scaramouch so forcefully, a tooth was knocked loose!"

"No!" Esther exclaimed, putting a hand to her face.

"No," Elizabeth replied. "But it was a thoroughly entertaining evening, nonetheless."

"Elizabeth Timothy, that was unkind. And after I gave you a necklace and everything." Esther appeared to be pouting.

Elizabeth briefly considered an unkind response, but she bit her tongue. In the publishing business, she reminded herself, relationships were tantamount. Lewis would tell her to be nice to the customers, especially customers whose husbands bought newspaper advertising. Esther was the wife of one of Charles Towne's merchants, and her husband was one of the Timothys' best advertisers.

"You are right, Esther," Elizabeth responded. "Please accept my apology. The necklace was very thoughtful of you. May I offer you a cup of tea?"

The gesture seemed to assuage the woman's bruised pride.

"Yes, thank you, my dear," she answered as her sour expression dissipated.

The Crokatts' marriage was an equitable relationship in more ways than one. Esther relished wearing Europe's latest fashions—one of the benefits of being a storekeeper's wife—and she also enjoyed the social standing her husband's success afforded. In return, Esther, a Gaillard, brought prestige to the marriage as one of the colony's leading Huguenot families. Perhaps more importantly, however, she was a walking placard for Charles Crokatt's new fabrics and a constant verbal advertisement in her women's circles concerning new items just received.

When the Crokatts' shipment of anodyne necklaces arrived from London, Esther had given one to Elizabeth for her youngest son. Paul Lewis was having a difficult time breeding teeth, and the poor child cried constantly. Esther swore that doctors abroad highly recommended the necklaces, made from dried henbane root, to ease the pain of tooth cutting.

Elizabeth would never refuse it, but in her heart, she believed a crying baby meant sound lungs, and the necklace was merely a huckster's charm. She had accepted the gift, however, knowing

Esther would consider it an affront if Elizabeth did not sing its praises, regardless of its curative powers. She put it around Paul Lewis's neck and continued to silently count the days until he turned three in March. By then, she could safely say he had made it through teething, the benchmark for survival.

"Well," Esther continued, "how is your boy?"

Elizabeth smiled and turned toward the woman with a look of resignation.

"How is it working, my dear?" Esther asked.

"Like a charm, Esther," she honestly replied and took a sip of tea.

"I am delighted to hear it," Esther said. "Now what is this about your Negro?" Esther was reading an ad on the proof page for the next edition. "It says here your boy London has run away."

The boy had belonged to a vintner in town, and while Lewis needed the help, he could never bring himself to hurt him.

"He just wants London back," Elizabeth said curtly. "The ad asks only that whoever meets with him should be kind enough to return him to us."

"Well," Esther replied, "I hope he is caught and flogged within an inch of his life. Should you recover him, you might consider selling him at public vendue for ready money. A friend of Mr. Crokatt's plans to sell a stock of horses and cattle, as well as a house wench."

Elizabeth ignored her completely, feigning to be absorbed in proofreading so as not to become more aggravated than she already was. She had traveled this road with Crokatt's wife before, and she saw no benefit in arguing with her.

"Suit yourself," Mrs. Crokatt responded, shrugging her shoulders.

"But mark my words: any chattel smart enough to run away once will likely do so again," she said, handing Elizabeth her tea cup and making her way to the door. "And next time he might take the silver."

The door closed with a satisfying thud. Elizabeth took a deep breath of print shop air: varnish and soot and sweat and wet linen. Not a smidge of onion.

Returning to her work, Elizabeth let her mind wander to their discussion to move to the double house on Union Street last year. Lewis's mind had been set, but his wife had put a quill to the numbers.

"It is not a prudent business decision," she told him, but he refused to look at her arithmetic.

Undeterred, Elizabeth reminded him of their ultimate goal to buy the business, including all equipment, from Franklin after the six-year agreement was fulfilled. But when she realized another baby was on the way, Elizabeth could not deny that the additional space was a blessing.

She allowed her gaze to wander out the window, where St. Philip's steeple seemed to pierce a hole in the cloudless sky. She recalled her first impression of the church from *Britannia* and the feeling of protection it offered then.

There was no protection from Charles Towne's heat, however, she thought, and wiped perspiration beads from her upper lip. Already the morning threatened to become a miserably hot day. She set her tea aside, determining it was just too warm for it.

Her first summer in the colony last year had made her less enthusiastic about the change of seasons. She closed her eyes and tried to summon a tactile memory of Philadelphia's wind-whipped, freezing temperatures so reminiscent of Holland, but the image gave her no relief. The heat and humidity of Charles Towne's moist climate permeated all pleasant thoughts, drowning out even her enthusiasm for trying.

Elizabeth located her feather fan, always at the ready these days. When George Chicken Jr. came in to place an advertisement, she was already employing it with one hand and restocking pamphlets with the other, on the shelves behind the counter.

Everyone in town knew the Chicken family, either by personal introduction or by reputation. George's renowned father, Colonel Chicken, and his Goose Creek militia had turned back the Indians at Wassamasaw and turned the Yemasee War in the colonists' favor. The colonel died eight years ago, a young man, but having made his mark in his short life. His son, George Jr., inherited his father's estate and lived on the Goose Creek plantation. He owned plantations in Santee as well. It was part of this land that he now wished to advertise for sale.

"Shaping up to be a scorcher, aye, Elizabeth?" he said as he entered.

"It most certainly is, Mr. Chicken. I have no idea how we will survive the summer if it is to be this hot now. What can I do for you today?"

"Here to place an ad in your newspaper. I have a thousand acres at Santee I wish to sell."

"Of course," she replied and went to the desk for paper and quill. "And how do you wish the advertisement to be worded?"

Chicken dictated the verbiage to her, describing swamp as well as cleared areas for planting.

"Are there structures associated with the land?" Elizabeth asked.

"Yes, several outbuildings and a barn, and a very good dwelling house," he told her. "I am willing to rent two hundred acres for a peppercorn but must receive 12d per hundred for the remainder."

Elizabeth carefully wrote everything down.

"I assure you, Mr. Chicken," she said, finishing her notes, "we will place a nice advertisement for your land, top right-hand page if possible."

Their business concluded, he bowed deeply, and she walked with him to the door. They talked lightly of temperatures and rainfall and the weather's effect on Chicken's stand of corn.

"Is it any cooler at Santee?" she asked as they stepped outside onto Union Street. Chicken hesitated a moment before answering, as if deciding how best to describe a hopeless situation as kindly as possible.

"I always feel I can breathe easier in an open space, Miss Elizabeth," he replied, adding that it was agreeable to have a change of scenery, even if the temperature was just as unrelenting.

She nodded, and the two of them stood at the threshold for a moment, relishing the early morning sanctity of relative soundlessness. Soon the streets would echo with hawkers and the noise of commerce: wagons and carriages, women emptying pots of human excrement into the city streets and sweeping children—late for free school on the west side of town—out the front door.

Elizabeth sighed. Near the water's edge she watched a reclusive moorhen ducking in and out of cattails. Her slate-black body seemed ridiculously perched on two stalks of yellow legs; her red bill glinted in the sunlight as she bobbed, pigeon-like, in search of something to eat. A whimpering fuzz ball of a baby wandered aimlessly behind her.

Without warning a hawk swooped down, snatching the baby in its talons. The infant was suddenly gone, lifted up and off to a place of safe distance where the hawk could tear its flesh from bone.

The mother, helpless, made the most mournful sound Elizabeth had ever heard from a bird. It reminded her of a succession of spasms that had collapsed into three soul-cleaving cries. Elizabeth clutched her chest, recognizing the heart-assaulting moment of an irreversible event.

"I should consider myself fortunate to have such a change of scenery, Mr. Chicken," she said. "I wish you a very good day, sir."

Mr. Chicken tipped his hat to her. "And I wish you a gentle breeze when you most need it."

Chapter Twenty-Seven

Elizabeth fingered the folds of her baby's chubby arms as rigor slowly took control.

Dale had paid another visit last night, his second call just this week—and how many since Lewis had first fetched him to examine Paul Lewis? *The pivotal events of life always seem to catch us with our proverbial pants down*, she thought.

Lewis had gotten up that morning before sunrise, intending to get a jump on the day's activities. The air had been cool and fresh: an agreeable time to do one's business, as it were. He planned to call round to the Council chambers to inquire if yesterday's meeting had resulted in new resolutions. He planned to meet with several tavern owners, including Shepheard and Breton at The Pink House. Crokatt's store had been robbed by one of his own Negroes. And there was the subscription office at Ashley Ferry and the one at Dorchester to visit. While he was there, he intended to survey the two hundred acres that had been granted to him just this month on the Pon Pon River and take a look at the half-acre town lot in Orangeburgh that accompanied the grant.

But sitting in the privy until his legs fell asleep had not been on his agenda.

Someone had used the last of the corn husks, again, and had not replenished the privy supply. Charles had been playing in the yard, chasing bantams around and catching several of the hens, when Lewis realized there were no husks for wiping. He yelled to the boy to run inside and bring him several.

Fecal matter simmered in the August heat a few feet below him, and the smell was becoming unbearable. He took short breaths through his mouth while flies, finding the courage to land on him, relentlessly explored his orifices. Lewis swatted his ears, accidentally hitting himself in the head. He checked the time on his pocket watch.

What could be keeping that boy? he wondered, fanning his face to keep air circulating.

He took his pocket watch out again; ten minutes had passed according to his silver timepiece. Just as Lewis was considering using the back of his hand, he heard the anguished cries of a child nearby and the sound of someone running into the yard.

"Father!" Charles yelled as he came to an abrupt halt at the privy door. "Mother says come quick. Paul Lewis is burning with fever."

By the time Lewis had buttoned up and thrown open the privy door, his little boy's feverish sobs seemed to reverberate off nearby houses, amplified by their own echo. He ran in the back door and up the stairs, taking them three at a time. The cries grew louder, assaulting him, surrounding him, pounding his ears, and bruising his heart. When he reached the second floor, he found Elizabeth pacing and rubbing Paul Lewis's back. She did not turn toward him; she did not stop pacing or patting.

The soothing tones she had been using to comfort the child were now laced with words for Lewis: "Go. Get the doctor. Yes, I know, sweetheart. You do not feel well. Tell him he is on fire with fever. Tell him we have tried the cool-water bath. Yes, my sweet boy. I know. I know. Tell him he will not eat, and there is a rash on his chest and back. Yes, angel, Mama will help. Go now. And *hurry*."

Lewis had turned to run down the stairs but felt the floor sway underneath him. Before he collapsed, he managed to shout to Charles to run for the doctor.

Elizabeth, not noticing what was happening with Lewis, had closed her eyes on the horrible memory of yet another dead child, as if shutting her eyes could provide a different outcome.

Mindlessly, she continued tracing around her dead child's alabaster wrist, up to his armpit, across the clavicle, and down to the well where the umbilical had once been attached. She smiled. He was a ticklish little thing who drooled from the corner of his mouth.

Paul Lewis, John's twin, had survived when his weaker brother failed. He survived—flourished really—to make the trip to Charles Towne. He had grown stronger each day he took breath. She smiled, remembering the swaddled infant who quickly developed into a kicking, screaming toddler: willful and constantly hungry. He had learned to walk the summer before his father left for the province, and he was completely uncontainable on the trip to South Carolina the spring of 1734. As maddening as Paul's behavior was to Elizabeth, she knew that pernicious quality would serve him well. Fighters fight: for position, for land, for wealth, for family. And for life.

Some mothers might disagree. Some might lecture her, or scold her, or at the very least click their tongues and discuss her at length behind her back. *An infant needs a strong maternal bond,* she could hear them say. *Babies need to know they are loved. Safe. Protected.*

Elizabeth had heard it all. But over the years she had developed her own philosophy, tried and true. Babies must learn that life can be hard. And the sooner they learn it, the better they can defend themselves against those forces that will most certainly come against them. Fight, not flight, is a choice, borne of instinct.

She felt her face become warm: a prelude to tears that, if allowed to begin again, might not stop. Swallowing her emotions as if weakness were strong medicine, she turned away from her youngest child. She drew herself up to her full height, smoothed the front of her skirt, and used the back of her hand to dab her eyes.

She knew from experience: with enough practice, enough pain in childbirth, enough dutiful intercourse against dry vaginal walls, enough watching a child throwing up kidney fluid and defecating blood, enough of holding cold, stiff babies at arm's length, and the mind could distance itself from life's little losses.

Life and Death are like conjoined twins, wanting nothing more desperately than to be free of one another, yet all the while bitterly aware that they cannot exist apart. They need each other in the most desperate, despicable way, and so, they must respect one other. But at every opportunity either Life, or Death, must prove itself worthy to retain the upper hand. *It is a dance really*, Elizabeth decided. Life can never completely let go of her partner's hand. The two keep time, rhythmically moving to the beat of Life as they step closer and closer to Death, bending and bowing gracefully across the floor like the perfect little pair. They spin apart, and Life begins to think she dances alone, no longer bound by the whim of her partner.

But in the end, Death leads. Always.

Elizabeth sighed and pushed it down—the goiter in her throat where so many raw emotions collected, festering. She swallowed it, feeling it sink heavily into her belly, knowing it would never digest.

She decided that it never profited a mother to develop too sinewy a heartstring with a child. The stronger the cord, the more likely it would affect maternal health if severed. She had given birth to nine children since wedding Mr. Timothy—a good stand of offspring, to be sure. Many other families had fared far worse. Her family would go on. The business would go on. That was what mattered.

Elizabeth glanced away from her son's body just long enough to watch the sun burning off whatever vestige of cool air there was to be claimed for the day.

August, she thought with contempt. So dreadfully hot and humid: the height of the sickly season.

"Lewis," she said loudly, noticing her husband on the floor.

Lewis managed to sit up and was rubbing his eyes when Charles arrived with the doctor.

Elizabeth said in simple terms: "It's too late. The baby is dead."

Chapter Twenty-Eight

When the funeral service was concluded, the mourners made their way to the church burial grounds. Esther, uncharacteristically silent, walked out with her friend into an overcast August day.

Outside, a woodpecker drummed against a tree with the *rat-a-tat-tat* of a soldier on his drum, while Reverend Garden read from the *Book of Common Prayer*. The words—of love and loss and reunion with the Father—were weak medicine to Elizabeth's soul.

If she tried hard, she could feel her baby in her arms. It was just a memory, but she could evoke the physical sensation of Paul Lewis squirming to get down: giggling, kicking, pushing himself away in a determined effort to get into mischief of one kind or another.

If he were here, she thought, *he would be toddling around, gathering crackly magnolia leaves as if they were redware.*

It made her smile sadly, imagining him presenting the "plates" to mourners of his choice. No rhyme. No reason. Just a three-year-old playing a game, blissfully unaware he was an odious distraction at such a somber occasion.

The reverend droned on. Elizabeth could hear his words, but she chose instead to focus on anything but them. With great effort, she listened to the background noises—bringing them to the forefront and relegating the graveside service to the back. Several streets over, children were playing. Fishmongers called out fresh catch along the bay. Insects roared, drowning out the buzzing of scriptural readings.

Elizabeth willed herself to remain distracted. On the far wall of the cemetery, sunflowers lined up in church-school rows to bow their heads in prayer. There was no sun today, and only the green tops of their spongy heads were visible. She imagined leafy ribbons tying their bonnets under bright yellow faces. They dared not look up until the sun instructed them to do so, and bees, so much louder in their busyness by virtue of her concentration on them, flew among the penitent stalks.

Things were changing.

She could feel it. Certainly not a change in temperature; there had not been one day in the last three months that was even mildly bearable. The chalky perspired residue left behind on her skin was confirmation that she had not drunk enough water. No, Charles Towne was just as hot and humid today as it had been every other day since mid-May, with few exceptions. But somehow, she knew things were changing.

If they had been wealthier, the Timothys would have visited Philadelphia while the South's oppressive heat and humidity had its way with the townspeople, making them weak and often cross with each other. They had hoped the land on the Pon Pon River, recently granted to Lewis by Thomas Broughton, would offer some relief. But in point of fact, the stifling heat and humidity were worse inland, even on property with river access.

And if the heat does not get you, the mosquitoes will. And if the mosquitoes get you, it might just be the preamble to something worse: yellow fever or malaria.

There was no homestead yet on their tract in Orangeburgh's western township, just a few modest lodging huts. Lewis, the Timothys' Gambian slaves, and their overseer had made the sixty-mile trip via the road to Orangeburgh several times to work the land, but it was a slow and arduous process. The government had put incentives in place to encourage outward settlement by Whites with White servants, but it was clear that Black labor was preferred, even by the Timothys, and it was shifting the racial balance. Negro shipments had escalated in the port city since 1732, with more than ten thousand slaves coming to Charles Towne in the last four years alone. They were the port of entry for almost half of all the colonies' slaves.

As much as Elizabeth disliked the designation, she could not deny that laborers were required to work the land, and she believed that Negroes were built for brute work. They were also accustomed to the climate and often offered some knowledge of rice cultivation from their native land.

Demand creates supply, Elizabeth thought to herself, *and there was good money in peddling human flesh.*

When Lewis told James Crokatt of his intentions to become a rice planter, James had commented on the governor's plan to create White settlements outside of Charles Towne.

"It is a worthy endeavor," James had said, "and a good plan for shoring up defenses and ensuring the province's prosperity, but surely you cannot deny the reports in your own paper, sir."

Lewis knew the slave ships were arriving in greater numbers, bringing more and more Negroes into the colony.

"There will come a tipping point," James told him with a frown. "I have heard it said that Negroes are the bait for catching a Carolina planter, as certain as beef to catch a shark."

Lewis replied, "You imply that the prey we attract will become our predator."

He thought about that for a moment, as if he was giving the remark its due contemplation: "You think we pay too much for our whistle."

Crokatt smiled at Poor Richard's reference.

"No," James decided after some reflection of his own. "The price for the whistle is fair, and we certainly do need whistles, if we are to prosper as we certainly desire. Someone must do the work which we, ourselves, will certainly not be doing.

"But," he added with a one-upping grin, "'Beware of little expenses. A small leak will sink a great ship.'"

Things were indeed changing. Their slave London, with his predilection for running away, was already at Pon Pon, under a White overseer, along with three other male slaves estimated to be in their twenties. There, London and the others would be worked so hard that they would not have strength enough to mount an escape.

South Carolina rice prices were at an all-time high: 8.64 shillings per hundredweight. Even rice flour, the worst quality of all, and the quickest to spoil, was valuable if only to feed slaves. And several merchants, including James Crokatt, accepted rice in payment. Carolina Gold was just that to the Timothys, or as good as.

Reverend Garden's nasal baritone voice rose and fell with intonations. Had he said a prayer? She wondered if anyone took notice that she had not bowed her head. Quite the contrary, Elizabeth had been concentrating on a thin vertical cloud stretching way overhead—from the rooftop line up as far as she could see in the sky. It had moved from the center of her vision, where she first noticed it, to the left at a fairly good clip. When she focused very hard, she could tell that it was she who was moving, and not the cloud. Feeling a little dizzy, she looked away.

Below, on the horizon, birds massed. Things were changing: time to seek the company and comfort of the flock. Grackles, birds so black as to appear iridescently purple, gathered in numbers, their yellow eyes threatening corn crops. Even the moorhens, reclusive marsh birds, now sought the company of others.

How far removed we are from the brute animals we command, Elizabeth thought. *And how terribly similar as well.*

She took a small amount of comfort in it: moving forward, increasing the flock, perpetuating the species, and willfully shut out the fact that she was standing at her son's graveside. Some things cannot be changed.

But some things are changing, she thought again.

She could feel it in the breeze. A mere whisper in the ear, a lover's hot breath on the back of her neck, sending a chill among beads of perspiration, in murmured promises. It made her feel curiously alive at a time when something inside of her was dead.

She almost wished she could just be an observer of life, watching things change. How pleasant to just look in, from outside. Not interacting—just watching, making notes. Something for tomorrow's front page.

Observers are safe, she decided. *Their hands never get dirty. Nothing stains. Nothing hurts. They keep their heads low, hoping to escape one day, and wing their way homeward in death.*

The participants in life charge into the messiness of it all, falling down so many times. So many callouses and scars, she thought. So many wounds and wrinkles and sad knowledge in eyes that reflect the risks—and the rewards—of drawing breath and giving it back, exchanging air with every other living creature.

She decided that these imperfect souls are God's chosen, taking nothing for granted, least of all the gift of life. Participants put life to their lips, taste and chew, swallow and consume it. And in return, they are consumed by it. These souls make the most mistakes. Some learn, but not all.

And when God judges them, which Christendom teaches us that He does, then surely it must be on the veracity of their hearts. God does love a sinner: cleft heart, feet of clay, crawling toward the throne in submission. For such people, God cannot help but love, and forgive, even for their poor choices.

Elizabeth wondered if perhaps an early death was merciful. Perhaps Paul Lewis is with God at this very moment—never to be touched again by pain, or sorrow, or want. Fear, anger, hopelessness, failure: none of it would curse him now.

Or, perhaps, he was taken from her as punishment. A reminder that God is omnipotent and will not be bargained with.

When the burial service concluded, Elizabeth wished to be anywhere but there, politely thanking people for their condolences. But of course, there was no place else to be. She could not hide from friends who felt required to offer some comfort, none of which was comforting, because there was no comfort to be had.

Her boy had made it past teething, to three and a half years old. And yet she would never know if he would be an observer or participant. He was not given the chance.

After the service, the mourners dispersed, each to their own business for the day. Her husband took the children home, but Elizabeth stayed there, at the fresh grave, for some unknown length of time. Only Esther Crokatt remained, a few paces away.

Holding an object in her left hand, Elizabeth stood resolute as the gravediggers began to close the hole in the earth that swallowed her son. She felt a welling-up of something that threatened to swallow her too, as each spadeful of disturbed dirt was thrown back into the gaping grave. The sound of it reminded her of blood splatter.

She could feel herself getting dizzy, unable to breathe. The rhythmic confirmation of her boy's short time on earth overwhelmed her; she was on her knees before she even knew she had fallen.

Esther was there, on her knees in the dirt next to her, her own eyes bleeding clear tears as she searched her friend's face. Without comment, she offered Elizabeth her gloved hand. Elizabeth took it, and cautiously, the two stood up together. When Elizabeth had regained her footing, she swallowed hard, squared her shoulders, and turned to her friend. She placed a small something in Esther's palm, brought Esther's hands to her lips, and backed away.

When Esther opened her hand, she found the anodyne necklace coiled up inside.

Chapter Twenty-Nine

Lewis's sudden burst of enthusiasm startled the napping calico cat tasked with keeping mice out of his shop. Napping in the rafters, the feline was frightened when Lewis swung the ladder around abruptly to retrieve two newly completed volumes—Trott's *Laws of the Province of South-Carolina*—his opus. Lewis opened the shop door and encouraged the cat to leave with a swift kick of his boot, nearly catching her tail in the closing. Their new home was too small for her to be under his feet; her work could wait until his was finished. He did not want to keep the French Club members waiting.

Lewis would never admit it to his wife, but she had been correct to question their move to Union Street. It had been beyond their means; ultimately, he had decided to move the family to their present location on King Street.

The single house, a two-and-one-half story wooden structure like so many others on the thoroughfare leading to the broad path, was configured similarly to their first home on Church: one room wide and two rooms deep, connected by a door in the center wall. The front entrance opened into the press room with the composing room in the rear. Stairs from the back room led to bedrooms on the second floor, and continued to an additional half story above, where the boys slept. Two dependencies beyond the back door took up most of the small plot of ground in the rear. But unlike the house on Church, the Timothys had no neighbors across King Street. From their front windows, the view was of vacant, swampy land owned by the Huguenot Church. Brackish streams circulated in watery veins on the low ground where mosquitoes, one of Charles Towne's most insipid pests, bred.

Elizabeth had been quick to point out that Benjamin Franklin would never have advocated the move to Union.

"You and he are partners," Lewis recalled her saying. "Perhaps it would be wise to discuss your decision with him."

Lewis countered that a message sent by postrider would take months to get to Pennsylvania, if it arrived at all.

"Then send it by sea," Elizabeth had insisted.

He had agreed that sending a letter by sea was generally less of a gamble but could take even longer than an overland dispatch.

"No," he had said emphatically, "Franklin is in Philadelphia, and I am here. This opportunity must be acted upon decisively before it is lost."

Lewis insisted that the extra space would allow him to expand the book binding business.

"And you can keep a larger inventory of stationery supplies," he offered. "Franklin has endowed me with decision-making responsibilities here in South Carolina, and I will make those decisions as I see fit."

It was clear that his mind was fixed. Elizabeth continued to object, reminding him of their plan to purchase the business from Franklin for Peter's inheritance at the end of the six-year term. To that end she quoted three of Franklin's virtues, which she insisted Lewis was ignoring.

"'Order,'" she began, "'let all your things have their places; let each part of your business have its time. Frugality: make no expense but to do good to others or yourself; waste nothing. Moderation—'" at which point Lewis raised his hand to stop her.

"'Silence,'" he countered, putting a finger to his lips and extending the palm of his other hand as if to halt her verbal assault.

He knew she would quote every applicable virtue, and he had had enough of being lectured by his wife. Elizabeth reluctantly submitted and withdrew to let the dispassionate language of mathematics make her argument for her.

There was one variable, however, which the numbers could not account for, and that was her husband's kind heart.

When *Gazette* subscribers continued to ignore his notices politely requesting payment for subscriptions and advertisements, Lewis was forced to use stronger language. He made it clear that the *Gazette* would accept no advertisements without money down, but of course, the exception ultimately gave authority to the rule. Finally, Lewis had decided, as if it were somehow a novel idea, that it would be a good business decision to move to smaller accommodations. He would not admit, however, that it had been a *bad* business decision to move to the larger facility. Elizabeth allowed him his pride and resisted quoting the virtue of humility to her husband: imitate Jesus and Socrates.

The family had no sooner moved to King Street when Elizabeth became pregnant again. Lewis prayed that this baby would survive to adulthood. The toll on his wife was already too great, and he needed her back at work.

He had shared his concerns with several friends who met regularly at a Tradd Street tavern run by a fellow Huguenot. The group's numbers had grown to several dozen since last year, when a few men of French descent had agreed to meet at the tavern to conduct business. When there was no business, they met there anyway, sometimes as often as several times a week. They met with such regularity that they began calling themselves the French Club. Lewis suggested that "members" contribute fifteen pence—a mere two bits—at each meeting for the greater good of charity and brotherly love. The idea had been germinating for quite some time, since Philadelphia. It was an agreeable way to enjoy the camaraderie of other Frenchmen while helping Charles Towne's less fortunate.

The group was gathering there today. Lewis quickly reshelved Trott's *Laws* next to his other masterpiece, John Wesley's *Hymn Book*, and left the print shop.

When he arrived at the tavern, Lewis walked briskly to a large plank table in the rear of the building where the others were waiting to celebrate his accomplishment. Someone had bought him a pint already, and Timothy arrived just ahead of the barmaid.

"I tell you," Lewis began, as tankards were placed in front of each man, "Elizabeth does not seem to be coming 'round. Paul Lewis has been dead more than a year, and she still grieves."

"Women are of a different humor," one man responded. "Are you sure it is not the pregnancy that is causing it?"

Lewis shook his head.

"No, I should not think so. Her melancholy began when Paul Lewis died, and she has not been the same since. Dale says she suffers from hysteria, and he is treating her accordingly. I must wonder, however, if it is a ploy to pare back on her duties."

The barmaid—semi-toothed with red-veined cheeks—set the last tankard in front of Timothy roughly.

"Tell ye one thing, Mr. Timothy, and no disrespect. Your wife is a dear friend a-mine and a stronger woman I ain't never knowed. Next time you give birf to a bouncing baby boy who makes it frew teevin' and then dies of a pestilence just as you begin to breave easy thinkin' he be out of danger, you let me know how *you* feel."

Lewis started to object and then to apologize, but she had already turned her ample backside to him and bustled out of earshot. His sleeve, resting on top of the table, began to feel wet as it absorbed the hard cider she had spilled in front of him. Perturbed, Lewis held his arm over the side of the table and wrung out the fabric.

No matter, he decided. Today he felt like celebrating. Right this minute he knew he should be setting type for the Saturday issue of the *Gazette*, but he allowed himself a moment's celebration with friends in the completion of Judge Trott's *Laws of the Province of South-Carolina*.

"These two volumes represent a three-year undertaking between the good judge and me," he announced. "Without this work, subsidized by the provincial government, I wonder if I could have continued to put food on the table."

French Club members raised their cups to celebrate his achievement.

"Drink a toast!" one member offered. "To Timothy's success in 'trotting' out all the inscrutable avenues—now set in stone, or more to the point, in type—by which we may leave the straight and narrow pathway of virtuous living!"

Chapter Thirty

Elizabeth stared vacantly out the front room window and wiped the tears from her eyes. She heard the baby's cries, rather like a muffled, distant sound that had no bearing on her. For a brief, foolish moment she thought about walking out the door. She thought about breeching the city walls, like an escaped slave, and running until she was home—into the arms of her mother. The thought bolstered her momentarily, but then she remembered there was nowhere to go. She felt heavy, as if a magnet were keeping her iron feet immobile. She wondered if it was merely a passing sadness, or if perhaps a veil had been lifted for a moment, allowing her to see things as they really were. She wanted so badly just to crawl back in bed, but inertia kept her there, at the window. Even the decision to decide to move required too much effort.

The baby cried.

Outside, snow continued to fall. It was mesmerizing, allowing her to see it without seeing anything. It had been falling for days; how many, she could not say. But the once-invigorating bite in the air now seemed more like an all-out feral attack, impossible to fend off. Dirty snowdrifts, awkwardly piled high, made the streets difficult to navigate. Gutters were swollen with solid waste. She imagined herself imprisoned in white walls that grew higher with each flake.

The baby cried.

From the window Elizabeth watched dispassionately as bundled-up town folk, more accustomed to heat and humidity than to freezing temperatures, hurriedly ducked in and out of doorways. The stinging, wind-whipped winters in Holland—so cold it burned—would lay waste to these southern residents, she thought. But Elizabeth admitted that she had forgotten how those winters *felt* and remembered only that *fact*.

Shivering, as intermittent blasts of cold air whistled through window gaps and around door seams, Elizabeth decided that every body, even her own body, seeks its absolute stasis around which all else becomes relative.

The baby stopped crying.

Louisa, Elizabeth's "Little Mother," had wrapped a shawl around her mother's shoulders and picked the baby up. Holding her mother's swaddled infant, she dragged a chair closer to the fire and wordlessly encouraged her mother to take a seat. Elizabeth obeyed, letting her mind wander to the cold, early December night of the baby's birth.

Lewis had sent Peter for the doctor. The doctor had sent Peter for Sarah Nader.

Elizabeth recalled Dale's recount of Peter's arrival: the boy had burst into the front room of his home late that night, startling him awake so abruptly that Dale ran down the stairs wearing nothing but his shirt and carrying his hunting rifle. It certainly was not uncharacteristic behavior for the boy, but it must have unsettled Dale, especially considering the hour.

But when the doctor heard the fear in Peter's voice, he knew he would need help delivering the baby. He dispatched the boy posthaste to the Naders' house, cautioning him not to make the same grand entrance there as he had done at Dale's.

"I do not need Sarah Nader filling you full of buckshot and sending me another patient to tend to," the doctor warned.

Elizabeth and Sarah had acknowledged early on in their friendship that they were an odd pairing. Both women were certainly working class and proud of it, but Elizabeth was also educated. Sarah had received her education the hard way: from the other side of a pewter cup. Her husband, John Nader, had owned a tavern on Queen Street before disease took him away. After John passed, Sarah ran the establishment, better than John ever did. Sarah had seen just about everything there was to see from the working side of a tavern stool, and she refused to run away from a fight. And to Sarah's way of thinking, everything was a fight. Dr. Dale trusted her more than anyone to deal with a difficult birth.

Elizabeth had proven herself to be a fierce friend as well. When Sarah's daughter Abagail was diagnosed with smallpox, she wasted no time calling 'round the Nader home. Sarah had offered the requisite cup of tea like any good hostess, but it was clear she was worried by the way she kept nervously wringing the apron tied around her ample waist.

"Blimey," Sarah said, her voice faltering when she opened the door. "Most others make a wide path around a working-class sick house. Elizabeth, so good of you to come."

"How is she, Sarah?" Elizabeth had asked.

"Better, I think. She seems better. I have been giving her tar-water at regular intervals, and it seems to be helping."

"I am so pleased to hear it," Elizabeth had said. "Is there anything I can do for your family?"

Sarah bit her lip and took up Elizabeth's hands. "Would you say a prayer?"

"I will do that and more," she said. "I will be back with dinner, and no protests from you."

Sarah smiled. "Abagail loves your rice griddle cakes."

"Done and done," came the reply. "Plan on it for tomorrow's evening meal, along with a hearty fish chowder for the rest of the Naders."

Elizabeth had hugged her best friend before leaving, promising the girls would be picking wildflowers again soon.

Sarah had stood by to assist when Dale had been called to the Timothy home to deliver Elizabeth's baby. When instructed to do so, she used a sharp kitchen knife to cut the cord. After swabbing the child's nose and ears, she wrapped a blanket tightly around the squirmy red infant and presented him to his mother.

But Elizabeth had turned away.

"You have a baby boy," Dale announced, hoping to elicit some maternal reaction. "And a healthy one at that. What Christian name shall he have?"

"He will not have a Christian name," Elizabeth answered.

Sarah stepped up to the bed with the baby.

"Doctor," she said, "them Timothy children might like to hear the happy news of another bruvver."

Dale nodded, indicating he had gotten the hint. When the doctor had left and the door was firmly closed behind him, Elizabeth repeated her decision.

"I will not give him a Christian name, Sarah," she said, expecting a fight.

"I understand," her friend said, not taking the bait. "So many babies, so soon taken. John, Michael, Paul Lewis. It ain't been easy for you. I know." After a pause, Sarah continued, "Only women is given this honor, but it don't come wifout a cost, do it, dear?"

Elizabeth shook her head, using her sleeve to wipe her nose. Sarah took her friend's hand.

"When a child dies before you do, part of your soul goes wif it," she said.

"A man could never understand," Elizabeth said haltingly, as if acknowledging that fact made the hurt so much worse.

Sarah nodded in agreement.

"But that ain't their fault, girlie," she said with a sad smile. "They cannot know what they cannot know. This boy is here. Now. And God give him to you and your Mr. Timothy. You are gonna have to call him somefin, if only so he knows when he be called fer supper."

With that said, Sarah put the infant gently but firmly in Elizabeth's arms.

There was a timid knock at the bedroom door; a turn of the knob followed, and a slice of light crept in from the hall.

"Lewis," Elizabeth said.

"Yes, my dear?" her husband answered.

"Lewis. We shall call him Lewis."

The baby, now several months old, was finally beginning to gain weight. It was merely an observation, nothing more.

Suddenly the front door opened, dousing the front room with a blast of cold air strong enough to extinguish the struggling fire. The baby, who had been almost asleep in Louisa's arms, was startled awake and began to cry spasmodically. Lewis stamped his shoes at the threshold and shook off his hat.

"Elizabeth!" he said with loud bravado. "You are going to love my idea!"

Elizabeth, taking the wailing infant from her daughter, made no response as she tried to soothe the baby.

"James Crokatt brought in seeds of all kinds and has been experimenting with growing saplings to sell for town lot cultivation."

Lewis said he had heard of encouraging prospects from other colonists and decided to surprise Elizabeth with a fig tree.

"Several of his brown turkeys are almost ready to transplant, one as tall as Peter. I told Crokatt I would trade him for advertising space. We struck a deal."

"Where do you propose to plant it?" Elizabeth asked half-heartedly.

Lewis said he had studied the possibilities and decided on a location directly outside their bedroom window.

"In a few years we should have figs the size of seed potatoes."

The pronouncement made it sound as if he had cured smallpox. Elizabeth offered a faint smile.

"If it survives, perhaps the girls and I can make preserves," she said dutifully.

"That is the spirit," Lewis said, happy his surprise had brought her 'round.

Chapter Thirty-One

Ben had sent a letter in advance of his sailing to Charles Towne, informing Lewis that, after four years, he would finally be taking him up on his offer. He planned to visit the Southern colony, stay with the Timothy family, and impose upon Lewis to show him the lay of the land with particular regard to postal routes.

Ben's arrival, however, beat his letter to Charles Towne by several days, and Lewis was not there to greet him.

"Precisely why we need a better system," Franklin grumbled to himself.

He waited a full hour after the schooner docked before deciding no one was coming to conduct him and his satchel to a place of lodging. Porters were available to help passengers, but Ben disliked spending money on work that he was capable of performing himself.

He would, however, need the help of a local man to find the Timothy home. To that end, he hastened to the public house, Shepheard's Tavern, for information.

It was a short, insect-infested walk from the Bay Street pier to Broad Street, oppressively warm for mid-May. Philadelphia was never this unbearable so early in the season, Franklin thought, swatting bugs away as they buzzed near his ears.

"Dear Lord," he mumbled, wiping his forehead with one of Debby's monogrammed cambric handkerchiefs. "I have sailed to the tropics by mistake."

Rounding the corner onto Charles Towne's main thoroughfare, it was not far to the bustling establishment known as Shepheard's Tavern. Shepheard's was as vital to the pulse of life in Charles Towne as St. Philip's, and just as full of sinners. Franklin knew the tavern by way of its Masonic designation; it was one of the first Masonic lodges in America, established just two years ago. Franklin, a Freemason himself for more than five years, had been instrumental in establishing the rite and was delighted well beyond self-satisfaction to see the organization flourishing in the South.

As in the cities up north, ordinaries were far more than their name implied. In addition to being brotherhood lodges, taverns often served as centers of government, including civil and criminal courtrooms and, almost parenthetically, grog shops. Franklin laughed to himself at the thought as he entered the establishment: take away the *libation*, in the legal term *deliberation*, and all that would be left were the letters *de* and *er*: deer. Stepping into Shepheard's, Franklin looked up and smiled. The first thing to catch his eye was a right fine buck head, displayed prominently over the bar counter.

All unclaimed mail was taken to the tavern keeper in large cities such as Charles Towne. Franklin stepped quickly to a long sideboard near the door and rummaged through envelopes and packages hoping to find the letter he sent to Lewis Timothy four weeks ago. Indeed, he did find it, momentarily dashing his resolve that a mail system would ever be worthy of the public's trust.

"I suppose, as postmaster general," he said to himself, "I should be prepared to hand deliver my own correspondence," and he stowed the letter in his inside coat pocket and took a seat at the bar.

"What's your pleasure, gent?" Mrs. Shepheard asked, wiping down the counter where a patron had recently spilled a pint.

She was a stout woman, buxomy and orbicular, with man's hands down to the dirt under her fingernails. A dreadfully stained cook's apron failed to cover the dingy brown-checked gingham dress underneath. Her checks were rosy—not from good circulation but from too much grog—matching the tip of her bulbous nose. Her sparsely populated teeth did not deter her from offering a wide grin.

Franklin liked her immediately

"Certainly not a shot of anything, my good woman," Franklin mused, pointing to the deer head above the bar, "since that is likely what landed him here."

He smiled, pleased with himself at the symmetry of it all.

"The kinda shot I offer ye will not get your head on the wall," she chuckled, "but it might make you feel a bit stuffed in the morning."

"Touché, madame," Franklin said, and took a seat. "May I trouble you for a tall glass of water?"

"'Tis a good deal of trouble, sir," Mrs. Shepheard would have him to know. "Finding potable water is one o' the most troublesome things about livin' here. Most water ain't fit to drink. If I was to offer you some, it would stink of sulfur and likely make you run at both ends before nightfall. No, mate, whiskey's what you want."

Franklin had no mind to offend the woman by announcing that he was a teetotaler. After all, the woman was running a business, and he could not ignore his parched throat.

"Would you have something appropriate for a Pennsylvanian unaccustomed to this oppressively hot weather?" he asked her.

"I thought I heard a Northern bend in your tongue!" she laughed. "Where you be from?"

"Philadelphia, here to meet my business partner and friend Lewis Timothy."

"A fine man, he," she said, hearing that her patron was affiliated with Timothy. "And for Mr. Timothy's friend, I have just the thing."

She bustled off toward the other end of the counter. When she returned, it was clear she was so pleased with her ingenuity that he would have no choice but to accept whatever was offered. To do anything less would have been an insult to her hospitality.

"Let's have a refreshing mug of Fish House Punch, shall we? And later, if you still fancy a glass of water, it won't bother ye so bad when the dysentery sets in."

She poured a generous cup for her patron, unaware that Franklin was a teetotaler.

Fish House Punch, Franklin thought. *Sounds just the thing to wet my whistle.*

He swirled the liquid around in his cup, not knowing that the main ingredients were Jamica run, cognac, and peach brandy.

"Entirely appropriate," Ben said. "To what shall we drink?"

She thought about that for a bit, cocking her eyes to the left and pursing her lips.

"To water," she declared, raising her mug to tap his. "May it always be bad enough for the rum to be better!"

Spoken like a shrewd businesswoman, he concluded, deciding he could very easily fall in love with her.

Chapter Thirty-Two

It had been routine for some time now to leave to Elizabeth the composing room work of setting type, transferring it to a galley, and planning the type form. The baby was old enough to be alone with Louisa, and Lewis had his hands full with bindery work and philanthropic endeavors as a founder of the reputed forty-three-member Two Bit Club.

Elizabeth did not mind. In fact, she rather preferred it this way. It had helped her to get back to work: she knew who she was there. And Louisa was a fine little mother; a fitting substitute to care for the younger children.

Walking down King Street from Crokatt's, Elizabeth stepped off the sidewalk several times for the women who refused to yield. She knew she was difficult to quantify—neither lady nor laborer. While it had been hurtful in her formative years, now she determined to give it no weight. She enjoyed everything about their trade: the smell of the place, the fellowship of working alongside people straining toward a common goal to produce something tangible and important. The work was not tiresome to her; while it was the same process week in and week out, each newspaper was different. There were new items to report and new advertisements. She especially enjoyed keeping the books. Her father had trained her well, for everything except the ostracism that accompanied her education. A fair exchange, she decided, for work so important, silently pitying the parasoled women.

"She who learns must suffer," she could hear her father say, changing the philosopher's pronoun for his daughter.

Still, Elizabeth considered herself fortunate to have a few good friends. While most women in Charles Towne thought of her as less of a lady because she got her hands dirty, Debby Franklin had been an exception. Ben's wife had tradesman's hands just like her husband, but Debby was too simpleminded to feel threatened by Elizabeth's education. Socratic paradox aside, it was an agreeable companionship for that very reason.

Her friend Sarah Nader was similarly oblivious, although what Sarah lacked in formal education, she made up for in business acumen. A true friend is the best possession, she remembered Ben saying. Elizabeth consoled herself with the thought of having *two* true friends.

She quickened her step, anxious to be in the familiar surroundings of wordless sanctity. Here, she felt most like the person she was meant to be, among the freshest advices, both foreign and domestic. She relished being the first to hold a freshly pressed sheet of each edition—the first to view each unique verbal portrait of time in those printed words: calls to action and offers for sale, Council minutes, and news from abroad. It would never come again, not in exactly the same way. She felt as if she were creating something of value that could not be taken away. She understood the power in that: wielding the chronicler of such a force in nature as Time and Tidings. She knew that she knew things, and she knew that fact alone was enough to distance her from others.

If knowledge itself is power, she thought, then the printed word was the most under-sung weapon in any arsenal, because it held the power to sway men's minds.

That power was far more effective than any sword, she decided. And when the sword was employed to forcibly change men's minds, the written word was there too, to report it.

Elizabeth turned the knob on the Timothy Print Shop and walked into the darkened room. She stood in the doorway, allowing her eyes to adjust.

Jonathan was nowhere to be found.

Where could that boy be? Elizabeth wondered.

Amsterdam was there, pounding pulp with a large wooden pestle and swirling the milky contents in a large bucket.

"Amsterdam, have you seen Jonathan?" Elizabeth asked.

"No, ma'am" he replied, "not since he went back to the composing room to work on the next week's edition."

Elizabeth walked briskly through the finishing room where freshly printed papers had been hung from the rafters to dry. She found the boy in the back corner, asleep on the floor.

"Jonathan," she said, trying to arouse him.

Louder, she called his name and touched him on the shoulder. With some difficulty, he opened his eyes; she put her hand to his forehead. He was burning up with fever.

"You must stand, Jonathan," she told him. "We need to get you home."

She called Amsterdam to help her.

"Jonathan is sick. Can you support his weight?" she asked, knowing full well the huge man could have carried both of them home on his shoulders.

"I got him, Miz Elizabeth," he said, and bending at the knees, the hulking figure scooped up the frail young man and laid him across his back.

Jonathan, dehydrated and on the brink of delirium, was too weak to even hold on.

"Take him straight home, Am, and then fetch Dr. Dale. Quickly now!"

Elizabeth walked him to the front door and firmly shut it tight behind him.

The next issue was not on deadline, and most of the print shop work was preparatory. Truth be told, Elizabeth could work faster with Jonathan and Amsterdam out of the way. Over the years, she had spent many hours alone, setting type. Even when she had helped Ben and Lewis at the *Philadelphia Gazette*, she often preferred to steal away by herself, after the children were in bed and her husband was busy with Library Company duties, to work alone in this familiar and comfortable environment. The smell of ink—a mixture of lampblack and varnish—was reminiscently soothing to her. Just as some people have deep-rooted memories of their mother's eau de toilette going all the way back to infancy, Elizabeth's earliest memory was the scent that clung to the proliferation of words. Even before she knew how to read and write, she could smell the words in her father's shop: mysterious, dark, and earthy.

Stringing the cold metal type on a stick and selecting initial letters and ornamental blocks for the columns was equally exciting to her. It was an activity that never seemed dull or rote, although she had been doing it all her life. Rather, she felt that the more she did it, the better she got at it. And the better she got at it, the more she loved doing it. The more she loved doing it, the more it sank into the very sinews of her existence and defined her.

It was comforting to know who she was.

Elizabeth fondled one of the metal Caslon letters from the upper case in her fingertips. In the printing business, there were several typefaces that were used with regularity, but the most common was the one developed by a dutchman, William Caslon. She could not help but appreciate the Dutch artistic influence as she held a capital *A* in her hand, ready to slide onto the stick as part of the headline for "Foreign Affairs."

When she had finished, Elizabeth looked over the galley one last time, checking for inaccuracies and misspellings in the reverse metal blocks before tying off the page form. Miss something now, and it would be too late to correct later.

Reputation was everything in this business.

When she was satisfied, Elizabeth stood up, stretched her back, and walked into the finishing room where ghostly broadsheets, still wet, hung from the rafters to dry. It occurred to her that she could barely remember what a proper ceiling looked like; so much of her life overhead had been bound up in the printed word.

Taking the wet broadside sheet up by its corners, Elizabeth walked to the narrow set of steps, pitched at a steep angle in the limited floor space. With one hand on the ladder and the other holding the wet sheet, she climbed up into the rafters. The ceiling above her looked like so many broadsheet ghosts, waiting to dry. It reminded her of a dirty winter: white sheets speckled with the words of sleet and snow. Threatening. Always threatening. She wrapped her shawl around her and shivered despite the climbing May temperatures.

An abrupt knock at the door startled her from her thoughts. She hoped it was not bad news. There was no room for it.

Chapter Thirty-Three

Bright and early the next morning Lewis was up and out the door. He kissed Elizabeth curtly, saying he would pay Judge Trott a visit.

"I hope I can entice him to dinner with our Philadelphia visitor," her husband said as he grabbed his hat. "I will return shortly to open the shop."

Lewis insisted that Ben spend a leisurely morning after sailing from Pennsylvania.

"You have only just arrived yesterday," he said. "You should rest and enjoy a good breakfast. When I return, we will have plenty of time to discuss your proposition."

Grabbing a cathead biscuit stuffed with salted pork and promising he would only be gone a short while, Lewis rushed out of the kitchen dependency into the yard before Ben could say another word.

Stepping onto the busy street, Timothy could not have been happier that Benjamin Franklin had finally come for a visit. It was like a tonic to be in the presence of his old friend again. Lewis whistled as he walked the short distance to the judge's Cumberland Street home, thinking about the shared history of their families. The Franklin/Timothy friendship went back now almost two decades. Lewis owed Ben a debt of gratitude he could never repay:

for his influence in placing him in the Library Company position, for hiring him as a tutor, as well as for writing and editing Ben's German newspaper and taking him as partner to be the King's Printer in Carolina and editor of the *Gazette.*

To that purpose, there were business matters to which they must attend, such as Lewis's accounting of their printing agreement and the condition of the press and accoutrements, as well as payments due. But there would also be much time to talk of news from Philadelphia and especially news from abroad, including Ben's proposal that Lewis take on postmaster responsibilities for Charles Towne.

Business notwithstanding, Lewis was grateful that they had always also been stalwart friends, almost like family in a place so far removed from their blood relations. Debby had been such a helpmate to Elizabeth, embracing the Timothy children as she would her own. Ben and Debby had stood by their side at christenings and burials, celebrating birthdays and grieving deaths. It was Debby who helped deliver more than one little Timothy, and it was Debby who had quickly carried more than one dead child away from his wife, who was consumed by grief.

The Timothys were deeply sorry to hear that the Franklins' son, Francis, had died of smallpox at such a tender age. Lewis knew Elizabeth wished she could have been there for Debby. Should they have remained in Philadelphia? He wondered if having such a dear friend close by would have made a difference to both women. He recalled how he and Elizabeth had argued about the contract. Though Lewis had not died in the Southern wilderness, he also could not say that he had prospered greatly either. Making a life here certainly had not been easy on their family, particularly Elizabeth. She had suffered her share of heartbreak, he knew. With each baby's death, she seemed to drift further away from him.

After a visit to secure the judge's acceptance for dinner, Lewis walked back down King Street to the print shop. He stood at the door fumbling for the key in his pocket and taking shallow breaths as he searched. The nauseating stench of the city streets was bad enough on any given day, but in wicked heat, it was more than the stoutest constitution could handle. Not a breath of breeze stirred, except from the occasional wafts of swine that ran loose in the streets. Wagon wheels, rolling over horse piles and human waste, released pungent odors into the brackish morning air. Lewis reached for his hanky in his trouser pocket and covered his nose before resuming the search for the key. Retrieving it from his inside left jacket pocket, he breathed deeply into the freshly laundered cotton cloth and unlocked the door.

Once inside the dark room, he quickly closed the door behind him. The familiar scent of the print shop greeted his grateful nose. He was safe here.

Lewis walked with purpose to the composing room and shoved his handkerchief into his trouser pocket, letting his eyes adjust to the diffused light. The galleys Elizabeth had prepared the day before were waiting for him. Lewis read the type form, right to left, line after line. When he reached the bottom of the metal frame, something on the floor caught his eye.

"Must have fallen out of my pocket," he mumbled aloud, and he reached down to retrieve his hanky.

The crumpled cotton was oddly stiff—unyielding to his touch— as if it had been soaked in marl and allowed to dry. Lewis lit a lamp and examined it closer. This was not his handkerchief; clearly it had been used to apply some sort of varnish, judging by the yellowish stains. It was stiff as a board.

A pity, he thought, as he examined the intricate scalloped embroidery along its skillfully hemmed edges.

He walked over to the water bucket and dunked it in, swirling the fabric around to soften the substance's hold.

Not varnish, he thought. Varnish would require turpentine to thin it. Perhaps a lung infection of some sort.

When the mucous had loosened enough, he wrung the hanky out and examined it closer.

"Peter's," he mumbled with disgust, noting the monogram in the corner.

He laid it out to dry on one of the paper-drying ropes, and he determined to speak with his eldest son for taking such poor care of Deborah Franklin's gift.

Just then the print shop door flung open, hitting the wall with deafening force and scorching the dark place with sunlight as Peter ran in at full bore, almost knocking over a vat of pulp.

"Peter!" his father yelled. "Have you no common sense at all, boy?"

"Sorry, Father," the robust thirteen-year-old boy said as sullenly as possible through labored breathing. Studying his shoes in contrition, he said, "I am late for helping you again, so I ran as fast as I could."

His father glared at him. "Do you imagine that running to be slightly *less* late, and knocking over a vat of rags in the process, is an equitable exchange?"

"No, sir," Peter replied, adding another mumbled regret.

Lewis determined to use the opportunity to warn Peter, yet again, that inheritance was not guaranteed.

"Printing is a serious business, young man. Just as 'Cleanliness is next to Godliness,' 'Timeliness' infers a sense of pride in one's work. And speaking of cleanliness, if I ever catch you leaving your filthy handkerchief on my print room floor again, I will have you disemboweled, disowned, and distributed down the center of Broad Street," he added, pulling the hanky down from the rope it had been drying on and waving it under Peter's nose.

"This is not mine, Father," the boy said as he studied it, turning the damp cotton over in his hand.

"Clearly, it is boy," Lewis replied, turning his back to Peter and returned to his type stick. "It has your monogram. I found it when I opened up this morning, on the floor over there."

Peter looked in the direction his father was pointing. Never one to miss an opportunity for posturing where the family business was concerned, but careful not to make his father look like a fool, Peter reminded him that he had learned his lessons well.

"'When setting type,'" he recounted from his mother's lessons, "'the lower case p and t look very much like a b and f when viewed in reverse. Perhaps it is Mr. Franklin's," he said. "I saw him leave around four o'clock yesterday."

"Mr. Franklin was here?" his father asked.

"Yes, sir," Peter replied, strapping on his leather apron and taking a seat at the composing table. "He arrived while you were at the Two Bit Club meeting. Mother was here. I stopped 'round about four o'clock to help her and just caught sight of Mr. Franklin as he left."

Curious, Lewis thought. Elizabeth had not mentioned seeing Franklin before he arrived at their home yesterday evening.

Chapter Thirty-Four

"**B**en," Lewis said as he gently shook his friend's shoulders, "it is time to get up."

Franklin's tall frame was stretched diagonally across the boys' beds, which had been pushed together in an effort to provide some vestige of a good night's sleep for their guest.

Ben sat up and yawned.

"Quite right, my good man," Ben responded. "Early to rise, as it were."

The rest of the house slept in the predawn morning as Lewis and Ben set out for the Timothy land on the Pon Pon River. Elizabeth had prepared hominy bread for the men's breakfast the night before. Boiled eggs, several slices of goats' milk cheese, and some salted fish were packed in a sack for their meals until they returned to Charles Towne the following day.

Stepping out into vacant streets, a crescent moon was still visible in the cloudless sky. No sound greeted them save the crescendo of cicadas—high-pitched and frantic—and the sorrowful sound of a larger red-crested woodpecker crying out like the very last Indian warrior making a battle stand. The air, fresh as May with morning dew, was already beginning to wither under another oppressive Carolina summer day.

"Are you sure you are up for the travel, Ben?" Lewis asked.

"Never felt better, my man. I am anxious to see some of the Carolina wilderness," Ben assured him. "But are you sure *you* are up for it? You seemed a bit fatigued last night."

"Nothing more curative than fresh air and amicable companionship," Lewis replied.

"It has been too long since I have enjoyed a good ride," he said and winked at Ben as men do when conveying a shared secret.

It was the better part of a day's ride by horse and carriage from Charles Towne up the main high road to the Timothys' land: two hundred acres granted two years ago by King George II. Lewis had made the trip many times, but seeing the wild beauty of inland South Carolina through Franklin's eyes made it seem as if he too were seeing this subtropical region of America for the very first time.

By the time they reached Parker's Ferry, where the main high road from Charles Towne crossed the Pon Pon River at John Jackson's plantation, they could smell the bream beds. Black water, lapping and slapping against breeze and current, reminded Ben of a woman enjoying a sponge bath. Hanging above their heads, her curled tresses were the Spanish moss, unpinned and ready for a soak. He felt like an intruder in a private moment. Without comment, the men tied off the horse and sat under the shade of a large magnolia tree while they ate. When they were finished, they quietly slipped two canoes into the dark water.

They paddled some distance before Franklin broke the silence.

"Quite the piece you have, Lewis," Franklin said, pushing the paddle in long, slow strokes on alternating sides of the canoe. "I can see you are a rich man, in more ways than one. Would that I were in your enviable situation."

"I have much to be thankful for," Timothy replied. "As do you, my friend. I do not recall 'Envy' appearing on your list of virtues." He added with a smile, "Have you perhaps added it since we spoke?"

Ben cut a sideways glance at his friend but, seeing the jest in his face, he smiled back.

"No," he replied, "Envy is something I try not to cultivate in my garden."

Lewis laughed. "It can be a rank weed at that, choking out more virtuous growth. And speaking of virtues, how is your list coming along?"

Ben thought about his answer as he surveyed his surroundings: *such a lovely place*, he thought, *but so oppressively hot.* Patting his pockets for his handkerchief but not finding it, he resorted to using his sleeve to wipe the Carolina humidity from his brow.

A large crested heron, barking disapproval at having been disturbed from his fishing hole, rose up from his tree perch like a mythical dragon and startled Franklin. The great bird's wings unfolded as if two gray sheets were catching wind; languidly and with broad, heavy strokes, he beat the sticky air toward another location downstream, grumbling as would an old man.

Cypress knees, wading into the water like young girls with their skirts raised just enough to taunt, seemed to enjoy the rhythmic undulation caused by their canoes. Formally known as the Pon Pon river, the Edisto's water slapped playfully in a pulse of retreats and plunges as gentle waves made their way to shore. Sun-dappled and diffuse from the leafy limbs above, the murky river seemed to be a private place of intimacy, as if two lovers joined, and parted, in a fluid motion.

In the years to come, who would win the battle? Ben wondered. Would the sturdy tree trunk remain erect, standing against the relentless lick of liquid? Or would the knees bow and separate and succumb?

"I have mastered several of them," Ben finally answered, "and am hopeful that one day I shall master them all, rather than allowing them mastery over me."

Lewis stopped paddling, keeping one oar in the water to turn the boat toward his friend. He smiled in response.

"No man has all that his heart desires," he said. "Not even in the Garden of Eden."

Carolina was certainly not Eden. From what Ben could see, the colony was a land full of dangers. But there were certainly many pleasures as well, where everything seemed to be yours for the taking.

While it offered much, however, Carolina required more: land, success, power, position—all of which came at the price of hard labor, and to Ben's mind, at the expense of the Black man. Ben knew all too well: to thrive, this Eden required connections with influential men. It meant defending what you have against all aggressors, and always fighting to keep it. Life was short, and hard, and often merciless. Love was an arrangement, a convenience, a social standing. When the heart followed its own path, this Eden became an even more unkind mockery of its sardonic promise.

To be cast out might well, then, seem a blessing.

Ben considered a response.

"I should not wish to have all that my heart desires," he offered at length. "The end of passion, after all, is the beginning of repentance."

Lewis made a study of his friend, looking him in the eyes. It was the tell again, that curious way Franklin had of unintentionally tipping his hand. But this time it felt different, as if the tide of the game had turned, and Franklin was already in position for checkmate.

Chapter Thirty-Five

When Dr. Dale was summoned to the Timothy home one dark December night in 1738, he was unprepared for what he saw. He remembered thinking how greasy the dead printer's hands looked as he examined the crumpled body. Those hands haunted him: with ink imbedded under the fingernails and in the folds, creases, and crevices of his palms, they seemed to be the hands of a lower-class working man, not this gentleman who had spent so many years turning pages in the classics. Ultimately, though, the dirty work of making a living was what remained.

Over the past four years, Dale had come to recognize that Lewis Timothy was born to be a writer, a speaker, a teacher, or a linguist—someone who conferred with other gentlemen over mahogany table tops. He was not born to be a newspaper printer, although he had been a good one. He had allowed his gentleman's hands to become marked by the newspaper's ink, but his bearing, dignity, and speech was that of a scholar, an intellectual ready to distill from the opportunities in the Carolina Colony all the advantages possible for himself, his ever-growing family, and his intellectual wife.

As a member of the committee that had approved Lewis Timothy's appointment to the Charles Towne printing position,

Dale had liked the chap even before he met him. Timothy had received Ben Franklin's approval, after all, and there was little else above that recommendation to be earned.

The good doctor enjoyed writing copy for Timothy's *Gazette*, especially as the debate raged over smallpox treatment. Many residents found it difficult to believe the medical premise that a dead virus could protect a living organism from infection. In desperation, a large number of townspeople ignorantly turned to bloodletting and, perhaps less invasive but certainly just as ineffective, tar-water as treatment when pox symptoms developed. Lewis, convinced that tar-water was the "anodyne necklace" of pox, used the *Gazette* to sway many townsfolk who had been skeptical—even fearful—of the variolation procedure. Timothy had been a stalwart proponent of variolation; the *Gazette* continued to promote its use even as infection rates reached half of the town's citizens.

The printer showed his true mettle, however, when he and his son Peter were among the first to receive variolation in October, barely two months prior. Dale wondered if the loss of his eight-month-old son Lewis Junior to smallpox had prompted Timothy to put his faith, as it were, in medical science. It was a bold leap, to be sure: choosing variolation for their head of household *and* for their first-born son. But his decision led the way for more converts and doubtless saved many lives.

It had been a difficult year for most Charles Towne residents, including the Timothys. No sooner had the sickly season begun than Lewis came down with yellow fever just last May. Dale shuddered at the memory of Lewis's battle against the insipid disease. Symptoms did not manifest themselves for as many as six days; by the time it showed its hand, the game was almost over. Within a week, his patients either died or got well. At that point, medical science seemed powerless to intervene.

Dale advised Timothy to rest, knowing his words would go unheeded. Lewis had been spending most of his time in the print shop in a desperate attempt to finish John Wesley's *Collection of Psalms and Hymns*. He was equally determined to finalize colonial mail routes prior to Ben Franklin's visit and refused his doctor's orders to rest while his friend and mentor was a guest in their home.

Symptoms showed up in earnest after Franklin returned to Pennsylvania. Timothy fought through a week of severe head and muscle aches, fever, dizziness, and nausea. It was another week before his wife would let him return to work. Thanks to her insistence, Lewis had persevered and lived when countless others had not. He had lost the better part of May and June at work, but he had not lost his life.

At least, not then. And not to the disease. *We are fooled with hope*, Dale thought, remembering his Dryden.

The good doctor could not adequately express the sympathy he felt for the Timothy family as he personally took the silver watch from Lewis's rigor-mortised body and assumed the duties of a late-December burial. As intensely as he felt for Mrs. Timothy, dangerously close to premature delivery, he moaned aloud for Peter and the other children. But had he attempted to offer words of consolation, he was sure Elizabeth would have put a finger to his lips. This is the time spoken of in Romans, when we do not know what we ought to pray for, but the Holy Ghost himself intercedes for us with groans that words cannot express.

After the funeral, Dale had stopped 'round the Timothy home. He used the excuse of returning Lewis's watch, but it was not the real reason for his visit. Dale knew the toll that grief could take on a pregnant woman and her unborn infant. It was not uncommon to keep the gravediggers busy when the head of household died.

Dale was startled to find her in the composing room. Her husband's printer's apron, loosely tied over her belly, seemed more to call attention to her pregnancy than hide it. Elizabeth was sitting on a high stool at the work bench, by rote putting letters together on Lewis's printer's stick. The good doctor had not her talent for backward reading, but it was clear, even to him, that the large letters on the page identified her oldest son as printer now. At least on paper.

The doctor put his hand on Elizabeth's shoulder and looked at a wet impression of the upcoming January 4, 1739, issue hanging to dry. He scanned the columns of advertisements quickly: A Negro girl, fourteen years of age, who had already had smallpox, to be sold by the printer. Below that, an appeal from the real printer of the *Gazette*, until Peter reached majority:

> *Whereas the late Printer of this Gazette hath been deprived of his Life, by an unhappy Accident, I take this Opportunity of informing the Publick, that I shall continue the said Paper as usual; and hope, by the Assistance of my Friends, to make it as entertaining and correct as may be reasonably expected. Wherefore I flatter my self, that all those Persons, who, by Subscription or otherwise, assisted my late Husband, in the Prosecutions of the said Undertaking, will be kindly pleased to continue their Favours and good Offices to his poor afflicted Widow and six small Children and another hourly expected. Eliz: Timothy.*

"An unhappy accident, Elizabeth?" Dale asked softly.

She stared at him with deep, moist eyes—pools to drown in—that begged answers he could not give, to questions too painful to ask. Her visage, ashen, looked as if it could slide off her face under the heavy pull of loss. Her mouth parted, feeling the tug of words to be spoken at its corners, but offered no reply. She continued feeding letters, as though hypnotized, onto the lengthening column of print … double-spaced … in her hand. She was not crying. She was not talking. She was not there. Only her agile and animated hands betrayed a desperate attempt to bring order to her life's chaos. She was in shock, he knew. What good could be gained from bringing her out of it to the more horrible reality of widowhood?

Chapter Thirty-Six

At the funeral, Elizabeth discreetly tugged at the high collar that seemed to be tightening around her neck. The air hung heavy with the weight of words unspoken; she sat up taller in retaliation. Small shafts of sunlight through stained-glass windows caught fragments of dust and colored them with rainbows; thousands of rainbows drifting carelessly about the room. Elizabeth imagined that the stained-glass rainbows alighted on the mourners' hair, giving them a fairy-like quality. She took a deep breath, praying that those dusty shards of refracted glass would make tiny incisions as they passed through her circulatory system. Only then, when the doctors could find no reason for her internal bleeding, would she be free to cry. Free to fly away.

A sound brought her back to the present moment. Now that she focused on it, she could barely hear the rector's words. It was the sound of her son's shoes, scraping the church floor as he swung each leg out, pendulum-like.

She looked around. Peter was disturbing everyone. She would have to apologize to Rev. Garden on the way out. She resolved to give the boy a good lashing when they got home. A thirteen-year-old was certainly old enough to understand death and the decorum required in its attendant societal obligations. People die. He had seen it with his own siblings.

In a hushed but firm tone, she said, "Your father is dead. At least have the decency to sit up straight."

When the service was over, the friends and family who had gathered at St. Philip's to pay last respects stood up silently and opened their pew gates. It was a church full of creaking, scuttling noise, like emboldened cockroaches seeking the dark. Wooden pew gates clapped closed as mourners stood up to leave. The floor beams creaked under the weight of so much grief.

Their own pew box was like a coffin to Elizabeth, a suffocating enclosure that penned her like an animal. She wanted to burst out of it and run down the broad path until she reached the city's walls, and keep running until she reached the hills of Holland.

With heads bowed and handkerchiefs in hand, the mourners passed single file, like mute little soldiers, out the rear door of the church and into the graveyard. Lewis's coffin was carried by six of his friends and business associates. Elizabeth shielded her eyes as she passed through the doorway from sanctuary to cemetery into the bright, brisk late-December day.

What a beautiful day for a funeral, she thought.

When the graveside service concluded and quiet, mandatory acknowledgments were made, Elizabeth grabbed up her son's hand and bade the other children to fall behind. Down the cemetery pathway and onto the bayside street, people were coming and going like any other day. No one outside the church confines seemed to be aware that she had just buried her husband. People strolled along, some linking elbows, some chatting amicably, others in a rush to complete this errand or another, at the beef market perhaps, or the courthouse, minding carefully to step out of the way of carriages and men on horseback as they crossed the cobblestone streets.

Everyone was enjoying this lovely, clear day, unusually brisk and clean, no less than one week after Christmas. No one—not a soul on that street—had any notion just how bad she felt at that moment.

"Peter, come along," she told her eldest boy, who was dawdling behind them. "We must get you home. Your shoes are dreadfully scuffed. I sincerely hope no one noticed them in church. You will be minding to them first thing."

Peter began to object, but Elizabeth snapped his hand up to get his attention.

"Your father is dead," she said harshly. "You are the man of the house now, so stop your pitiful mourning and hold your head up."

Peter instinctively pulled his hand away from his mother's grip and moved to face her. A resolution came over his young face, and the two of them stood toe-to-toe in the middle of the street; the other children turned to find out why they had not followed them to the other side. But no one moved. No one dared move.

"I am sad, Mother," Peter said. "I am so sad he is gone, and I miss him. Do you not miss him?"

"Yes, of course I do," Elizabeth responded, glancing around at who might be observing them. "What an absurd question. But death is a fact of life, and you may as well learn that."

She reminded him harshly, "'He who learns must suffer, and even in our sleep, pain that cannot forget falls drop by drop upon the heart.'"

Peter knew his mother expected him to finish the quotation and cite its source. He did not want to—the words scared him. He feared his father's ghost would haunt him at night, bleeding dark-red drops onto his nightshirt until he drowned. But he knew his mother's temper, and he dared not exacerbate her.

"'And in our own despair, against our will, comes wisdom to us by the awful grace of God,'" he replied, wiping his eyes.

"And the Greek tragedian who said it?" Elizabeth asked her petulant son.

"Aeschylus," the boy said sniffling, studying his shoes.

Elizabeth straightened and smoothed her widow's weeds over her latest pregnancy. This was an unpropitious place to carry on a private family conversation. She took a quick survey of passersby. No one on the street seemed to have taken notice.

"If you promise to stop crying," she said in the gentlest voice available to her at that moment, "I will let you record your father's death in the family Bible. But you must promise to stop crying."

Peter nodded and rubbed the cuff of his sleeve across his nose. "Yes, Mother."

"And you must promise to use your best cursive," Elizabeth added.

Chapter Thirty-Seven

The unseasonably nice weather of the funeral inevitably succumbed to drizzling rain the next day. As January began the following week, temperatures plummeted, and Charles Towne became an icy, brittle place where everything from doorknobs to the fingers that grasped them felt as if they would snap off from the freezing temperatures.

Dale delivered Elizabeth's son just as February got underway.

Elizabeth rubbed her frozen fingers briefly and grabbed a wooden bucket from the hearth. It had begun to snow overnight, and the fire was dying.

Best not let it burn out, she thought, and hurriedly threw her husband's coat on and wrapped a shawl around her neck.

With a determined chin, she grasped the doorknob and prepared herself for the blast of cold air.

There was no other sound in the world like the *absence* of sound in the presence of falling snow. For a moment, Elizabeth was back in Holland, in her childhood. Closing the door tightly behind her, she stood on the snow-covered stoop, watching small white dots blow straight into her eyes. All she could see was swirl, like angel dust, lightly encircling her. Protecting her. She tried not to blink, afraid it would break the spell and she would wake from the dream.

She loved this reverent time, the moment of snow when gray sky erupted in the cacophony of pure silence, and everything—even the troubled soul—pauses to acknowledge God's magnificence. She closed her eyes, opened her mouth, and stuck out her tongue. Light shavings, delicate and ethereal, clung there and dissolved immediately. She could taste the cold flakes, metallic in her mouth. Like a trinity of ellipses slugged for the press. Hope of things to come, or at least the hope of hope.

For one brief, silent moment, human inadequacies and failures were set aside in the presence of something larger, more important, and everlasting. The quietness slowed everyone's tongues.

Soon, though, children would erupt from their homes dragging scarves behind them and rushing to pellet one another with snowballs. Laughter would overwhelm the raucous quiet, and God would retreat.

She would be exposed again.

Feeling the chill, she wrapped her woolen shawl tightly around her nose and mouth, breathing warm, moist air into it. Each step she took in her inadequate shoes let in spoonfuls of snow over the tops, which settled and melted around her ankles. She loved the crunch, though, despite the discomfort of her feet now burning with cold. Every deliberate footfall made the sound of a fist being driven into a sack of cracked corn—rhythmic and deep—as if a man's large hands were scooping feed for livestock. Elizabeth walked quickly to the woodpile, gathered as much kindling as her numb fingers could hold, and put it in her bucket.

Carefully, she retraced her steps to the front door, wary of exposing her numb feet to more snow over her boot tops. When she reached the door, she stamped first one foot and then the other, knocking the iciness off the sole. With a raw hand, she reached for the door handle and, using her backside, shoved open the entrance. She laid the bucket off to the side, where a dying fire now struggled to consume morsels of glowing hardwood like the last light of an animal's ravaged eyes. She removed her boots, one at a time, spilling the slushy contents on the stoop. The door was shut with determination.

One arduous step at a time, Elizabeth held tightly to the rail as she climbed the staircase to the second floor. After placing two fairly good-sized limbs in the hearth upstairs, she reached for the infant, lifting him out blankets and all, and sat down in a chair by the fire. She juggled him handily while she unbuttoned her bodice and put him on her breast.

As Joseph suckled, Elizabeth had no choice but to be motionless, kept company by her own intrusive thoughts. With her eyes wide open and unblinking, she stared at some distant point without really seeing it. Here, within this ethereal sojourn, she could feel the planet spinning.

After Lewis's funeral, Dr. Dale had insisted that Elizabeth take some time for herself. She dismissed that advice, these inane instructions from a man with little sensibility of what it was like to be a pregnant widow and mother to half a dozen children under fourteen years of age. Between feeding and educating her children and keeping the business running without Amsterdam after her husband's death, she found it difficult to do much else. Now that Joseph was born, she had a newborn to take care of as well. The days were so short—and so interminable at the same time. If she could have spent all day and night in the print shop, there still would not be enough time to do all that the business required. And yet the days seemed to drag on forever, one long, dreary trip around the sun after another. She wondered if it would ever be different.

At length, however, Elizabeth had capitulated to Dale's demands under her own terms. She agreed to suspend publication of the *Gazette* for one month—much less time than polite society required—to grieve and rest and care for her infant. But she secretly began work on the next edition, choosing to set the "Universal Prayer" in type for the February 1 issue. Pope's poem was more remedy to her than anything else could ever be.

Elizabeth was well aware that most local news got around much quicker than the newspaper, especially with correspondents like

Esther Crokatt sharing gossip. There was much talk of the historic meeting between chiefs of the Choctaw and Chickasaw Nations. In the middle of Broad Street, each man smoked the pipe of peace, followed by an elegant dinner at James Crokatt's home.

Let them discuss that news, she decided, not the cause of a printer's unhappy accident.

She looked down at her baby while he nursed. In the soundlessness, her thoughts screamed, a constant, silent assault.

It had been kind of her friend Sarah to insist she attend service the first Sunday after Lewis's funeral, before Joseph was born. Sarah and all the little Naders, including Abagail, whose permanently scarred face was the cost of her living, had appeared at Elizabeth's door an hour prior to the ringing of St. Philip's bells. Sarah was fully prepared to dress her friend herself, by brute force, if required.

"Well, as I live and breathe, Sarah Nader," Elizabeth said, answering the door in her bedclothes.

From under her cap, pinned wisps of unkempt hair crawled like dull brown veins along her forehead.

"I will not sing you a song this morning, Elizabeth Timothy, and there is no sense in your asking it. If you wish to hear me carry a tune, put on a frock and wash your children," Sarah said, hands on her hips as if to confirm the matter had been decided. "You are coming to Sabbath service this morning. I will not take *no* for an answer, and neither will the Lord your God."

Elizabeth had stood resolute in the doorframe, arms folded atop her ripe belly in defense against her dearest friend; Sarah chuckled at that.

"Have you forgotten, dearie," the ale seller asked, "that I have pushed my way past bigger men than you in this town, and shoved many of them out into the street past closing? I suggest you get yourself dressed, or me and your oldest boy will carry you there against your will. I mean it. You know I do."

Sarah held Elizabeth's stare and did not blink. She had learned that even women could have a right fair pissing contest, and among dickless females and eunuchs, Sarah was an undisputed urination champion. Even while her husband was alive, she had dealt with the business world of men the hard way: from the other side of a pewter cup. After John passed, Sarah had championed each and every day by refusing to run away from a fight. And to Sarah's way of thinking, everything was a fight. Elizabeth admired her for her petulance.

Finding her determination dissolved as much from knowing she could not win as from realizing she should not, Elizabeth stepped aside. Sarah bustled into the front room of the Timothy home, unpinned her hat, and laid it on the oak side table.

"I have no interest in hearing what the Bible says about my husband's untimely death," Elizabeth replied. "But people will begin to talk."

"They already have," her friend said bluntly.

"What are they saying?" Elizabeth wanted to know, but she neither expected nor required a response.

"What they are saying is of no consequence. But you are going to service this morning to put an end to the tongue waggers," Sarah said firmly. "Now get dressed. And mind you cover up; that baby is due any day now. You take care of him and you; I will handle the rest of the children."

Without further comment, Elizabeth obediently retreated upstairs to dress.

When all seven Timothys were present and accounted for, Mrs. Nader pronounced them satisfactory for public display.

"None of you will set them women to talking as much as me though," she said, pinning her hat back on her head.

Strutting and twirling around like a whirling dervish full circle to give them all a proper look, she asked, "How do you like it?"

"Like *what*?" Elizabeth asked, willfully vexing her friend. She had not failed to notice Sarah's new hat. Elizabeth kept her eyes on her children to ensure their silence, and dutifully, none of them gave Sarah even the satisfaction of a glance.

"Like what?" Sarah asked, stepping up her theatrics.

From the corner of her eye Elizabeth could see the woman, hands on hips, strolling lengthwise across the room and back. Her head was erect, and her neck stuck out.

"Oh, my goodness!" Elizabeth exclaimed, pointing dramatically at her friend. "You have a *bird* on your head!"

Elizabeth walked briskly to Sarah's side and made exaggerated antics of trying to shoo off the feathered headpiece. Sarah ducked her friend's advances and stood sulking against the type rack, her arms crossed like sabers to protect her head.

"That is more than enough, thank you," she said, while Elizabeth and the rest of the Timothys did little to control their own laughter.

"Well, it ain't no wonder," Sarah said, unpinning the hat from her coiffure to reposition it properly. "You always been jealous of me."

"Jealous of you?" Elizabeth laughed. "You look like a peahen in that thing! How many beautiful birds had to die for that monstrosity?"

"Mock me if you will, but the colonies are making a handsome profit on these feathers. London milliners cannot buy enough plumes to keep up with demand, which works out nicely here, I am told."

"How so?" Elizabeth asked, as the group made their way out the front door and onto King Street.

"These birds are a farmers' pestilence," Sarah said. "George Chicken's wife was in town last week complaining about the devastation Carolina parrots wreak on his crops. They come in droves, she tells me, flocks of them like green waves, and devour everything. They are just as bad for corn as ricebirds are for rice. And Cockerel had a stand of apple trees too, Catherine said. They ruined the fruit just to get to the seeds. Everything ravaged. Just ravaged."

Sarah continued, clucking and shaking her head, "Chattering up a storm, too, they were, like it were sport. Mr. Chicken's overseer killed two dozen of the varmints. Each time one fell to the ground, the whole flock would fly to its rescue. He picked off as many as he could before his bird shot ran out and scattered the rest. Took a heavy toll on his corn, but he plucked the dead ones and sold the feathers to Mister Crokatt. James told Chicken he could peddle all he could get to British milliners."

"Just like a man to destroy beauty in order to obtain the very thing that makes it beautiful. And all so that homely women can hide underneath it," Elizabeth had observed, not bothering about how her comment might be taken. "What did he do with the plucked birds?"

"Who? Chicken?" Sarah had replied. "He ate 'em, I suspect. Parrot pie."

* * ★ * *

Elizabeth removed her son from her breast and laid him in his cradle. Even now, the memory of her friend's coquettish attempt at high fashion brought a smile to her lips.

Joseph was sleeping on a full stomach. Elizabeth crept quietly out of the room and closed the door behind her.

"Peter," she called out as she descended the stairs, "Run down to the wharfs and ask what ships have been received."

Her promise to the good doctor had been attempted long enough; the next *Gazette* was due for the press.

"And bring any news from the captains who have sailed from abroad," Elizabeth added.

She was editor now, and the only one qualified to finish her son's training. She would not have Benjamin Franklin renegotiating their partnership.

Chapter Thirty-Eight

Since Franklin's visit last May, regular mail service had begun, quite tenuously, in the colony. The Assembly gave two hundred pounds a year toward that end, and several private benefactors had agreed to fund the endeavor as well. The goal was to deliver post from the Northern colonies to Cape Fear, George-Town, and Edenton on the twentieth of each month with mail returning to Charles Towne in less than one month.

Elizabeth loved the idea. Written communications among colonists were good for the printing business, she argued, but Peter thought otherwise.

"I certainly hope you are correct concerning mail service, Mother," Peter said sarcastically when she again broached the subject.

Their oldest child's temperament had always resembled Elizabeth more than Lewis in several ways, not the least of which was butting heads with anyone who disagreed with him. When the boy of fifteen disagreed with his mother, it was like striking flint against char cloth.

"When we cannot even distribute the *Gazette* to the country outside our own town limits, I will freely admit I have my doubts," Peter added. "But if dependable mail service can be accomplished, Mr. Franklin is certainly the man to do it."

"When do you plan to propose it?" Elizabeth asked.

"Propose what?" Peter responded with a quizzical look.

"Your canonization of Franklin," his mother replied.

Peter glared at her. His father's death had rendered a formal education studying abroad out of the question now. He held hope, however, that one day he might at least return to Pennsylvania to study under the imposing shadow of Big Ben. Their reunion, albeit brief, in May last year, seemed to only exacerbate the situation.

Elizabeth did not wait for her son's answer because she did not expect one.

"I am aware it is Franklin, and not your own father, whom you most wish to emulate," she added. "Thank God he is not around to face this bitter truth."

She kept her head high and her gaze penetrating, which Peter, seething, returned.

After several intense minutes had passed, Elizabeth reminded him, "Distribution of the newspaper is your concern, Peter. It is incumbent upon you to fix it. Write a notice to *Gazette* subscribers concerning the matter and give it to me for the next issue."

The next day Peter handed her the notice to set.

"Your intent is well meaning," she said after reading it, "but you apologize too much. You must be stronger, Peter. You must present the demeanor of someone who is in charge, but who also wishes to please his customers, within reason."

"Always the school teacher," Peter mumbled to himself.

"You have something to say, young man?" Elizabeth countered.

Peter turned to face her. His expression conveyed contempt; his arms, held out wide, looked as if a different son might hug his mother.

"At what point will you leave me to run the newspaper I have inherited?" he asked almost rhetorically. "This enterprise is *mine*. *I* am the colony's printer now. *I* will decide what is best."

With the bravado of a child who was still nothing more than a boy to everyone but himself, he rummaged around in his pocket and withdrew five shillings.

"Here, Mother," he said, spitting the words out as if they tasted as bitter as they sounded. "I give you all the money I have—one week's pay. Take it. Fair compensation for the *Gazette*, if you will step away and leave me to make even one decision as its true proprietor."

He slapped the coins down on the composing room counter in front of her.

Elizabeth held his gaze. He was furious, that much was clear. When Lewis died, the contract had almost exactly one year remaining. The cold, hard fact was that Benjamin Franklin must continue to be satisfied with the arrangement, or Elizabeth would forfeit her oldest son's inheritance. It was imperative that she see to Peter's proper training so that the *Gazette* continued without interruption and with no cause for complaint. At the end of their contract term, she hoped to buy the business from Mr. Franklin and continue to run the newspaper, with Peter as printer in name only. When her son reached the age of majority, then, and only then, would he be ready to take over the business.

After an uncomfortably long moment, she drew a breath and broke the silence.

"It is my fervent prayer that this printing house will belong to you one day," she said in controlled, even tones that belied her anger. "And when you reach majority, it will be yours—God willing, if Mr. Franklin will accept my terms for purchase. I will hold your payment until that time, young man."

She slid the coins off the counter into her open palm.

"For now, I am in charge. Not you."

The words were as pointed as her outstretched index finger, punctuating her position with a fleshy knife that pierced his pride. Peter smiled the cocky smile of a pubescent boy, full of airs.

"Not according to the masthead," he shot back and walked out.

It was propitious that he had left the room. She had in mind to tell him a thing or two, and once said, she would not have been able to take the words back. Elizabeth breathed deeply to calm herself. And then she set the notice:

Whereas divers Complaints have been made by the Gentlemen who live in the Country, of not receiving their Gazettes regularly. This is therefore to inform them, that it is not through my Neglect, for I send them constantly every Week to Mr. Childermas Croft who informs me that he meets with Opportunities enough, but the Persons who go up to those Places refuse to carry them, and as I know no other Place, this is therefore to desire the said Gentlemen Subscribers to send me proper Directions where they may be sent for the future that they may have less cause of Complaint, and their Commands shall be obey'd by

Their most humble Servant, PETER TIMOTHY.

N.B. The Packets which are not so carried are the following, viz. For Dorchester to Mr. John Roberts and to Mr. John Stevens. For Goose-Creek, to the Rev. Mr. Millechamp. For Ashley-Ferry, to Mrs. Billiald, and for Georgia, to Coll. William Stephens.

When Peter read the printed and distributed June 2 edition, Elizabeth watched his face turn a hot red.

"Mother," he said between clenched teeth, his visage building pressure like a pustule ready to pop, "these are not my words."

Elizabeth gave him a smug smile.

"No, son, they are not. And until you learn the art of authoritative diplomacy like your idol Mr. Franklin, they never will be."

Peter was livid.

"You had no right," he began, but his mother drew herself up to her full height in front of him; she was still a knuckle-length taller than he, and she would use it to her advantage.

"Peter, surely you must know by now that you cannot believe everything you read in print, including the name listed on the masthead."

Peter retreated, choosing to fight the battle another day. He could not reprint the *Gazette*. His mother had won this round. But he had learned one thing, at least: the value of proofreading.

Chapter Thirty-Nine

Elizabeth gazed out the window at another summer come and gone—just as incessantly, just as lethargically as any other. The city streets, now the playground of dead brown leaves, resembled a cobbled sea floor where piles of scuttling fiddler crabs collected in corners. Even dragonflies seemed grateful to perch on decaying stalks, their translucent blue wings and bulbous black eyes lulled into a sense of calm by the husks' rattle. Beyond, on the Cooper River, buoyant coots gathered, as thick as ants on molasses. Hundreds of them took refuge in the company of others, clustering together in liquid islands of warm water. Their gray feathery necks and bodies blended seamlessly into the dark brackish pools, making each bird's stubby ivory beak stand out in stark relief. The collection of single white dots bobbed up and down above the water's ripples like a ponderous grouping of ebony ace dominoes that had been stood up vertically.

Autumn, the season of dying. In accordance with the nature of things, Elizabeth buried Charles.

Lacking any other prospects, she now needed a compositor. She turned away from the window and made her way back to the print shop.

Sitting on a stool, she fed the metal cubes one by one before transferring it to a galley:

NOTICE is hereby given, that there is wanting *at the Printing-House in Charles-Towne, a Person who understands the Part of Composing in the Printing Business. Any Person who understands the same, may apply to the Printer hereof, where he may meet with Encouragement.*

When Peter read the proof copy, he looked at his mother disdainfully. "Is that it, Mother?" he asked. "Has your heart grown so hard? I have learned to expect very little emotion from you, since you treat me less like a son and more like an apprentice, but I find it hard to believe that even you could be this callous."

Elizabeth turned to face him. Her son was becoming a man. It was a delicate balance for her, trying to raise Peter as head of household while continuing to retain the upper hand. To that end she had often involved Charles in the business. Louisa was by far superior to either of her brothers—the boys knew it, and so did Elizabeth—but it would be the boys who would continue in their father's footsteps. Charles had proved to be quite adept at setting type already, even at nine years of age. He was not old enough to send on information-gathering errands to the wharfs and taverns, and certainly not to the Council, but he had already been helping at the counter, accepting advertisements and tendering change. Charles also took the initiative to proofread the *Gazette* behind Peter's back. As second in line to succession, he had worked harder than his brother, which encouraged Peter to work harder too.

Elizabeth had held hope that one day the Timothy boys would run the *South-Carolina Gazette* together. She dreamed of the newspaper becoming the Eastern Seaboard's most trustworthy news source, containing the freshest advices foreign and domestic. In parlors from New York to Florida, men of great learning would read every word the Timothy boys printed. They would quote from Peter's essays. They would refer to Charles's astute turns of phrase as if they were their own. Seats of government would read proceedings from far-flung colonies while businessmen kept apprised of political events in the world's most important cities: London, Lisbon, Madrid. The *Gazette* would become a mouthpiece for the world, more trusted than any other printed piece and the flagship of all newspapers, everywhere.

"Yes," she answered. "That is it. And this is business."

Peter shook his head and smiled a condescending smile. In it was bound up years of disgust, resentment, and anger for pushing him toward excellence, and for pushing him away from a relationship between a widowed mother and a fatherless son.

Elizabeth could not hold her tongue any longer. Her recalcitrant man-child, still growing into his father's breeches, was vainly confident he was ready to wear the pants. If she did not meet him head-on, she would risk losing the upper hand prematurely. She could not let Peter suffer the victory that, later, and too late, would be his ultimate defeat.

"Do you believe that my unwillingness to display grief for your pleasure in any way translates to a lack of it?" Elizabeth barked, returning his glare.

"Your father's relationship with Benjamin Franklin expires in less than three months," she reminded him. "It is my intent to purchase the *Gazette*, the printing press, typeforms, and every tool necessary for print work *from* him, for *you*. Now, the question you must ask yourself is this: are you man enough to accept this opportunity I have fought so hard for, under condition of my deciding when you are ready for it?"

Peter took a step back to drink in the full portrait: his stoic mother, this bitter woman, continuing to treat him like a schoolboy. He had had just about enough of it.

"Yes, Mother," he replied after some contemplation. "I will accept your conditions. And I will have my birthright—this 'opportunity,' as you put it, as if it is *your* gift to me. I just never thought it would come at the cost of our relationship."

He might have stayed, but when she returned to her work without comment, he left, leaving her to consider his words.

Chapter Forty

Elizabeth counted them on her fingers: six boys. Only Peter remained now, with his sisters Louisa, Mary Elizabeth, and Catherine.

"Poor little soul," she whispered as she kissed Joseph's still-warm cheek. "Brought into this world through no fault of your own."

Gently, she unclenched his tiny fingers before rigor hardened them forever into cold fists. She laid her baby down, removed his damp soiled clothing and began to bathe him with warm water from the basin. Carefully, she sponged away his tears before they could dry into salty scars. She cleaned in and around his mouth, crusted with yellow vomit. Where he had thrashed against the crib, disheveled wisps of corn-silky brown hair were smoothed back into place.

From a drawer she took out a clean napkin, gown, and cap. Reverently, she dressed the infant. When she was finished, she folded the yellowed monogrammed handkerchief in half, and then half again, and tucked it inside Joseph's clout.

Why she had never gotten rid of it, she could not say. Perhaps this was her sponge, offered to a savior thirsty for answers she could not provide.

Perhaps, she admitted, it was simply not mine to dispose of.

High upon a shelf in her bedroom, out of the reach of young fingers, she retrieved the wooden box that had held Charles's pinwheel prize so many years ago. Rummaging inside, she pulled out Lewis's pocket watch. It had been years since she had looked at it. It was a handsome but modest timepiece. She took it to her high-post feather bed and sat down, opened it, and traced the engraving with her finger. In the grooves were shadows of black ink, deposited there over years of her husband's soiled fingers opening and closing the cover.

She missed him so.

Elizabeth clutched the watch. She closed her eyes, fearing that this time the levy behind them would not hold. She let her head fall forward in surrender, allowing memories of buried events to bubble up. She held her stomach as spasms of hot tears boiled over the embankment she had erected, and brackish tributaries traced a path down weak clay. Clear, warm tallow bled from her nose as if the recollection of ponderous events were melting. She groaned under the weight of things she did not know to pray for.

Gasping under her own sobs, the emotions she had kept pent up—too muddy to sort out—now burst through and crowded her mind. She surrendered to them as they traveled up from the place where she had buried them. She shook under the crushing weight of it, unable to breathe.

When it subsided, Elizabeth lay on the bed, curled up, wet and tired, for some undetermined amount of time. At length she sat up and blotted her eyes, blew her nose, and put a hand to her tear-stained hair to smooth it back.

The innocents who are harmed by another's wickedness are the lucky ones, she comforted herself. *The guilty must live with their burden.*

She could never be rid of it.

Standing, she smoothed her skirt. She was so tired of wearing black. It seemed she had spent most of her life covered in it. She wondered what God saw when He looked at her. She wondered if He saw black and found it fitting.

Elizabeth replaced Lewis's watch in its box, and the box to its hiding place. Outside her upstairs bedroom window, the autumn day was clear and bright. Across the street in the Huguenot Church land, bald cypress trees towered over smaller trees and shrubs, their roots creating loose, uneven stitches in the thick brown plough mud fabric below. Elizabeth stood at the window. She could almost conjure the illusion of Lewis striding down the street, checking the time on his pocket watch with no mind to the uneven cobbles beneath his shoes. The thought made her smile. In the distance, she heard the call of Catesby's largest white-billed woodpecker, like an aboriginal savage summoning tribesmen to the hunt. She strained, first left and then right, out of the window, hoping to catch a glimpse of the magnificent black-bodied bird speaking in his native tongue.

From the south, a flock of hungry green birds suddenly converged on the cypress trees, fluttering and squawking loudly as they vied for branch space nearest the ripe kernels. Standing in the shadows of the afternoon sun so as not to frighten them, Elizabeth estimated at least a thousand, their emerald-green bodies creating the illusion of lush foliage on the bald trees. Those that fluttered in search of a perch filled the open spaces like phyllobolia. Their raucous chatter, like so many rusty bed springs under a restless sleeper's weight, created an atmosphere of discontent until, in an instant, they took flight as if one hive collective. Elizabeth closed her eyes and heard mimicked waves crashing to shore in the sound of so many beating wings.

This is a decision, she concluded: *to seek the comfort and protection of one massive flock. So many individual birds choosing to follow the instinct God gave them. People are not capable of that much intelligence. Least of all I.*

She reached up to the shelf again and retrieved Volume One of Catesby's *Birds of Carolina*. Turning to the page where the Carolina parrot, beautifully illustrated in a cypress tree, was depicted, she read the description in French. English would be too heavy, too grounded for these iridescent winged creatures, she decided. The beautiful French word for bird—*oiseau*—was perfectly suited for the species: barely more than breath, as weightless as a feather above her whisper.

The book's description of *perroquet de la Caroline* confirmed that she had just seen a flock of Carolina parrots. This was the bird George Chicken had killed and sold so peahens could wear their glorious feathers.

Elizabeth closed the book and sat heavily on the bed, fingering the dark tooled leather of her most cherished volume. She had used this book to discipline Peter so many years ago—he had found the printing error, but only after tricking Louisa into pointing it out to him.

Elizabeth opened the book again, this time to the page where Mark Catesby's typeset genuflection to the queen, who had sent him on his seven-year expedition, was printed. The printer had selected a lovely initial letter *A*, decorated with what looked to be a Carolina parrot perched on the letter's bar—the horizontal stroke in the center of the capital A. To the left and behind the capital letter, a pelican sat contentedly on a wooden log, as if resting on a Charles Towne wharf. Flourishes of feathers were carved all around the block letter, in intricate detail:

> *As these Volumes contain an Essay toward the Natural History of that Part of your MAJESTY'S Dominions, which are particularly honoured by bearing YOUR AUGUST NAME, CAROLINA; this, and YOUR great Goodness in encouraging all Sorts of Learning, hath embolden'd me to inspire YOUR Royal Protection and Favour to my slender Performance, I hope YOUR MAJESTY will not think a few Minutes disagreeably spent, in casting an Eye on these Leaves; which exhibit no contemptible Scene of the Glorions Works of the Creator, displayed in the New World; and hitherto lain concealed from the View of YOUR MAJESTY, as well as of YOUR Royal Predecessors, tho' so long possessed of a Country, inferior to none of YOUR MAJESTY'S*

*American Dominions, Wherefore I esteem it a singular
Happiness, after several Years Travels and Enquiry in so
remote Parts (by the generous Encouragement of several
of YOUR MAJESTY'S Subjects, eminent for their Rank,
and for their being Patrons of Learning) that I am the
first that has had an Opportunity of presenting to a
QUEEN of GREAT BRITAIN a Sample of the hitherto
unregarded, tho' beneficial and beautiful Productions of
YOUR MAJESTY'S DOMINIONS.*

Her eye was again incontrovertibly drawn to a careless
typesetter's mistake in such a precipitous work. *It was regrettable
that Lewis was not given the honor of setting the book*, she
thought. *He would never have made the error of placing the "u"
in "Glorious" upside down so that it spelled "Glorions." Peter,
yes, but not her Lewis.*

She slid the wooden tray holding her noon meal over to her
quietly, and she nibbled on a piece of bread. She took a sip of corn
chowder but was unable to muster any enthusiasm for eating it.
Instead, she poured a cup of tea from the kettle. Sipping it gingerly,
she returned to the window where, below on King Street, the
boisterous birds had moved on to other feeding grounds.

Here, in the sanctity of her bedroom, she was an observer only—
not a reporter, editor, or publisher. She could quietly watch the
world turning from her upstairs window, with no responsibility
whatsoever to say or do anything in response. With that certitude,
she took a deep, long breath, and let it out, as if fear, anger, guilt,
and so much sorrow had been expelled with it.

The November day was breezy and clear, sending gentle gusts
through her open window and billowing out the sheers like
sailcloth harnessing God's breath. On the street below, men, some
in powdered wigs, held tight to their chapeaus while coattails went
flying half-mast behind them. The heels of their shoes, troublesome
on Charles Towne's uneven paths, tried to force a stumble while
walking canes counteracted in an eternal conflict.

Wisps of vapor floated past her window, almost unnoticeable at first, but becoming more visible as the minutes ticked by. People below were becoming agitated. And then panicked.

Charles Towne was on fire.

Elizabeth opened her bedroom door to find Peter standing there.

"The city is burning," she told him hastily. "Go and get details."

In characteristic fashion, Peter was gone before the last syllable left her lips—in a blind rush as if his own tail was on fire.

Elizabeth found Louisa, the calm and steady one, in the print shop, ready to receive her instructions too.

"Look after the children," her mother said as she also prepared to leave, headed for St. Philip's where families with no other resources would go for shelter.

As Elizabeth was on her way out, Esther Crokatt rushed in the Timothy Print Shop.

"Elizabeth!" Esther said, her frantic voice lilting incongruously, "We had word that the Naders' home has been completely consumed by the fire!"

Dismissively thanking Esther for the information, Elizabeth hurried out the door in search of her friend. Elizabeth knew the Naders would be totally reliant on charitable aid if what Esther said was true.

When she arrived at St. Philip's, hundreds of the fire's victims already spilled out into the churchyard. Many, wrapped in wool blankets to protect them from the November chill, presented an ironic parody as hot flames wrapped around Church Street's crowded wooden structures. Rooftops, smoldering in the setting sun, looked like an evil fog descending. She found Sarah and her four children near the street.

Abagail, Sarah's oldest daughter, stood next to her mother. She was a lovely dark-haired young lady now despite her pox scars. Her brother John Jr., however, was the spitting image of his dead father right down to the space between his two front teeth and the broad nose overhanging his upper lip. The two oldest children helped Sarah with their younger brother and sister, Rebecca and Paul, red-headed twins aged six. The two little Naders were sitting on an upping stone with their knees bent under their chins and their arms clasped around both legs, foreheads resting against their knees. The tops of their auburn heads looked like two small, simmering fires, side-by-side. While it was clear everyone was trying to be strong for everyone else, the Naders' sagging lips and sorrowful eyes belied fear and exhaustion.

"Oh, my dear girl," Sarah cried when she saw Elizabeth.

"How is it with you?" she asked as she stood to grab Elizabeth's hands in her own. "Everyone safe?"

"Yes," Elizabeth told her friend. "Our home is spared. And I insist you stay with us."

Sarah began to object, but Elizabeth would hear nothing of it.

"The children can sleep on pallets. We have more than enough to eat, and besides, you can help me in the print shop until other arrangements can be made."

Sarah looked into her friend's eyes and began to cry. Elizabeth put an arm around Sarah's shoulders, now heaving under the weight of fear and grief. Together the two walked toward the Timothy home with little Naders trailing behind.

"We shall put the charitable generosity of that Two Bit French club to the test, shan't we?" Elizabeth asked, hoping to get at least a chuckle out of her weary friend.

Sarah managed to turn the corners of her mouth up slightly.

"But Elizabeth," she said, "I ain't French."

Elizabeth had to laugh at that and was pleased to see a small vestige of her friend's spunk left in her.

"Perfectly fine, my dear," she answered. "I was married to one. And if those old curmudgeons refuse to help the best friend of the wife of a founding member, I shall give them good and fair warning that my friend Sarah Nader will sing for her supper if necessary."

"Oh, bless me!" Sarah exclaimed. "If you threaten them with that, I might just find myself in better circumstances than before the fire!"

Chapter Forty-One

Elizabeth had grown accustomed to her son taking credit for her work over the decade since Lewis's death. That did not concern her; Peter was editor now and must be viewed as the strong, capable inheritor of his father's thriving enterprise. What she could not tolerate, however, was that he also took credit for Louisa's work.

Elizabeth had brought up the subject with her daughter only once. Louisa interrupted her with familiar, forgotten words: "'There is no limit to what you can do if you do not care who gets the credit.'"

Putting her index finger across her mother's mouth, she said in Low Dutch, "That is my secret. I give it to you for your secret too."

Smiling at the memory, Elizabeth was proud that her eldest had learned the lesson well so many years ago. Peter never quite grasped that secret, to his mother's regret.

Elizabeth knew Peter would blatantly deny it, but his older sister had been a measuring stick that encouraged him to try harder. Louisa never viewed her printing education as anything more than familial obligation, and everything she did, from slugging type to proofreading to running down to the taverns for the latest gossip and even soliciting rags, she did out of genuine desire to contribute well to the family. Elizabeth held to the belief that Louisa would have made a better editor and publisher than her younger brother. But she had not been born male. That fact, and that fact alone, meant the business would pass to Peter, as first-born son.

Perhaps it was a blessing in disguise, Elizabeth decided as she closed and locked her shop door on King Street for the very last time. Peter was well-respected in town. He had proven himself to be a competent newspaper publisher even before he officially held the position. Elizabeth, happy to be released of the obligation, had set up shop next door on King Street and had been content for a time, selling books and stationery items. Peter had taken his place as a reputed gentleman and recently had completely thrown himself into organizing a lending library in Charles Towne similar to Franklin's in Philadelphia. He and sixteen of his friends pooled their own resources and were working toward acquiring books for the edification of Charles Towne's residents. Elizabeth knew Lewis would have been proud.

Peter had thrown himself into another pursuit as well, and had convinced a girl to wed him, although Elizabeth was unsure whether by hook or by crook. She was a fine young woman of Irish descent, and fair skinned to prove it. It was her nature that was even more fair, however, a fact Elizabeth had known since she met the girl several years ago. It was thanks to a ship, ironically named *Loyalty*, that had brought her daughter-in-law to Charles Towne.

Once in port, Captain John Fowler had wasted no time coming to the *Gazette* office to place an ad to the attention of one subscriber in particular. Elizabeth took up a paper and quill.

"As a general rule, Captain Fowler," Elizabeth explained, "advertisements are published to all *Gazette* readers, not to the attention of one specific person."

He insisted that the type be set according to his directions, however, and Elizabeth understood his reasons when she heard what he had to say.

"I have brought relatives of his from Ireland," the captain said. "One Mr. Henry Donovan, a house carpenter and joiner, and his wife and daughters. Their passage is now due and payable, and unless this particular relation pays me for their passage, I will be forced to sell the man and his family as servants to pay for their voyage."

Elizabeth quite understood his meaning. The Timothys had known passengers on *Britannia* in similar circumstances.

"Tell me more about the girls," she said.

Before the captain left her shop, the ad had been revised to read "daughter," instead of "daughters." Elizabeth had bartered with the captain to purchase the younger girl, figured to be around sixteen, for the price of the advertisement.

In retrospect, she was glad. Ann Donovan had been a capable worker in the print shop. She learned to set type as well as any Timothy, but she excelled at taking subscriptions. The fair-skinned girl, so diminutive and friendly, was positively infectious at the counter. Elizabeth noted that the girl's disarming manner encouraged longer advertisements, fewer accounts unpaid, *and* an increase in subscriptions.

Elizabeth could not have imagined a more caring, Christian, hardworking girl than her indentured servant, and now daughter-in-law, Ann Donovan. Peter had received full control of the *Gazette* at the time of their marriage, but Elizabeth had her reasons for not making it official until the following May. Peter protested, of course, asserting he was ready for the responsibility. He demanded to know why his mother would withhold what she herself had worked so hard to provide for him. Elizabeth refused to give him an answer, but she admitted to herself that she would miss the work, which had become a source of pride for her. And that, alone, was reason enough.

Peter and Ann were now the proud parents of their first child: a girl named Elizabeth Ann Timothy. Elizabeth's adult children had their own lives now; it was time she got on with hers as well. Facts required reporting—even if it meant disclosing information she would prefer not to share.

Elizabeth made deliberate steps toward the waterfront. King Street was positively bustling with townspeople on their way from here to there, causing others she met to step into the street quite a few times. Thank goodness her trunk was already at the dock; Peter had seen to that.

When she arrived at the wharf, the ship was already boarding. Pausing a moment, Elizabeth turned back toward Charles Towne. It would be a while before she would return, and she wanted to remember it. This place was more home to her now than Holland or Pennsylvania.

They say home is where the heart is, Elizabeth thought, but she decided that was not entirely true. The heart—fickle, fleshy thing that it is—can rarely be trusted with the heavy business of making and maintaining a home. No, home is harder won than a heart can handle. Home is will, and determination, and living through it all. Home is an indivisible number, the value with which the heart has very little to do.

Home, she decided, remembering her Crusoe, is where you keep things exact, impartial—like debtor and creditor—making an accounting of the comforts enjoyed, against the miseries suffered.

Chapter Forty-Two

Elizabeth kept drifting in and out of consciousness.

Awake had become shards of time that sliced at her insides, as if she had swallowed glass. She remembered Lewis's funeral some two decades ago, and wondered if perhaps the refracted light had finally overcome her as she had once prayed it would.

Asleep had become waves in which time had no meaning and, as such, held no power to harm her as her spirit floated gently toward the horizon.

From a partially reclined position, she turned her head slowly toward the window. So much had changed in the living painting outside. She could see the fig tree Lewis had planted for her; it had been so much smaller then. But now it was an old brown turkey, with arthritic branches that swept low across the ground. Roots, searching for years through dusty ground, occasionally broke through the soil and dived back down again, reminding her of the back of a mythical sea serpent.

The business of roots is heavy work, she thought. *Always looking for some way to support itself and the rest of the tree. How tiresome it is to put down roots.*

She suddenly felt very old herself, and very tired.

In an adjoining yard, birds perched in a row like a little abacus on the horizontal counting bar of someone's fence.

What were they counting? she wondered. The remainder of her days?

No matter, she told herself. *Only God knows the sum.* There is no miracle cure for death, no anodyne necklace that would protect her from judgment, no tar-water that could get her safely past the disease of her soul. It had been nothing less than hard work and perseverance that had gotten her to this point in life, but her works would not trumpet her into God's presence. She only hoped her sins would not keep her out of it.

She closed her eyes. In her mind she was walking into the newspaper office. It was several years ago; Peter was holding the latest *Pennsylvania Gazette* open to its full width. Her son and his wife, Ann, and Elizabeth's Negro, Amsterdam, were discussing Benjamin Franklin's curious drawing of a snake, dissected into eight pieces.

"He calls it an 'editorial cartoon,'" Peter had explained to his mother as she walked around the group to see what was so intriguing. "Every newspaper in all the colonies is reprinting it."

Elizabeth remembered studying the drawing. Each section of the snake was labeled with the abbreviation of each colony. New England was the first section, followed by New York, New Jersey, Pennsylvania in the center, then Maryland, Virginia, North Carolina, and South Carolina. Underneath the snake were the words, "JOIN, or DIE."

"I should not wonder that Ben made South Carolina the arse end," Elizabeth scoffed.

"Interesting observation, Mother," Peter said. "I had in mind he meant to represent South Carolina as the southernmost tip of the colonies, and since a rattlesnake brandishes his saber from the 'arse end,' as you so eloquently put, I postulate that Ben intended a compliment: that we are not afraid to fight, though we are the most open to invasion and farthest from protection, and that we, as gentlemen, give good and fair warning that we will follow the strike of the head if necessary."

Elizabeth began to argue the point, but her son interrupted.

"Besides," he said, "I believe you miss the point of the illustration. Ben intends to suggest that we combine to form one complete body. He did not intend that we quibble over which section is larger, or more important, or has a place of priority like ill-tempered children fighting for attention. It is precisely this way of thinking that impedes us from defending ourselves, Mother. Hence the need and, I would argue, the moral imperative to unite."

Elizabeth always enjoyed a good debate, and she was not about to back down from her eldest son despite the fact that he had been running his father's business for the better part of a decade now.

"I have known Ben Franklin much longer than you, and I will thank you not to lecture me, young man. I can assure you, he was laughing with each cut of the wood he made on that drawing. The New England colonies are the head of the beast because they are the intellectual seat of power.

"And he grouped them thusly to imply that they, the wiser colonies, already demonstrate cooperation. 'The New England colonies.' 'Oh my!'" she said with exaggerated gestures like something she had seen on Charles Towne's stage, "'How shall the rest of us ever measure up?' At least he was honest enough to draw in a forked tongue. But poor, old South Carolina, bringing up the rear! Trying desperately to keep up, you see, just following the others' lead because we cannot think for ourselves."

"Oh, Mother, you exasperate me. By your logic Maryland would take umbrage at being the belly. 'All we seem to be good for is devouring whatever comestibles are sent our way and sending the bile down to poor old South Carolina!'"

"Precisely! I am delighted you are at least wise enough to concede my point," she'd said.

Elizabeth felt a hand on her shoulder. Had she slept? It was Louisa, standing by her bed. It had been her eldest who had borne this last agony with her, now that their repertoire of home remedies—from

Ireland, Holland, the colonists and Indians, even the African slaves—
had failed. Louisa had taken care of her mother's most personal
needs in the sickroom, protecting her dignity always even when the
misery was more than she could endure.

"I have something for you," Elizabeth whispered as if the words
clawed their way up her throat on the way out.

Louisa held her mother's hand.

"Go to the bureau," she said. "Bring me Pope's poem."

Louisa did as instructed and returned with the handwritten pages.

"Here, Mama," she said, gently guiding her mother's hand to
the document.

"I met him, you know," Elizabeth struggled to say.

Her daughter nodded, squeezing her hand.

"His prayer has always been a comfort to you, especially when
Papa died."

"It is yours now," Elizabeth whispered.

"Mama, no," Louisa objected, but Elizabeth stood firm. It
had been her eldest who had made sure the covers were orderly
above the messiness of dying. When Elizabeth had broken the
bedpost writhing in agony, it was Louisa's voice that comforted
her. Elizabeth had drawn strength from her Little Mother even as
unrelenting pain tossed her body from side to side in a mad rhythm.

"Take it," she said. "*Please.*"

Elizabeth felt a cool cloth on her forehead.

"Get your rest, Mama," her daughter urged. "You will be getting
your strength back soon."

Elizabeth knew better. She had watched Death dance with
other partners too many times before. There was no mistaking
his outreached hand inviting her now. She lay there, exhausted,
watching herself in reverie the day Dr. Dale told her Lewis was dead.
That very hour she had pied the type in the standing masthead of
the *South-Carolina Gazette* to read "Peter Timothy, Printer." This
was the nightmare she had planned for, when she and Ben Franklin
changed the contract that sent Lewis to the Carolinas as the King's

Printer. She had meant to save her son. She had not meant to lose her husband.

She had come to detest the irony of it all long ago. The cold arithmetic was not lost even on Franklin, the central figure in the equation, despite the fact that he had always had difficulty with "figures" of one kind or another. She had thought about it many times, reliving the decision in her mind. It seemed the more she tried to think of something else, the more the single memory intruded. She was too tired now to fight it.

Lewis had been so weak from the fever. It was not his failing that he could not manage an erection.

She closed her eyes a moment, remembering the last time they had tried to make love. She had rubbed his flaccid penis, like a pinch of dough between her fingers, but it would not stiffen. When the pregnancy began to show, he still might not have suffered the knowledge of its origin had it not been for Peter's unwitting testimony and that handkerchief, the only token from a father who never even knew he had a child.

So long ago now, but always just yesterday in her haunted memory. Too exhausted to open her eyes, she saw herself in the print shop, watching an unspoken event unfold. So much of life is bound up in small decisions. The big choices pale by comparison, it seemed to her. It was utterly frightening—and exhilarating—how the Almighty pivots the course of human lives on our own free will.

She could not relive that day. She could not change her decision. And the hardest part about those facts was wondering if she would. Fools rush in, her favorite poet had tried to warn her.

* * ★ * *

She had been pulling characters for page 4 advertisements. Her eyes had been fixed blankly on the door, but they were not focused there as her mind wandered through the next day's schedule of activities. When the door opened and her old acquaintance walked in, it had taken some effort for the actual event, too unbelievable to accept, to register upon her brain.

"My old friend!" she exclaimed when the realization took hold.

Composing stick in hand, she ran to him with the unbridled delight of a woman reunited with a loved one.

He had immediately scooped her up in his arms and spun her around, twirling her skirts in a furious circular motion and sending her shawl, and the line of type, clattering across the wooden floor. When he set her back down, her head was spinning. He held her to him, letting her catch her balance.

The two chatted mindlessly about the nature of his visit. When he had arrived. What he had done. Whom he had seen. The printer in him, however, could not resist pushing against her to read over her shoulder. His breath stirred the small hairs on her neck, emoting a curious tingly sensation that made her shiver. His lips were almost on her skin as he whispered the backward words aloud. And almost at the same time, she felt his desire for her—stiff and unrelenting—on her inner thigh. She pulled away slightly, just enough to read his blue eyes. In that breathless, eternal moment, consent passed wordlessly between them.

Her heart was pounding. This was treacherous ground, the nirvana where a single decision can change a life. Lives.

She did not care. With her left hand, she reached up to the nape of his neck. With her right hand at her side, she lifted the hem of her skirt and raised her leg to the first rung of the stool where she had been sitting.

He knew he must move swiftly. There could be no time for second thoughts. He unbuttoned his trousers, bent his knees, and skillfully navigated the yards of fabric.

He looked into her eyes as his mouth found hers. There was no regret there. He had fantasized so often about this moment. And every time, in his fantasies, it was never quite so pleasurable as this reality, this very moment.

In her expression he found what he was looking for: the certainty of mutual consent. But it was in the arch of her back that proved beyond a shadow of doubt: at this moment, she was his.

And what a prize.

He knew his passion for her would now become his obsession. And that obsession would be the death of him. He knew, when her eyes opened, the spell would be broken. He kissed her neck. He lifted her head. He kissed her lips and probed her with his tongue.

She responded by allowing it. And then she opened her eyes.

With that single action she communicated not only that it would not happen again, but that it should not have happened at all. Her unspoken regret wounded him deeply, but it was pointless to speak in rebuttal.

Words. Words can be so meaningless. So dismally superfluous and unnecessary.

He withdrew, and took his monogrammed handkerchief from his pocket, trying to swab the semen. When he had finished, he remained for another moment, wanting to say, or do, something. But her shoulders were squared now, and her back rigid—she had pulled herself up to her full height and was busy at the easel again.

He had put his handkerchief away and walked to the door. Pausing there, he had heard a moorhen's mournful cry emanating from the waterfront in the vacuum of silence. He had put his hand on the door knob and then left.

Elizabeth could see the scene playing out in her mind, over and over again, until the involuntary need to "black ink" her eyes broke the spell. Neither of them had been aware at the time that his handkerchief—as pitifully inadequate a sponge as a sheet of rag paper tossed in an ink bucket—had fallen to the composing room floor.

Though she had always been better at figures, Lewis had added it all up. By his own calculations, and with Peter's offered information, her husband had come to one unalterable conclusion: the handkerchief belonged to Ben, and so did the child expected soon. The pregnancy had begun while Lewis had been incapacitated with yellow fever.

Some part of him must have known from the moment he found Ben's handkerchief. He would have asked her to wash it if he were planning to return it. He would not have kept it, waiting for the moment it would corroborate his accusation.

Elizabeth saw her husband, in her memory. When he confronted her that night, his expression had been quizzical: realizing, but still refusing to believe. For a brief moment outside of time, the brain can deny what it wishes where wounds that breach the soul are concerned. But when that moment has passed, something primordial takes its place.

As Lewis held the stiff, yellowed handkerchief, horrid comprehension crept across his face. It was just soiled linen, but the scrap of cloth could not absorb the awful truth. Her husband, the printer, with the help of their oldest son who had learned his lessons well, had placed all the characters in their proper order, and he had read backward to the undeniable facts.

When Lewis finally confronted her, he already knew. Her lack of confession only made her appear more guilty. A seed of doubt had been planted, and that seed was not his.

The first slug had been Peter's testimony. But the final slug had been a handkerchief that should have been pounded into paper so many months ago.

Lewis, uncharacteristically drunk, had picked up a length of cord and moved toward her with halted urgency as if propelled by a force he could not control. In her memory, he looked like a marionette loosely dangling at the whim of a wicked puppeteer, commanding him to do something he did not wish to do. His face was a tightly sealed pot, threatening to boil over. The pressure built until red rage colored not only his skin but the wild whites of his eyes as well. He raised his hands as he approached, the rope taut between two clenched fists, and lunged at her. With a seamless, circular motion he wrapped the rope around her neck and twisted it, using it as a fulcrum against her trachea to lift the heavy weight of her betrayal. She remembered uselessly putting her hands up in defense, as he tightened the hemp that cut into her neck—a fleshy cleat on which he would hang his rage. Dragging his chattel with him, he mounted the finishing room ladder and began to climb.

Had Lewis not been so weak—left alive, but feeble from the disease—he could have overpowered her easily. Combined with drink, her dependably docile husband had found himself in entirely new territory when faced with her infidelity. He was ill-equipped to handle the rage that consumed him, and it put him at a disadvantage.

Elizabeth's heart raced at the memory of it, and instinctively she raised a hand to her throat. Ligatures—mere temporary scars—could be hidden beneath widow's weeds until they healed; would that it were not so. But the ligatures of life: two characters, bound together at their core, could not.

Elizabeth, scrambling helplessly to keep her feet on the floor, had smelled her own blood even before it trickled into the folds of her neck. Still holding the rope tight with one fist, Lewis worked awkwardly with the other hand to swing the rope's loose end over a high rafter. With each attempt, he yanked her head roughly, and she felt sure her neck would break. Lewis had almost reached the top rung when Amsterdam came in through the rear door. The huge man lifted Elizabeth high enough to ease the choke hold Lewis had on her. With the extra slack, Lewis managed to swing the rope's loose end over a ceiling joist. If he could just reach the end of the—

Suddenly Peter, always in some blind rush to finish whatever it was he had put off, burst in the room at full bore. The door swung open violently, knocking his father off the top of the ladder and sending him plummeting to the floor eight feet below.

Dazed and disoriented, the three of them lay in a heap with Amsterdam standing over the tangled bodies.

Lewis, his eyes unblinking and his head and arms bent at right angles, lay prostrate. His legs suggested a curious sort of running position, as if he meant to get away.

Elizabeth, coughing, had crawled to him and knelt beside him. She closed her eyes, hoping he was still alive, praying he was still alive.

Hope.

Prayer.

Ridiculous concepts, she had thought. *Facts are facts. Hoping and praying will not change the facts.*

The facts had already been played out: either Lewis was dead or he was alive. Whichever the case, she just did not have all the information.

Hope is nothing more than ignorance of the facts, and all the prayers in the world cannot change the facts.

The rest of the Timothys, roused from sleep by the commotion, came downstairs haltingly. When Peter came to, dazed and bloodied, he struggled to his feet. Elizabeth remembered telling him to take his brother and sisters back to bed immediately, and to stay there.

By the time the constable arrived, she had already wrapped her neck and shoulders in a dark shawl. She reported that Peter had run in to find Amsterdam overpowering his father. Lewis, still weak from smallpox, could not fend off the massive slave.

The slave, she said, had gotten away. Those "facts," in addition to the word of Elizabeth Timothy, would preclude any investigation.

Amsterdam would not swing for his intervention. He had merely acted out of instinct on her behalf. But he had to go.

The slave was given a note to be delivered to his Pon Pon overseer. It contained instructions to put Amsterdam to work on the property and destroy the note. He left immediately on foot.

The next day Elizabeth arranged for a family acquaintance, John Hammerton, to purchase the gentle Black man. Hammerton, personally sorrowed by her situation, would collect Amsterdam from Pon Pon and take him immediately to his North Carolina plantation, where he would be worked hard, but he would be safe. The fact that Amsterdam was not a murderer, but her savior, could never be shared.

Other facts, in retrospect, which seemed indisputable to her now, were at the time nothing more than poor choices. Out of weakness, she had made her own bad decisions. Maybe Providence permitted weakness in some to allow others to grow strong. Certainly, her own weakness had forced strength on her son so long ago.

Elizabeth looked out her bedroom window to the bustling street below. Draw from others the lessons that may profit yourself. Her bad decisions had become facts, and those facts could not be changed.

What is truly true, after all? It was a fact that she loved her husband, but other facts kept him from being convinced of it. That fact now stood in stark contrast to all others.

She had learned another terrible lesson, and she would not forget it. Not all facts are germane to the topic. As the *Gazette*'s publisher until Peter was of age, Elizabeth would not only have to verify facts—immutable and absolute—but also determine which facts to include in the newspaper's limited space. The irony of it all was that it was now her job to decide which facts were relevant to her husband's death—an unhappy accident—and print only those facts in the newspaper's columns.

Lewis was dead. That was a fact. The *Gazette* would continue without interruption, and Peter would take his father's position when he was old enough. That too was a fact, and she would ensure that fact remained unchanged. No other facts were relevant to readers, nor to Benjamin Franklin, save the one she had already shared.

Thirteen-year-old Peter believed the facts that were fed to him. But the truth was something entirely different. The truth was that Lewis lost his life while she kept hers. And the truth was that Peter—whose testimony concerning a scrap of monogrammed linen had precipitated his father's death—was the one who profited most.

There was no undoing what had been done. One of the most troublesome tenets of Christianity was that this power, only, is denied to an omnipotent God: the power to change the past. Elizabeth could reconcile this sole limitation only by reasoning that it was not a limitation. An omniscient, omnipotent, and omnipresent deity is not bound by time, past, present, or future. The only logical conclusion, then, is that He either causes, or allows, events to happen.

Either way, the fact was that she would bear the stain.

She had won the battle to have Peter's name on the front page at age thirteen, but it was a battle she continued to fight, as the newspaper's true publisher, until the business passed fully to him some years later. For most of that time, it was a battle she had fought against Peter, the very person for whom she was fighting.

Elizabeth closed her eyes. She was tired. Soon this business of dying would be over, and it would be sweet not to have to hate any more. Peter would have the Timothy enterprise—all he ever wanted from her, anyway—as well as her books of account and the bond John Hammerton owed her.

"Peter is here," Louisa said gently. "He wants to read the document you prepared. Do you hear me, Mother?" Elizabeth nodded.

"Read it, Peter," she instructed him.

He read the document aloud to her: "Be it known to all whom it may concern that I, Peter Timothy of Charles Towne in the Province of South Carolina, printer, do hereby acknowledge and declare that I have been fully satisfied and paid by my mother, Elizabeth Timothy, administratrix of the estate and effects of my late father, Lewis Timothy, for all claims due or demands which I had or might have upon or against the said estate, and that I do therefore hereby forever acquit, release, and discharge her, her heirs and executors, and administrators from all and every such claims and demands they may be. Witness my hand this twenty-ninth day of March, 1757."

Peter looked at his mother with the expression of someone who had hoped his worst fear would not be confirmed, only to be disappointed. He waved the paper at her, rattling it audibly.

"What is this, Mother?" Peter asked. "What claims would I have against you that prevent my inheriting Father's estate?"

"Look in the chest of drawers," she said. "There is a brass mortar containing a bond and some money. Bring it to me, please."

Peter began to argue but thought better of it. After so many years he knew his mother would have her way. He walked briskly to the chest, retrieved the mortar, and delivered it roughly to her.

Elizabeth took out the bond and stuffed it in Peter's folded hand. "You hold John Hammerton's note now."

Peter knew Hammerton, the prominent citizen: secretary of South-Carolina and a Freemason. When his father died, Peter remembered that Hammerton had purchased their slave, Amsterdam. Apparently, his mother had never received payment, since the bond was still in her possession.

"I will collect on the bond for you," he said, a bit calmer now.

"You will tear it up," she directed him. "When I am gone."

Elizabeth's trembling fingers reached once again in the mortar and extracted a sum of money, which she handed to Peter along with a slip of paper.

"Now, on to one last business item. I want you to accept this payment and sign this receipt."

Peter, perplexed, took it without comment. She was weak; her face looked tired, ashen. But the fight was not gone from her. She had lived a methodical life, and she would die with order. He looked at the receipt.

"What is this?" he asked.

Louisa intervened: "Mother wishes to purchase the *Gazette* from you so that she has clear title to leave you the business in her will."

Quietly, Louisa took Peter aside and whispered forgotten transactions into his ear.

"I should have known," Peter said, smiling contemptuously. "She learned that from Benjamin Franklin. Put it in writing and keep it legal."

He read the receipt aloud: "Received April 1, 1757, of my Mother Elizabeth Timothy five shillings in full satisfaction of all demands whatsoever to this day."

Peter dropped his arm and let the paper hang from his hand.

"All right, Mother," he said, depositing the coins into his pocket and taking up the quill Louisa offered him.

Leaning over his mother's bedside table, he signed his name at the bottom of the page.

"I have signed it in big letters, 'PETER TIMOTHY,'" he announced with exaggeration. "You have officially paid me back the money I gave you for the *South-Carolina Gazette* so many years ago. And now you can leave it to me as my rightful inheritance."

He asked, not expecting a response, "Is that good enough for you?"

"*Peut-être*," she answered in French.

"'Maybe,' Mother?"

"'Can be,' son."

Peter gave her a smug smile.

"I believe, in this particular instance, '*will* be' is a more appropriate translation."

Elizabeth reached out to take her son's hand.

"After all those years of working on that paper, after all the work I did for your father even before we came here, I cannot risk any possibility of my will being contested, especially over such a trivial matter. It is a comfort to me to know that I may now legally pass your father's business to his son, as successor to the *Gazette*."

Peter held his mother's hands. How weak they felt now, compared to the hands of his boyhood memories. These hands looked strangely unfamiliar to him now; there were no ink stains on her fingers, no dark edges to her nails. During his formative years, *those* had been his mother's hands, not these. But in recent years she had confined herself to the stationery shop, leaving the dirty work of printing to him. The skin of her hands was less alabaster than his boyhood recollection and dotted with brown spots, but just as rough. Still printer's hands, he decided with relief. It was tired skin, loose and deeply grooved, with crusty dry patches at the knuckles. Large blue veins ran below the surface of her translucent skin, tracing over and around the delicate bones of her hands. Her fingers, at one time thin and straight, were thicker now, and slightly bent.

How many words they must have set in her lifetime.

"Mother," he tried to begin, but Elizabeth stopped him, using her free hand to pat the top of his.

"You and Ann have been running the newspaper for years now anyway," she said. "I do not like leaving things to possibility. I have worked too hard to protect your legacy."

She closed her eyes momentarily and swallowed, as though even words were difficult now.

"*Et peut-être maintenant,*" she said in French again, "*il serait sage de signer le papier.*"

Peter signed the document and handed it to his mother. She looked it over, mentally setting the type in reverse, a force of habit she had been unable to break. When Elizabeth had signed her will, Louisa insisted everyone leave her mother's bedroom so she could rest.

Chapter Forty-Three

When Elizabeth awoke, her children were by her side. She had no idea how long she had been asleep. Time was becoming irrelevant to her. Blinking back tears, Elizabeth gripped the covers in pain. Once again, she set the word *delirium* in imaginary type to describe her bed muslin. Much more appropriate now, she thought, looking at the two berms she had made in her shallow grave of loose blankets.

Soon enough, Elizabeth. Soon, but not just yet.

She could see the rector there, standing beside her bed. He would hear her confession now if she felt it necessary to offer one.

"He who learns must suffer," Elizabeth could hear herself tell him, as if she were listening to another person talking. "And even in our sleep pain that cannot forget falls drop by drop upon the heart," she mumbled.

"She is out of her head," Louisa said gently. "Peter, she is out of her head, and she does not know what she is saying."

"She knows," Peter responded. "She made a point of quoting Aeschylus when my father died."

"Drop by drop upon the heart ... drop by drop upon the heart," she repeated in her delirium, becoming more agitated.

She wanted to remember.

Her husband touched her face, caught her tears with his finger. She closed her eyes.

"And in our own despair," Lewis answered, as if a teacher helping his student. "And in our own despair ..."

Someone was holding her hand.

"Can you forgive me?" Elizabeth asked, her eyes searched wildly for him. "Lewis?"

"No, Mother," Peter replied. "It is Peter. I am here."

Elizabeth swallowed hard.

"And in our own despair," she repeated.

"Against," he prompted.

"Against our will," Elizabeth recalled the phrase.

It was Peter's turn: "Comes wisdom to us ..."

"By the awful grace of God."

Elizabeth exhaled the words like a satisfying sigh. It felt good to remember that.

"Aeschylus," Peter said.

Elizabeth smiled and patted the top of his hand.

"So you had your classical education after all," she told her son, swallowing hard and giving in to the delicious desire to close her eyes.

"Yes, I suppose I did," he said, reassuringly.

She moaned as pain seized her again, leaving marks against his skin. Her agony overwhelmed him.

Through his sobs, Peter told his wife, "She has not wept like this since that awful day Joseph died. Not even when my father died." Peter used his free hand to wipe his nose. "The pain must be hell."

Elizabeth opened her eyes and looked at her son.

"Bring me the wooden box," she said weakly. "Top dresser drawer."

His mother's life was nearing its end. Peter found himself oddly overwhelmed with the urge to say things now. Ask for her forgiveness. Ask her for answers to questions that haunted him. But now was not the time for selfish pursuits; he would not burden her with things that would only benefit himself.

Louisa fetched the box and handed it to Peter. He opened it; Elizabeth's fingers fumbled inside for Lewis's silver watch. Peter gently took the timepiece from her grasp.

"Father's watch," he whispered.

"It is not for you," Elizabeth spoke plainly.

Peter tried to stifle a recoil but found it difficult.

"Who is to receive it then, Mother?" he managed to ask without too much sardonic inflection.

"It is for *your* son, Lewis," Elizabeth said. "Keep it for him until he is old enough to know the fine man to whom it belonged, and for whom he was named."

"I will, Mother," Peter replied.

At his side, Ann cried softly. He offered her his monogrammed handkerchief, which she gratefully accepted.

Elizabeth smiled.

"Promise me you will tell my grandson about his grandfather."

Peter swallowed hard.

"I will. I promise, Mother. And I will tell him about you as well."

Elizabeth smiled again and said with a wink, "Be kind."

A tear slid down his cheek.

"I will report the facts of your life, fairly and accurately, just as you taught me."

"Nothing in the *Gazette*, promise me. It is my final wish that you do not set my name in type. *Elizabeth* looks too much like 'Heber the kenite' set backwards. Besides, I will not have the Frenchmen in town reading my obituary and discussing me at their next Two Bit Carolina Club meeting," she said.

"Careful, Mother," her son chided. "It is a venerable society now, and not just for Father's French friends. I plan to join as well. Were they to discuss you, it would be done by many more influential men in town than merely the French."

Elizabeth appreciated her son's attempt at levity. He brushed a lock of damp hair away from her forehead, bent down, and kissed her there. Elizabeth looked at her son with an expression that asked forgiveness, and offered it. Behind him, the rector from St. Philip's was lurking in the doorway. Her dimming eyes could see prisms of light, a rainbow.

"Last rites," Elizabeth murmured.

Peter moved back, and the specter moved toward her. Obediently she closed her eyes and opened her mouth.

She tasted the wafer on her tongue, and it immediately began to dissolve. She heard someone mumbling in Latin. A watery fingertip made the sign of the cross on her forehead. A single drop trickled down the bridge of her nose and pooled behind her nostril. She felt like she was floating on calm swells, in a place she could almost recollect. The canals of Holland perhaps. A gentle breeze brushed her cheek, a reminiscent whisper ready to breathe her home when her own breath was gone. Vague shadows waiting on the distant bank seemed friendly and familiar, as if they knew and loved her. She felt as if she knew and loved them too. They were waiting, waiting to welcome her.

All that remained now was the crossing.

Epilogue

In 1733 I sent one of my journeymen to Charleston, South Carolina, where a printer was wanting. I furnish'd him with a press and letters, on an agreement of partnership, by which I was to receive one-third of the profits of the business, paying one-third of the expense. He was a man of learning, and honest but ignorant in matters of account; and, tho' he sometimes made me remittances, I could get no account from him, nor any satisfactory state of our partnership while he lived. On his decease, the business was continued by his widow, who, being born and bred in Holland, where, as I have been inform'd, the knowledge of accounts makes a part of female education, she not only sent me as clear a state as she could find of the transactions past, but continued to account with the greatest regularity and exactness every quarter afterwards, and managed the business with such success, that she not only brought up reputably a family of children, but, at the expiration of the term, was able to purchase of me the printing-house, and establish her son in it. I mention this affair chiefly for the sake of recommending that branch of education for our young females, as likely to be of more use to them and their children, in case of widowhood, than either music or dancing, by preserving them from losses by imposition of crafty men, and enabling them to continue, perhaps, a profitable mercantile house, with establish'd correspondence, till a son is grown up fit to undertake and go on with it, to the lasting advantage and enriching of the family.

   —Benjamin Franklin, *The Autobiography of Benjamin Franklin*, 1791